Starting Over in Cariad Cove

Darcie Boleyn has a huge heart and is a real softy. She never fails to cry at books and movies, whether the ending is happy or not. Darcie is in possession of an overactive imagination that often keeps her awake at night. Her childhood dream was to become a Jedi but she hasn't yet found suitable transport to take her to a galaxy far, far away. She also has reservations about how she'd look in a gold bikini, as she rather enjoys red wine, cheese and loves anything with ginger or cherries in it – especially chocolate. Darcie fell in love in New York, got married in the snow, rescues uncoordinated greyhounds and can usually be found reading or typing away on her laptop.

Also by Darcie Boleyn

A Very Merry Manhattan Christmas
Love at the Italian Lake
Love at the Northern Lights

Conwenna Cove

Summer at Conwenna Cove
Christmas at Conwenna Cove
Forever at Conwenna Cove

Cornish Hearts

The House at Greenacres
The Cottage at Plum Tree Bay
The Christmas Tea Shop

Cariad Cove Village

Coming Home to Cariad Cove
Starting Over in Cariad Cove

DARCIE BOLEYN

Starting Over in Cariad Cove

CANELO

First published in the United Kingdom in 2022 by

Canelo
Unit 9, 5th Floor
Cargo Works, 1–2 Hatfields
London, SE1 9PG
United Kingdom

A CIP catalogue record for this book is available from the British Library.

Print ISBN 978 1 80032 381 0
Ebook ISBN 978 1 80032 380 3

Cover design by Cherie Chapman

Cover images © Shutterstock

Look for more great books at www.canelo.co

Printed and bound in Great Britain by Clays Ltd, Elcograf S.p.A.

1

MIX
Paper from
responsible sources
FSC
www.fsc.org
FSC® C018072

For my family, with love always xxx

Chapter 1

Hannah Marlowe pushed her hair off her face and blinked.

What time was it?

The hotel room was flooded with golden July sunlight, the curtains fluttering softly in the breeze, and she could hear birdsong from outside. She reached for her smartphone and saw that it was just after eight, so she closed her eyes and pulled the duvet up to her chin, hoping that she'd drop off again. Unfortunately, her brain had other ideas and after ten minutes of trying to relax, she gave in and sat up.

The room was very pleasant, and from what she'd seen of the rest of the hotel after her arrival last night, the rest of it was too. As a freelance travel writer, she'd stayed in a lot of hotel rooms over the years but not in this part of the world. The Gower Peninsula in West Wales had never really appealed and so she'd jetted off to foreign climes instead, visiting historical landmarks including the Parthenon in Athens, Machu Picchu in Peru, the pyramids in Egypt, and more modern sites like the Grand Canyon Skywalk in Arizona, the Burj Khalifa in Dubai and The Vessel in New York. She liked to get as far away as she could for as long as she could and her contacts in magazines, newspapers and online publications meant that she was able to do so.

Over the years, she'd learnt a few tricks like the importance of selling articles in advance of each trip, landing press trips to destinations where companies wanted publicity and keeping her out-of-pocket travel expenses as low as possible. There were ways to manage expenses and also, whenever things had got tight, Hannah had rolled up her sleeves and worked, whether it was helping with the grape harvest in France, vegetable picking in Zurich or cleaning hotel rooms in Lanzarote. The advantage of working said jobs had given her a wider range of experiences where she got to see the destinations from a different perspective, as well as giving her more to write about. But now, she was in Wales for four weeks spanning the end of July and the beginning of August, courtesy of two online publications who wanted articles on the Summer Festival at Cariad Cove. Initially, these jobs hadn't been hers and had been commissioned from another writer, but when that writer had fallen pregnant, she'd recommended Hannah as her replacement. The fact that Hannah had a sterling reputation as a reliable writer – who produced good quality articles and met deadlines – meant that the editors didn't mind the change. Hannah knew she was lucky in that she had regular offers of work and didn't struggle to make ends meet like some writers did, but then she could jet off at a moment's notice because of her lack of ties and this worked to her advantage. Plus, her domestic expenses were low and so she spent some of what she earnt on travelling for work and securing more jobs, and the rest went into her ISA to top up the inheritance her mum had left her.

She stood up, stretched, then pulled her green silk kimono on over her short pyjamas. At the window, she pushed open the curtains exposing floor to ceiling windows and her jaw dropped at the view.

'Bloody hell! It's gorgeous.'

The hotel was nestled in the cove with cliffs and trees in one direction and the beach spreading out for as far as Hannah could see from her first-floor room. She opened the curtains at the other window and found that it over-looked the hotel grounds and the winding road she'd driven along last night. Everything looked fresh and green and the grounds were bright with a rainbow of summer flowers. An elderly couple were sitting at a table in the grounds having breakfast, the hum of their conversation and the clinking of their cutlery reaching her ears.

She returned to the window with the beach view and gazed out at the sea, following it with her eyes until she reached the cliffs at the far end. If she remembered correctly from what she'd read, the cliffs separated Cariad Cove from Barddoniaeth Bay and when the tide was out, it was possible to walk from one beach to the other. She'd thought that the names were lovely, *cariad* meaning love and *barddoniaeth* meaning poetry, and knew that she'd find a way to weave both into her articles along with their meanings and possibly some history too.

Her stomach grumbled, reminding her that she hadn't eaten since yesterday lunchtime. She'd been too tired when she'd arrived last night and declined the night recep-tionist's offer to find her some supper. But now she needed to eat, so she'd dress and go down for breakfast before deciding upon her plans for the day.

–

'Please let me put your shoe on, Beti.' Will Hopkins fought the urge to check the kitchen clock again, knowing that seeing how late he was running wouldn't help him to get his daughter ready faster.

'Don't like them anymore, Daddy. I want new ones.'

Beti folded her arms over her chest and scowled at him. Will had to bite the inside of his cheek to prevent himself from smiling. In her blue and white checked summer school dress with her soft brown curls in bunches and her white ankle socks, his daughter was incredibly cute. Too cute for her own good at times because she often ended up getting her own way and Will knew that wasn't a good life lesson.

'Beti… we've been through this,' he said, trying to reason with her. He had always tried to appeal to her sense of logic, wanting to treat her with respect and patience, however difficult she was being. Most of the time, he was lucky, and she was happy to get ready in the mornings but some days, like today, she made things challenging. 'You can have new shoes for September. There are only three days of term left and there's no point getting new shoes now as you'll grow out of them.'

Beti sighed then held out her foot. 'OK go on then. But do you promise, Daddy?'

'I promise,' he replied, sliding the black leather shoe onto her foot then fastening the buckle. 'Right, go and grab your cardigan and I'll get our packed lunches out of the fridge.'

'OK, Daddy, did you put my apple in because—'

'I did!' He cut her off before she launched into a monologue about what her teacher said about the importance of eating fruit.

'Good. Miss Dix will be pleased.'

Will listened to Beti climbing the stairs to make sure she was doing as he'd told her then he opened the fridge and reached for the lunch boxes. He loved being a dad but school mornings could be challenging when he used up so much energy, especially when he knew that he had a whole day ahead of him teaching teenagers, so he was glad that the summer holiday was almost upon them.

He got out the lunchboxes – his clear one and Beti's purple one – and set them on the table then filled their water bottles. Once he'd loaded lunch boxes and bottles into his and Beti's rucksacks, he checked that he'd turned everything off and went through the hallway to the front door.

'Beti?' he called then waited. 'Are you ready?'

No answer.

'Beti?' He looked up the stairs and listened. What on earth was she doing now?

'Daddy...' His daughter appeared on the landing, a frown on her face. 'I had an accident.'

'What do you mean you had an accident?' Will dropped the rucksacks and shot up the stairs, his heart hammering with fear. He knelt in front of Beti and cupped her face, staring at the red splotches all over the front of her school dress as cold fear gripped him. 'What happened? Are you bleeding?'

'No, Daddy, I wanted to paint my nails to make them more pretty and I spilt the nail varnish on my dress.' Her eyes widened as if in disbelief at how this terrible thing had come about and Will suppressed a groan.

'It doesn't matter. As long as you're all right,' he said, as he led Beti to the bathroom. 'I'll get you a clean dress and we'll try to get the nail varnish off this one later.'

'Yes, Daddy,' Beti said, 'I really have no idea how it happened at all.'

Will shook his head. 'I'm sure you don't.'

'We'd better get a move on, Daddy, or we'll both be late for school.' Beti gazed up at him, her eyes wide with innocence, looking as if butter wouldn't melt in her mouth.

'Yes, we better had, and I'm sure Miss Dix won't care if your nails aren't painted.'

'Miss Dix always has painted nails. She's very pretty. You should marry her, Daddy, and then you'd have a lovely wife.'

'If only it was that simple.' Will left Beti in the bathroom while he went to get her another dress. Whenever Beti talked about him getting a girlfriend or getting married, she made it sound so straightforward. He adored her innocence but often felt guilty that she didn't have a mother around. Didn't have *her* mother around, more like. Will tried hard to be a good dad and all he could hope for was that he was good enough because Beti deserved the absolute best.

Chapter 2

In the dining room of the hotel, Hannah helped herself to some things from the breakfast buffet then she carried her tray outside to the garden where she'd seen the elderly couple sitting earlier. There were other people out there now – all adults, as the schools didn't officially break up for another few days. Hannah had checked because she wanted to know when the hotel's busiest times would be.

She'd only come to Wales for the summer festival because an acquaintance she knew from the travel writing circuit had contacted her out of the blue and offered her the jobs and the room that was booked. The woman had confessed that she'd got pregnant on her third round of IVF and wasn't up to travelling anywhere because her morning sickness was horrendous and her GP had prescribed plenty of rest. Hannah could have declined but she rarely turned her nose up at a job and it was why she'd been so successful over the years. Work came first for Hannah. Then again, she thought wryly, there was nothing else in her life to worry about.

According to the hotel's website, while the Cariad Cove Hotel itself was popular, the nearby self-catering properties that belonged to the hotel were even more so, as guests could bring their dogs on holiday too. There

7

were six cottages near the hotel and each one accommodated different group sizes. Hannah was impressed by that flexibility and would certainly include details of the other properties in her articles. After all, some people had friends and family to holiday with, as well as dogs, so they'd want to know about the group booking options.

Hannah located a smaller table beneath the shade of a large tree. She placed her tray on the table, pulled out a chair and sat down, then lowered her sunglasses because it was so bright. After she'd poured herself a cup of tea from the pot, she buttered her freshly baked croissant and sat back to enjoy the ambience. Eating inside this morning would have seemed like a waste when it was so beautiful out here. She snapped a few photographs of her breakfast on her smartphone, having left her Nikon D5600 in her room, then put it on the table face down. She'd filled a bowl with fresh berries and yogurt but she'd eat her croissant first while it was still warm.

As she bit into the buttery pastry, she looked around. The elderly couple from earlier had gone but there were two couples who looked like they were in their late twenties or early thirties, and two women who Hannah estimated to be around forty. Estimate was all she could do though because these days, she often found it hard to guess people's ages. Genetics and lifestyle played big parts in how someone aged and she often got it wrong. She had no idea if she looked thirty or if she appeared older or younger. When she'd been in her early twenties, she was always asked for ID when buying alcohol, but that had worn off in more recent years. It was funny, she thought, that when she was younger it had irritated her while now she'd have found being asked for ID flattering. Perhaps the fact that she never was asked anymore meant that she did actually look older than she was. Not that she minded that much because as far as she was concerned, ageing was a gift that not all people got to enjoy.

Like her mum, for instance.

The croissant suddenly seemed dry in her mouth, so she took a sip of tea then swallowed it down. She put the rest of the croissant on the plate and cradled her cup between two hands. Twenty years had passed since she lost her mum and yet it still got to her at times. She was able to keep busy and push it from her mind most of the time but occasionally, it hit her like a wave that stole her breath, the fact that her mum would never again share breakfast with Hannah, swim in the sea or walk along a sandy beach. It didn't seem right; was incredibly unfair, and all because of a bloody horrible disease. A disease that terrified Hannah and that kept her vigilant in getting her own regular health checks – even though she sometimes felt that she'd rather not know. She could still remember her mum crying as she lay in the hospice, telling Hannah that she was afraid of leaving her all alone, that she wasn't ready to go.

Hannah shook herself inwardly. It was a long time ago and she'd managed, had made something of herself and she was doing her best to grab hold of life with both hands. Well, some areas of life anyway. That was what she was supposed to do in honour of her mum. She was trying…

She picked up the bowl of fruit and yogurt and gazed out at the beach where the sea was lapping at the shore and where a dog raced up and down as its owner threw a ball. If she didn't travel so much, she'd love to get a dog, but right now it just wouldn't be fair to leave one behind so often. She didn't have a home of her own, and over the years she'd stayed in a series of short-term lets in Watford. None of the furniture was hers and she had few belongings, not seeing the point in accumulating things she would have to keep packing up when she moved on. She'd leave all that until she had a home of her own. If she ever got a home of her own. Sitting still left her too much time to think but travelling kept her busy, focused on the moment and the experience. It had been that way for the past decade and she suspected it would be the same for another ten years or more because she couldn't imagine living her life any other way.

At least, that's what she told herself when any doubts or the longing for a place to call home crept in. What was the point in wanting what she couldn't have?

–

'Morning all right, was it?'

Will looked up from the book he was marking to find his colleague and friend, Joe Thomas, standing in the doorway to his classroom.

'Hey Joe. Not too bad, thanks.'

Joe entered the classroom and rested against a desk near to Will's. 'You look tired, Will. Beti giving you a hard time?'

Will put his red pen down and sat back in his chair. 'When isn't she?' He laughed to show he was joking. 'I have no idea how I'm going to keep her occupied for a whole summer. She likes to be constantly busy, which is great, of course, but some days I'd like to go at a slower pace. Even just one day a week. Perhaps have a lie in and drink my tea while it's still hot.'

'I don't know how you do it.' Joe shook his head then rubbed a hand over his cropped blond hair. 'You're a real hero.'

'I'm just a single parent. Other people do it all the time and don't complain.' He winced. 'Sorry... I don't mean to complain at all. I love Beti and she's the most important person in my life, but I do worry about being enough for her. That she might be missing out, you know?'

'You're the best parent she could have.' Joe smiled. 'Stop beating yourself up. You're doing an amazing job and Beti is very lucky. Some kids don't even see their dads... look at some of the ones we teach.'

'I know. Some have it tougher than others.' He thought of his parents and how they'd always been there for him and for Beti, about how his older sister, Alice, had been a rock for him. 'Beti does have my family too so I'm sure that helps balance things out a bit.'

'Beti is a bright and bubbly child and she'll go far in life. In fact, after seeing her kick a ball at the beach recently, it's possible that she'll be a footballer. It seems that her strategy of taking down the players of the opposing team is quite successful... if a bit... scary.'

Joe laughed but Will flinched at the memory. He'd taken Beti down to Cariad Cove a few weeks ago and Joe had been there walking his giant rescue dog, Odin. Will had a football with him and Beti had insisted on showing Joe her best penalty shot. However, she'd also insisted that Joe be in goal, which consisted of Will's trainers set on the sand a few feet apart. Joe had agreed, clearly thinking it was all a harmless game, but he hadn't bargained on Beti having a strong kick that sent the ball right towards Joe and hit him in the crotch. He'd fallen to the sand clutching his groin while Odin had seized the ball and run off, Beti jumping up and down cheering the whole time. It would've been funny if Joe hadn't been in so much pain.

'I think we'll keep her away from football for now. I can't afford to be at the mercy of her... goals.' Will rubbed at his eyes and stifled a yawn.

'Three days, buddy, and you'll get a break from this place.'

'I always look forward to the end of term but after a few days, I kind of miss the routine.' *And the adult company*, he added silently.

'I know what you mean, but I'm still working on the garden at my cottage so I've got lots to do this summer.'

'With your lady friend?' Will winked at him and Joe blushed.

'Ffion will be around too, I hope.' He rubbed at the back of his neck then said quietly, 'I know I'm a lucky man.'

'She's lucky too. You make a very cute couple.'

Joe had fallen in love with the youngest daughter of the owners of the Cariad Cove Hotel. They'd met earlier in the year when Ffion had returned to the cove and she'd started running with Joe. They'd set up a local running club and Will went out with them when he could, usually on two Saturdays a month when his parents had Beti to stay over on a Friday night. He didn't run outdoors as often as he'd like these days because he had Beti at home, but he still used the treadmill in his garage and did what he could to stay fit. After all, he was the only parent Beti had around, so he had to stay healthy for her.

'You coming for a drink after work on Wednesday?' Joe asked.

'Probably not.'

'Shame. If you decide you want to come, Ffion said she'll pick me up afterwards, so she could give you a lift home too.'

'Thanks. I'll see how the land lies.'

'Right,' Joe went to the door, 'I have Year 10 set three last lesson and as it's their last PE lesson before the summer, they requested... *dodgeball*.'

'Sounds like fun.'

'It allows them to burn off some energy so that's always a bonus and gives them the opportunity to throw a ball at one another which always goes down well. Don't forget about Wednesday if I don't see you again this week. The offer stands.'

'Thanks, Joe.'

After his colleague had left the classroom, Will sipped his water and gazed out of the window into the courtyard of the city school. The caretakers had turned the space into a garden complete with a greenhouse and raised beds, and some of the younger pupils were out there now, tending the plants in their lunchtime or sitting on the picnic benches eating their sandwiches. It wouldn't be long before Beti would be their age, attending high school, preparing for exams and taking part in extracurricular activities. It was why he felt the need to treasure every moment with her now, to ensure that she knew she was loved and important to him. After all, her mother hadn't put Beti first and so it was up to Will to compensate for it.

He hadn't been out for a drink with his colleagues for a while and it would be nice to sink a few beers, feel the stresses of the term fade away, and spend time with them. But the thought of afterwards, when he'd be at home with Beti, turned the thought of the beers sour. He didn't like to drink much around her or to smell of beer because he was keen to set her a good example, so it wasn't an option unless she stayed at his parents' house, and as happy as they were to have their granddaughter stay, Will didn't like to ask too often. He never wanted to impose on them because they were so supportive and he valued them too much to take advantage. Besides which, he felt that the last day of term should be a celebration for him and Beti, a time to watch a movie and eat pizza and ice cream as they planned their summer together.

Nights out could wait, socialising could wait. Will had no place in his life or in his heart for anyone else, so everything, except for Beti, could wait.

Chapter 3

After breakfast the previous day, Hannah had read all the tourist information leaflets the hotel had to offer, added details to her research file on the location and mapped out the two articles about Cariad Cove and Barddoniaeth Bay. She'd worked in her room initially then taken her laptop outside to sit at the table under the tree. With the breeze rustling the leaves and the song of the tiny birds in the gardens lifting her spirits, she'd enjoyed working outdoors, inspired by the beauty of the location.

She'd been keen to walk along the beach but told herself she had plenty of time and that if she did the groundwork for the articles first, she could relax a bit later. However, following a delicious lunch of honey-roasted salmon and salad, she'd gone back to her room, stretched out on the bed and fallen asleep. When she'd woken in the late afternoon, it had been raining, so she'd taken a long bath in the en suite before heading down for dinner.

On her second morning in the hotel, she'd woken feeling refreshed; the sea air certainly seemed to be helping her to sleep soundly. She'd eaten a hearty breakfast, grabbed her camera bag, sunglasses, baseball cap and phone, then set off for a walk.

It was a perfect July morning. The tide was on its way out and the sand gleamed like a polished mirror under the bright sun. The air blowing in off the sea was fresh and briny making her feel instantly cleansed. She walked down a concrete ramp to the sand then toed off her plimsoles. Beneath her feet, the sand was damp and gritty and as she walked droplets of water flicked up onto her cropped jeans. Avoiding the coiled castings of lugworms, various shells and mounds of dark green seaweed, she headed for the water.

Out at sea, a boat bobbed along and she wondered who was on it and where they were going, if they were out there for work or pleasure. While she was here, if she had time, she'd like to take a boat trip so she could see the cove from another angle and get a variety of different photographs.

When she reached the water, she stepped into it, feeling the push-pull of the tide, the shifting seabed under her feet. Standing there for a moment, she closed her eyes and savoured a moment of stillness. Hannah spent so much time rushing around, trying to forget about the past and to prevent herself worrying about the future. Avoidance, she thought the experts called it. She was good at avoiding the things she didn't want to consider. But what was the point in worrying about things she couldn't change? She certainly didn't have the power to change the past and because she hadn't fully faced up to what she'd been through, she didn't really know what she wanted from her future. How could she when she was still trying to figure out who she was? In those rare moments when she did allow herself some time to reflect, she could admit that she kept moving to avoid everything that troubled her, everything that scared her. Travelling around gave her the chance to try to find somewhere she could belong, somewhere she could settle and become who she was meant to be, but it hadn't happened yet and at thirty, she wondered if it ever would. As a child, she'd thought she'd have it all figured out by the time she hit the big three-oh, but it hadn't happened and she was still drifting uncertainly.

The sound of feet slapping against the wet sand snapped her from her reverie and she opened her eyes to see a woman jogging along the beach. She wore dark running gear and her brown hair was pulled back in a ponytail that swung from side to side with her movement. As she got closer, Hannah could see that she had AirPods in her ears and a bumbag around her waist. The woman slowed, then stopped and bent over, one hand pressed to her middle.

'Hello,' Hannah said as removed her sunglasses. 'Are you all right there?'

'I'm fine, thanks.' The woman stood up and smiled. 'Bit of a stitch, which is very annoying, but it still happens sometimes.'

'Are you in training?' Hannah asked.

'I'm always in training.' She laughed. 'I'm a relatively new runner, having only started this year, and I'm still learning about how far I can push myself… and when to listen to my body.'

Hannah nodded. 'I used to run when I was younger.'

'Younger?' The woman frowned. 'You're young now.'

'Yes. Well… thirty, but I meant when I was a teenager and… well, that was some time ago.' She let her words fade away, not wanting to get into her reasons for stopping running, not wanting to let them infiltrate her mood.

'You can always start again. I mean… I'm in my thirties and I've only recently started so you'd probably find it would come back to you. Muscle memory, I think it's called.'

Hannah cleared her throat, lifted her feet in turn and swilled the sand from them before setting them back down again. The sea that had felt so inviting just moments ago now felt cold, the sand clammy, and she was gripped by an urge to return to the hotel, but she wasn't quite sure why. Was it thinking about her past that had made her feel differently?

'Are you staying locally?' the woman asked.

'Yes.' Hannah gestured in the direction of the Cariad Cove Hotel. 'There.'

The woman's face lit up. 'Fantastic! I'm Ffion. My parents own the hotel.'

'Oh wow! Hello, Ffion, I'm Hannah. I'm here for the summer festival. I'm a freelance travel writer.'

'Are you the writer doing the articles about the hotel and the festival?'

'That's right.'

'My mam and dad said that you'd be arriving this week. Gosh, it's great to meet you. I bet your job is fascinating.'

'It has its moments.' Hannah smiled. 'So do you live locally?'

'Kind of… I've basically unofficially moved in with my partner, Joe, who has a house in the village, although I still spend some nights at my parents' home. They have the cottage just behind the hotel.'

'I know the one.'

'The thing is, I only moved back this year after… well, that's a long story, but I'm glad I returned. It's such a beautiful place and I feel at home here now.'

'Where were you living before? If you don't mind me asking.' Something crossed Ffion's face and Hannah hoped she hadn't made Ffion feel awkward. 'I'm sorry... it's the journalist in me. I'm always asking questions, so I probably seem incredibly nosey.'

Ffion smiled and her eyes crinkled at the corners. 'It's fine. I lived in Scotland for a long time.'

'Scotland is beautiful too.'

Ffion rubbed at her belly and let out a long breath. 'That's better now. You distracted me from the pain.'

'You should take it easy on the way back though. A stitch can be nasty if you don't rest it.'

'I will. Look... uh... if you're going to be around for a while and you're looking for someone to show you the sights, I'd be happy to help. I know the area and while I help out my mam and dad at the hotel, I'm still not officially gainfully employed.'

A seagull squawked overhead making them both jump.

'Bloody things.' Ffion grimaced. 'They're so bossy. Anyway, as I was about to say... I'm thinking of setting up my own PR firm to support local businesses and making connections will be very useful. I'd love to have a chat to you and find out more about your job and to see if we can help each other out.'

'I'd like that.' Hannah knew the value of business connections and the fact that Ffion was the daughter of the hotel owners would be a good thing too. Besides which, although Hannah usually kept her distance from other people, Ffion seemed so friendly and down to earth that spending time with her would probably be quite nice. Plus, having a local guide was always a positive. 'Let me give you my number.'

After they'd exchanged phone numbers, Ffion gave a little shimmy. 'Right, well… I'm going to get going but I'll text you soon and we can arrange something.'

'Brilliant, thank you.'

Ffion broke into a gentle jog and soon she was running up past the hotel, disappearing from sight. Hannah could make out a road leading off to the side of the hotel then a wooded area. She spotted Ffion's head emerging from between the trees, bobbing up and down as she ran, and realised it must be the way to the coastal path.

Turning back to the water, she watched as it continued to recede, as if creeping away from the beach, hoping to avoid detection. She decided to walk a bit further along towards the cliffs then she'd head back to the hotel and have another soak in the giant bath before lunch. The food at the hotel had been excellent so far and she wondered what was on the menu today.

Chapter 4

Will collapsed into his chair and sighed. He'd just said goodbye to his Year 9 class and wouldn't see them until the start of the next academic year. The end of the summer term was always a strange one because it was something that Will and most of his colleagues looked forward to for ages then it seemed to arrive suddenly. The relief at finishing another academic year and having six weeks to wind down could never be underestimated. And yet, there was also a sense of anti-climax about it. Will felt exhausted, physically and mentally, and knew that if Beti let him he'd probably sleep in past his usual wake-up time of six a.m. tomorrow, even though it was only a Thursday. The school year was so busy that when he reached July, he was ready to drop. It would take a few days to unwind enough to enjoy being off school and then he'd start to feel more like himself again. Not that he didn't love his job, of course, because without it, he'd have struggled over the years. The camaraderie with colleagues, the pupils who wanted to learn and who enjoyed his subject, even the pupils who weren't big fans of History but who relied on Will as a source of pastoral support; all of these things kept him going and gave him a sense of purpose. Beti was his world, but his job helped to provide a sense of self-worth and another reason to get up every day.

And now he'd need to tidy up his classroom, collect the pens, pencils and rubbers that had somehow managed to fall under desks, to get wedged behind filing cabinets and to hang from the blinds, as well as file any paperwork that was confidential or that he'd need at the start of September term. He'd come back in for results day in August and probably on a few other occasions to update his wall displays and to get his books and photocopying sorted for September, but apart from that he'd have some time away from the school building.

Will's classroom went through its own seasonal changes, starting the academic year neat and tidy with clean surfaces and fresh new books, and by the end of the year it would look like winter winds had torn through it and destroyed all semblance of organisation. It was a bit like the pupils with their fresh new uniforms and shiny shoes in September, ties done up to the collar and blazers a bit too big; by the end of the year, blazer sleeves would be halfway up wrists, shoes would be scuffed or replaced with trainers and ties would be 'forgotten', 'lost' or suspiciously shorter because someone had thought it would be funny to cut the end off. But that was teaching for you. It was so busy that filing and tidying were things that took a back seat, staying on top of uniform checks fell by the wayside, and ensuring that the pupils were taught, their welfare considered and the essential admin was done was all that mattered at the end of the day.

His thoughts flashed to Beti for a moment. What would she be thinking and feeling now? His little girl loved school and he knew she'd miss the social element during the holidays, as well as the stimulation of lessons, though he always strove to do his best to provide her with learning opportunities and playdates with friends. Over the holidays, Beti would grow, but not as much as some of the older pupils did, especially the boys. Sometimes they left at the end of July as boys and returned in September as almost-men, their legs much longer, their voices breaking and hair and acne appearing in patches on their faces. It was like they went through a metamorphosis during August, or their parents planted them in growbags so they shot up for the autumn.

As Will went to straighten the blinds, he caught sight of some of his colleagues through the window, escaping from the building as soon as the pupils had gone, hurrying to car shares with their keys in their hands. They were off to the pub, to celebrate reaching the end of term. And so they should. For a few seconds, Will wished he could go too, to sit in a pub garden with the July sun beating down on his head, feeling the relaxing effect of a beer as the alcohol entered his bloodstream. But then, if he could do that, he wouldn't have Beti, and he'd be going home to an empty house. At times like this, he wondered what it would be like to have a companion, a friend to share his life with, to help him to raise Beti and possibly more children. But it hadn't happened so far and might never happen because he never opened himself up to the opportunities that, on rare occasions, presented themselves. Since Kayla, he'd shut himself down to romance and love.

Will shook himself and vowed to count his blessings, because he had so much more than many people out there. So, as he tidied things away, he went through a mental check list of things he'd need to get for Beti's birthday. She was turning seven on the 7th of August and he wanted to ensure that she had a wonderful day.

'Beti! Come here and put your shoes on, please.'

Another day, another shoe fight, but this time it wasn't Will battling to get Beti's shoes on.

Standing in the doorway to the back garden, Will smiled at the scene before him. He'd just arrived at his parents' house to collect Beti and it seemed that his daughter was giving his mam, Dorothy, the run-around in their large back garden.

'No, Nanny, I like running around in my socks.'

'Beti Hopkins, your white socks will be filthy.'

'Daddy will wash them. He's good with stain remover. Anyway, Nanny, I'll have new ones for Speptember.'

'*Sep-tember*, Beti.'

'That's what I said.'

Beti skipped off down the garden in the direction of the playhouse that Will's dad had built for his granddaughter. At her heels was Indiana Bones, his parents' three-year-old golden cocker spaniel. Whenever Beti came here, Indi was never far from her side.

Will bit his bottom lip to stifle his laughter. His knew his mam was perfectly capable of wrangling Beti, and that she'd be swallowing back her laughter too. Beti had brought his parents endless joy in her almost seven years and they adored her, as she did them. She attended the primary school within walking distance of their four-bedroom detached house in the Uplands area of Swansea, and while Will was able to drop Beti at breakfast club most mornings, his parents often picked her up at the end of the day if Will was running a revision lesson after school, had a meeting or a parents' evening.

'Hello, darling.' Will's mam walked towards him, arms open, a smile on her face. She embraced him then stood back. 'You all right?'

'I'm a bit tired and looking forward to having a rest but apart from that, I'm OK.'

'I remember it well.' His mam's eyes took on the distant appearance they got when she thought about her days as a primary school teacher. She'd loved her job but found juggling work and home a challenge, and so she'd worked part-time to have more of a balance. 'I don't miss the tiredness, but I do miss the joy of the last day of term. And there's nothing like that first Sunday of the holidays when you sleep better than you have done for months because there's no school the next day.' Placing a hand on his arm, she asked, 'Want a cup of tea?'

'Yes please.'

'And a slice of cake?'

'That would be perfect, Mam, thanks. I'll just go and wash my hands then I'll say hello to Beti.'

Will went back inside and headed for the downstairs cloakroom. He loosened his tie, washed his hands and face then peered at himself in the mirror over the sink. He did look tired, had dark shadows under his eyes but a few days off would get rid of them and he'd soon look more human again. Running a hand over his brown hair, he noted that he needed a haircut too or his curls would soon be obvious and he always thought they made him look too boyish, although that probably had to do with the fact that his older brothers used to tease him about them when he was young.

Back in the kitchen, he picked up the tray of tea things, carried it out to the garden, placing it on the table on the decking. He sat down and his mam joined him with a glass of juice for Beti.

As if summoned by the sound of the patio chairs being moved, Beti appeared from the playhouse and raced up the garden.

'Daddy!' She flung herself at Will, wrapping her small arms around his neck and smothering his face with kisses. 'I didn't know you were here.'

'Hello, baby girl.' He kissed her forehead then gently stood her in front of him.

'It's the holidays now so we can go to the beach and the animal sanctwy and the toy shop.' She bobbed on the spot, her pretty face lit up with excitement.

'It's *sanctuary*, Beti,' Dorothy corrected.

'Sorry, Nanny.' Beti grinned. 'Is this my juice?'

'It is.'

'Thank you.' Beti picked up the glass and took a sip. 'That's delicious.' She drained the glass then ran off down the garden, calling to Indi, already lost in some imaginary world.

Will sipped his tea, thinking about how his mam always corrected Beti if she said something wrong. It was probably the primary school teacher in her and never done out of meanness, just because she was teaching her granddaughter. She'd been the same with her own children but always reassured them that they were never wrong, just learning, and she was teaching them how to speak properly.

'Here's your cake, darling.' His mam held out a plate with a slice of her homemade Victoria sponge on it.

'It looks delicious.'

While Will ate, his mam chatted about her day and Beti roamed the garden. Will felt some of the tension in his shoulders slipping away, content to listen to his mam as a blackbird warbled in one of the trees and the afternoon sun warmed his skin. The scent from the roses his parents had tended over the years filled the air, sweet and intoxicating, like honey and cloves.

'What do you think then?' His mam was leaning her elbows on the table, two fine lines between her plucked brows. She pushed a hand through her short brown hair and the sunlight caught the silver at the roots.

'Sorry... I think I drifted off for a moment.'

'You're exhausted, Will. I asked if you'd like to stay for dinner.'

Will put his empty plate on the tray then picked up his mug. He had planned on getting a pizza for him and Beti but they had plenty of time to do that. His parents were good cooks and he knew Beti was happy there, so why not?

'That would be great, thanks, Mam.'

'Wonderful. I'll text your father and tell him to pick up some steaks on his way home from the golf course. You need some red meat to raise your iron levels.'

While his mam went inside to get her phone, Will sat back and closed his eyes, and within minutes, he was drifting into a doze as the stresses of the term slipped away.

Chapter 5

Hannah was sitting in the hotel garden at one of the tables. It was mid-morning and the day was already hot. Ffion had sent her a text the previous day asking if she wanted to go for a walk along the coastal path and Hannah had been delighted to accept. They'd agreed to meet at the hotel because Ffion said she'd be coming from Joe's house up in the village and wanted to pick up a few things from her parents' home first.

Hannah packed a small rucksack with a bottle of water, sunblock, a hat and her phone and hung her Nikon around her neck. The camera on her phone was very good too and photos taken on that saved automatically to her iCloud, so she'd take some shots on that as well.

'Good morning.' Ffion sat down opposite her looking fit and healthy in walking shorts, a T-shirt and trainers, her long brown hair pulled back into a high ponytail. 'I think it's going to be a hot one.'

'Definitely. I feel sorry for the hotel staff this morning, rushing around like ants in this heat.'

'Friday is changeover day at the hotel and at some of the cottages.' Ffion gestured at the lane that ran from the hotel grounds. 'The staff will be busy cleaning rooms before the new guests book in.'

'Is it because term ended this week?'

'That's right. The hotel and beach will soon be a hive of activity.' Ffion widened her eyes. 'My parents love this time of year, even though they claim it's too hectic at their age.'

'I don't know how they do it.' Ffion's parents had introduced themselves to Hannah the first morning of her stay and told her that if she needed anything, to let them know. Gwen and Aled Evans were friendly people with musical Welsh accents and ready smiles. They were clearly proud of their hotel and wanted all guests to feel welcome. Since then, she'd seen them around constantly, wondering if they ever went home.

'They're machines and always have been.' Ffion laughed. 'My sister, Mari, and I used to beg them to take some time off when we were young, but it was rare that we all had a holiday together. Not that we were neglected, I'd never want anyone to think that. We were loved and cared for and had a great childhood – who wouldn't living here right on the beach? But they were very busy and the hotel was like another child for them. It still is.'

'Does your sister live locally?'

'In Swansea. She has a house on the site of the old Swansea Institute of Higher Education. It's a lovely estate. She's married with two gorgeous little girls who keep her very busy. I'll introduce you to her soon.'

Hannah watched Ffion's face as she spoke about Mari and her heart squeezed. Ffion clearly loved her sister. Hannah had sometimes dreamt of having a sister or even a brother, someone she could rely on because she had no parents around. There had been no constant person in her life and sometimes she got tired of having to rely on herself.

'Do you have any siblings?' Ffion asked as if reading her thoughts.

Hannah sighed inwardly. 'I don't.'

'I'm not sure if that's a good thing or not.' Ffion chuckled. 'Over the years, Mari and I have fought like cat and dog, but she's always been there for me and I know I'm lucky to have her. There were years when we didn't see much of each other, when I lived in Scotland...' A shadow passed over Ffion's features and she frowned for a moment then shook her head and took a deep breath. 'But we've made up for it since I came home.'

Hannah wasn't sure what had happened when Ffion lived in Scotland but it seemed like there was something in her past that had hurt her. Looking at Ffion now with her glowing skin, her toned physique and pretty smile, it was hard to think that she'd ever been unhappy, but Hannah knew that everyone had their challenges in life. Goodness only knew she'd had her own.

'Are you ready to go?' Ffion asked, standing up.

'Just about.'

'I'll pop and see Mam for a minute then I'll meet you out here.'

'Great.' Hannah stood up and picked up her rucksack. She'd pop to the loo and then put some sunblock on her face and neck while she was inside because the last thing she wanted was to burn in the summer sun. It might not be the Med but it felt hot enough to be.

Hannah headed up to her room, a flutter of excitement in her belly at the prospect of the day ahead.

–

'This is incredible,' Hannah said as she gazed out over the cliff top. They had walked up the path that ran along the side of the Cariad Cove Hotel, through the wooded area where the ground was dappled with the sunlight that penetrated the gaps in the leaves, and emerged onto the coastal path. The sea spread out ahead of them, endless blue-green with darker patches in the shallows where rocks sat immersed in the water. To their left was Cariad Cove, its golden sands hugged by the curve of the headland that ended with the rocks of Barddoniaeth Bay. To their right lay the coastal path with its twists and turns, peaks and troughs, fields and woods that led inland.

'We could walk to Rhossili Bay from here but it's about 18k and that might be a bit much for one day with the return walk too, but it's a possibility for another time.' Ffion grinned. 'If you like walking.'

'I do. I like being active.'

'Have you travelled a lot?' Hannah could feel Ffion's eyes on her face, interested but not prying.

'Extensively. For work mainly but also because I like being busy.'

Hannah met Ffion's gaze. She'd forgotten what it was like to spend time with someone one-to-one. Not that there had been many times in her life when she had; a few college friends along the way and one kind foster mum. It was nice. And yet unnerving. Hannah was used to being there for herself and not opening up to others but a voice deep inside her – that sounded suspiciously like her mum – was trying to tell her that she should give Ffion a chance.

'Shall we walk a bit further then we can stop and have lunch?' Ffion asked.

'Lunch?'

'Yes.' Ffion reached around and patted the rucksack on her back. 'You didn't think my mam would let us go on a walk without sending food along, did you?'

Oh to have a mam who cared like that, Hannah thought.

'Your mam gave you a picnic?'

Ffion grinned. 'She might be busy but she's not going to let her star guest go hungry. This is Welsh hospitality at its finest, Hannah. Welsh mams like to feed their children and their guests, to make sure that they're being properly nourished.' Ffion paused. 'In more ways than one.'

Hannah wasn't quite sure what Ffion meant by that last bit but didn't want to ask in case it was something she didn't want to hear. Had Gwen Evans, a mother of two grown women, somehow seen through Hannah's carefully constructed façade? The years of building a wall around herself so she'd never get hurt, never be vulnerable, never need anyone else in her life? It made something inside her quiver. She didn't want to be vulnerable, open, raw or seen for who she tried not to be.

And yet… five days had passed at Cariad Cove and Hannah liked it there. She liked the hotel owners and the staff; they were all so friendly and accommodating. She didn't feel like she needed to be on guard all the time like she had in other locations she'd travelled to. It was, she realised, like she'd gone to stay at a big family home and everyone there was keen to make her feel safe and welcome. Cariad Cove was a place where people could belong, where they could be a part of a community, and as an outsider, Hannah could see that clearly. Her old longing was stirring and she wanted to squash it, to extinguish it before it rose inside her and became stronger, because her desire to belong somewhere had always been there, a shadow over the sun, a yearning whispering to her that there were other ways to live if she just took a chance.

A chance… The words seemed to be whispered on the breeze, but they disappeared quickly and Hannah dragged herself back to the moment. The sun was on her skin, the fresh sea breeze washing over her, the ground solid beneath her feet. She was here to work, to earn a living and nothing more, however much she might wish things were different.

–

Sitting on the grass, legs stretched out in front of her, Hannah took a bite of the crusty bread roll. The mature cheddar and apple and plum chutney was delicious and she had to stop herself from stuffing it all into her mouth at once. Ffion had opened her rucksack and set out a feast on the picnic blanket she'd brought rolled up in her rucksack. There was so much food that they'd had to sit on the grass next to the blanket but that was fine with Hannah.

It reminded her of one summer before her mum passed away. She'd have been nine, so it was before her mum got ill. They'd gone to Southend-on-Sea, just the two of them, as it always had been. Her mum had managed to save up for a week in a caravan and they'd both been incredibly excited. They'd spent their days on the beach making sandcastles, splashing in the sea, eating sandy corned beef sandwiches and salt and vinegar crisps then buying ice creams from the van that parked nearby. Hannah's skin had turned brown, her hair was lightened by the sun, and she'd felt so free. She'd thought her mum was the most beautiful woman in the world with her long blonde hair and sapphire blue eyes, long limbs and easy smile. If she closed her eyes, Hannah could feel her mum's arms around her as they sat and watched the sunset, its glow bathing the sky in candyfloss pink and blood orange, the sea sparkling like it was filled with precious stones.

That summer was her most vivid memory, her most vivid good memory at least. Every day had been wonderful and she'd fallen into bed at night with the taste of salt on her lips and a delicious lightness in her heart. Being near the sea was good for the soul and until now she hadn't realised how much she'd missed it. She'd travelled, of course, but even then she kept busy so sitting still like this, enjoying a picnic and being in the moment, was very different. As was allowing the memories to return because she often found it too painful to be reminded of what she missed.

'Mam's quiche is so good.' Ffion held up a slice of cheese, mushroom and tomato quiche. The surface was golden with cheese and the crust perfectly fluted around the edge.

'I'll try a piece now,' Hannah said, picking up a slice, her mouth watering at the prospect of how it would taste.

'Are you OK, Hannah?' Ffion asked without looking at her.

Hannah swallowed the bite of quiche. 'Yes… Why do you ask?'

'You seemed to go somewhere in your mind. Are they good memories?'

Hannah reached for her water bottle and took a drink.

'I do have good memories, yes. I was just thinking of a summer in my childhood when I went to Southend-on-Sea with my mum. We had a lovely week.'

There! She'd said it and it wasn't that hard. The sky hadn't crashed down around them and neither had Hannah burst into tears.

'Where does your mum live?'

Hannah coughed as her water went down the wrong way. Her eyes watered and she had to cough a few more times to clear her throat. 'She's… uh… she passed away when I was ten.'

'Oh god, I'm sorry.' Ffion's brow furrowed. 'That's so sad.'

'I never knew my dad.' Hannah rushed the words out before she lost her nerve. It was easier to tell Ffion before she asked. 'He was a fling, apparently, and he didn't even know I existed.'

'Wow.' Ffion put her unfinished quiche on a napkin and wiped her hands. 'I'm very sorry, Hannah. You lost a lot when you were so young.'

Hannah shrugged, an action she'd tried to break free of but one that remained from her teenage years when she'd tell herself she didn't care about anything. 'It happens. Or, as they say, shit happens.'

'It really does.'

Hannah glanced at Ffion and was shocked to see that her eyes were glistening. The last thing she wanted was to upset this kind woman.

'I'm fine, honestly. It was a long time ago and I've been fine. Just fine.'

Ffion reached out and took Hannah's hand, making her freeze initially, but Ffion squeezed her fingers gently and Hannah realised that it was quite nice to be touched by another human being. Not that Hannah didn't feel

36

awkward, because she most certainly did, but even so, she knew that Ffion was showing she cared.

'Finish your quiche then we can keep walking if you like. There's a beautiful hidden bay just along the path that not many people know about. It's a steep descent but we're both fit and strong so we can head down to the beach and even have a swim if you fancy it.'

'I don't have my costume.' Hannah said, looking down at herself, panic filling her at the thought. 'And I'm not much of a swimmer.'

Now it was Ffion's turn to shrug. 'That's OK. Perhaps you can just have a paddle.'

Hannah smiled through her unease. 'Sounds good.'

Chapter 6

Waking to a beautiful morning with the sun shining through a gap in the curtains, Hannah stretched out in bed. She'd slept like a log following her coastal walk with Ffion the previous day. They'd gone down to the private beach and Ffion had been right; there had been no one else around. Ffion had stripped off, making Hannah laugh at her boldness, then raced into the sea. For a moment, Hannah had stood there, indecision weighing her down, but as Ffion had splashed and called to her, she'd decided to paddle. After all, her mum had died aged just twenty-eight and Hannah was already two years older than that. What if her time was limited too? The last thing she wanted was to regret not having fun, not feeling alive while she had the chance and so she'd walked into the water up to her knees, gasping as it rushed over her skin, cold and refreshing.

While Ffion had swum further out, Hannah had sat on the beach and gazed up at the clear sky, watched a plane as it left a white trail in its wake, making her think of how even when people passed on, they left something behind. There was no escaping the fact that people died, but they left trails too, evidence that they'd been here, that they'd existed. Her mum would always live on in her heart and in her memories and therefore she'd never really be gone.

When Ffion had emerged from the water, Hannah had averted her eyes, giving her some privacy. Hannah gazed out at the water while Ffion dried herself with her T-shirt, feeling as if something inside her had lifted, that she had reached an understanding that she'd needed to find. It was as if the simple act of paddling in the sea had washed away some of her grief and when she emerged from the water she felt renewed.

She'd sat on the beach for a while with Ffion, eating what was left of the picnic before heading back to the hotel. Ffion was kind and open, not afraid of asking questions that others would shy away from and yet she seemed to know when to stop. It was as if she'd been through something traumatic too and Hannah, though usually reluctant to trust and confide in people, felt an affinity with Ffion that she'd never felt with anyone before. Perhaps it was the gorgeous location, the time outdoors, the fact that she had reached thirty or the fact that she'd opened up just a bit to Ffion, but Hannah felt something shifting in her outlook and in her heart. It might be nothing more than endorphins but she was interested to see where it went.

Hannah wasn't used to people being so kind or showing so much interest in her on a personal level. Sure, there were those interested in her work and keen to emulate her success (who wouldn't want free or subsidised travel and what seemed like a glamorous, nomadic career?) and people who found her attractive and wanted to spend time with her for those reasons, but Ffion was different. She actually seemed interested in Hannah as a person. It made Hannah feel… significant. Apart from her mum, a kind foster parent and a few teachers along the way, no one else had event been that interested in who Hannah was, in what made her tick, and in her hopes and dreams.

Back at the hotel, she'd showered then gone down for dinner, surprised at her appetite, enjoying the new lightness in her heart and mind, lighter just for telling Ffion about her mum – she did exist, she was real, even if it was a long time ago.

Sometimes, it seemed, talking really did help.

–

Will breathed deeply, savouring the air on his skin, the regular pounding of his feet on the coastal path, the sense of freedom that running gave him. He'd spent last night alone after dropping Beti at his parents' home. They'd had a Friday evening Disney marathon planned along with hotdogs, popcorn, ice cream and plenty of cuddles and games with Indiana Bones. His mum had asked if he wanted to stay too but he knew that Beti liked being left with her grandparents, knew that it was good for her to spend time with other people and that his parents loved the sleepovers too. His dad had seen him to the door, offered him twenty pounds to go for a drink at the pub then, when Will declined it, his dad had pressed it into Will's hand and insisted that he use it for a takeaway or for Beti during the week. Then he'd given his son a quick hug and a vigorous pat on the back. Will's dad wasn't one for showing a lot of physical affection to his sons but he showed he loved them in lots of ways.

Will's older brothers, twins Andrew and Anthony, had both gone into the army. They were away a lot with their careers and while they were both in relationships, neither had married or had children. They had military partners and their careers were paramount to them so it didn't seem like Will's parents would have any grandchildren from Andrew or Anthony, at least not any time soon. The same went for Will's lawyer sister, Alice, who was very picky about men and had no maternal yearnings whatsoever. Beti was the only grandchild and therefore the apple of her grandparents' eyes. When Will's family did manage to get together, Beti was showered with love and attention and it made Will's heart brim with happiness to see how many people cared about her. He tried to hold on to that thought when the fears about him being a single parent crept in; if anything ever happened to him, there were people around to love and care for Beti. She'd never be left alone, but he wanted to be there for her for as long as he could.

The coastal run was busy this morning with around forty people joining in. Since Joe and Ffion had set up the sponsored run in the summer, the club had taken off and more people were applying to join all the time. Joe had told Will that the membership fees paid for admin costs and that the rest was donated to the Cariad Cove Animal Sanctuary that was run by Gwyneth Parry. Will had taken Beti to the animal sanctuary several times and she loved it, saying that when she grew up she wanted to work there, and Will could imagine her caring for animals in need. Beti might be bossy, articulate for her age, forwards and stubborn, but she was also an incredibly compassionate little girl, and on the days when Will felt low and struggled to hide it from her, she seemed to understand. On those days, Will found that Beti hugged him more than usual and tried to do more to help him around the house. He felt certain that she would grow up to be a kind and caring adult and that she would make her dad very proud indeed.

'Lovely morning,' Joe said as he jogged at Will's side. 'Good to be out, isn't it?'

'It's the best. But even better is knowing that there's no school on Monday.' Will laughed.

'Too right!'

Joe's giant dog Odin was ahead of them, keeping pace with Ffion and her sister, Mari, who also ran with the club.

'Ffion and Mari getting faster than you now, are they?' Will asked. The sisters had started running earlier that year and that they were doing really well considering that they hadn't been runners before. That was the thing with running, you could do it at any stage of your life and reap the benefits.

'Can't hold them back now. I wouldn't be surprised if Ffion decides she wants to do the London marathon soon,' Joe said.

'You think?' Will loved to run but twenty-six miles was a somewhat daunting challenge.

'Nothing is beyond her. She can do anything she puts her mind to.'

Will glanced at Joe and saw the smile on his face as he watched his partner running ahead of them. Joe was absolutely smitten with Ffion and it was good to see.

They continued in silence, focused on their pacing and the incredible views. Will's eyes traced the curve of the coastline, the changing blue of the sea from the lighter shades in the shallows to the darker blues of the deep. The sun was high in the sky but the breeze was fresh and cool, carrying aromas of brine and occasionally a sharp iodine-like tang.

As they descended the path that ran alongside the Cariad Cove Hotel, they entered a wooded area and the scents changed to those of flora and fauna, the rich peaty smell of the earth and the mingling of flowers and shrubs, of bark and fungi. Light seeped through the foliage, dappling the ground with shadows, and birds and squirrels rustled the leaves and branches overhead.

Soon, they were back out in the sunlight again, passing the hotel then reaching the sandy beach. The planned run took the club along the beach towards the cliffs of Bard-doniaeth Bay and those runners who followed the full run would easily clear a good 6k that morning. The distance of the run could be adjusted depending on what had been agreed in the Cariad Cove Running Club WhatsApp group that week. The group was handy because when the weather forecast didn't look good, they could easily message the club's members and things could be tweaked to suit everyone or cancelled if things looked awful weather-wise.

Will ran close to the water, avoiding the tide but keen to be near the waves, to enjoy the sound of the sea as it lapped at the shore and to feel the water droplets that flicked up and landed on his bare legs. He'd have to clean his trainers later but he didn't care; this was what beach running was all about. He'd arranged to collect Beti late afternoon because his parents were taking her out for lunch, so he had all morning and most of the afternoon to himself. If he'd had no plans, the thought of time alone to fill wouldn't have been so appealing, but having the running club gave him something to look forward to on the Saturdays when Beti wasn't with him. He could run alone, and did on occasion, but there was something about the structure of the Saturday morning coastal path run that added to the enjoyment. He hadn't even spoken to every member of the club – new ones joined all the time and some left along the way plus there wasn't always time – but there was a sense of belonging in the club, in having a shared interest that meant that he didn't feel the need to speak to them all individually.

When they reached the end of the beach, they turned and headed back the other way. The sensation of heaviness began creeping into his limbs, warning him that his body was tiring; however, knowing that when they reached the Cariad Cove Hotel, there would be refreshments ready for them, he felt a spurt of energy. The hotel owners Gwen and Aled sponsored the club too and provided refreshments on Saturday mornings. The thought of a hot chocolate to boost his blood sugar helped him speed up, pushing himself hard to be one of the first to reach the concrete ramp that led up to the hotel.

When he neared it, he slowed his pace, glancing around to see who was with him. Odin was in the lead, Ffion and Mari not far behind, but Joe was way back along the beach running with a new club member. He seemed to be struggling a bit so Will knew that Joe would be encouraging him, supporting him on the final stretch. Joe had done the same for Will a few times when he'd found some of the longer runs challenging, the PE teacher in him ever supportive of those trying their best.

At the top of the ramp, Ffion and Mari were stretching while they waited for the others to catch up and Odin had gone into the hotel gardens to have a drink from the bowl of water that Gwen and Aled ensured was left out for local dogs.

Will looked back across the beach as he stretched. It was a good run and they'd made it at a fair pace today. He felt tired but elated and enjoyed the buzz that came as his system was flooded with endorphins. It was better than alcohol, better than a good meal, better than most good things he could think of.

Better than sex? popped into his head. Well… perhaps not but it had been such a long time that he couldn't remember what that was like. Or he tried not to because what was the point in yearning for something he didn't have?

Turning back to the hotel, his breath caught in his throat. Standing there talking to Ffion and Mari was a vision of loveliness. Her blonde wavy hair glowed in the sunlight, her skin was so clear it seemed luminous, and her eyes, when they glanced away from Ffion, were the colour of emeralds. When they landed on Will and caught him staring at her, they darkened, reminding him of rock pools when the sun went behind a cloud. He dragged his gaze away from her and leant over, pretended to tighten his laces.

Who was she? He felt sure he'd never seen her before and she was so beautiful that he'd certainly have noticed her. Petite with feminine curves, she'd been smiling as she talked to Ffion and Mari. As Will stood up, he looked at her again, unable to resist, and found her eyes still on him. Flustered, he turned away and looked out at the beach again, his heart pounding in his chest and not from the run he'd just completed. He felt, ridiculously, like a teenager caught staring at a girl in school – shy, awkward and embarrassed. But he was thirty-three years old and not a teenager so he shouldn't feel like this. And yet... although Will spoke to female colleagues on an almost daily basis, although he interacted with women in a variety of situations every day, he might appear confident but in reality, he was quite shy. Being a teacher was a role that was about acting; when he was in front of a class he wasn't Will, he was Mr Hopkins, History teacher, member of staff. It was like a suit of armour that he donned on weekday mornings, for parents' evenings and open evenings. Outside of that role, Will was different – softer and far less confident.

Getting together with Kayla had been a miracle, he sometimes thought. He'd been sixteen, had a few beers at beach party and they'd ended up talking. He'd fancied her for ages but assumed that the confident, beautiful Kayla Rosser would never go for someone as quiet as him. However, she'd seemed to like Will, had taken his hand then rested her head on his shoulder as they'd toasted marshmallows on sticks then laughed as they stuck to their fingers and lips. When they'd kissed for the first time, Kayla had tasted of marshmallows and Will's head had spun.

It had been a while before their relationship had progressed to a more physical level but to Will's surprise, Kayla had seemed to like him and been happy to be his girlfriend. She'd teased him about his shyness, told him that all her friends said he was hot with his muscular physique, brown curls, full lips and come-to-bed eyes. Will had been stunned by her words, filled with confusion that they thought this about him because throughout his teenage years he'd felt awkward as his limbs grew, his shoulders broadened and his voice deepened. And yet it seemed that Kayla and her friends saw something different than what Will saw in the mirror; they saw a young man and not a teenager trying to come to terms with his drastic transformation from boy to adult. He worked out because it felt good and kept him calm, and not because he cared about developing muscles, but the muscles that came pleased Kayla and she told him she was proud to be on his arm. Although it had worried him a bit when Kayla had seemed to flirt outrageously with other men over the years, he believed her when she said it was harmless, that she cared about him and their relationship. There had been rumours about Kayla's fidelity in the year before Beti was conceived, and while Will had heard them once or twice on nights out with mutual friends, he'd struggled to accept that the woman he loved would betray him. And then, suddenly, there had been a missed period and a positive pregnancy test. Will had only graduated five years earlier and found the fact that he was going to be a father daunting, but he loved Kayla and promised to support her and their child and so they had planned for the future. When Beti had arrived, Will had known love like no other and he'd been determined to create a happy life for his daughter, had believed that Kayla would want the same. However, in that first year of Beti's life, things had changed in ways Will not had foreseen, and Will had been left heartbroken and alone.

'Will!' He turned to find Ffion waving him over. 'Come here a minute. I want to introduce you to someone.'

He swallowed, pushed a hand through his hair then walked over to the three women, feeling every bit the self-conscious teenager uncomfortable in the body of a man.

'Will, this is Hannah. She's in Cariad Cove to write about the summer festival, the hotel and the area.' Ffion gestured at Hannah who stood at her side, her lips curved upwards into a smile. Will reached out his hand and Hannah took it.

Though her grip was firm, her hand was small in his, her skin soft and something jolted inside him as he met her gaze. The green of her eyes was so intense, he felt like she could see deep inside him. Yet, as he said hello, he realised that the smile on her lips wasn't echoed in her eyes and that there was something guarded in them, as if she was holding something back, fearful and wary as a wounded animal.

'Good to meet you, Hannah,' he said. 'So what do you think of the cove?'

'It's stunning,' she replied, the light in her eyes changing as she looked around. 'I've travelled a lot over the years but Cariad Cove has something special. I didn't expect to find it in Wales...' She placed a hand on her chest. 'Gosh, I really hope that doesn't offend any of you. What I meant is that I'd never imagined how truly beautiful West Wales could be and I haven't even seen that much of it yet.'

'I wouldn't want to be anywhere else,' Will said, feeling slightly affronted by her comment but willing to give her the benefit of the doubt. He had friends from university who'd come to stay with him in Swansea, and they'd said similar things. He'd gone to Cardiff university, not wanting to go too far from home because of Kayla – who hadn't gone on to higher education as she already had a job in a surf shop in the Mumbles at the time. Will's English friends from university had returned to Swansea with him many times over the years because it was such an incredible place. Once you'd fallen for the Gower Peninsula, you'd want to return, Will felt sure.

Ffion was talking to Hannah about the previous day now; apparently they'd been for a walk together and they already seemed to be getting on well.

'You OK, Will?' Mari asked. Ffion's older sister lived on the same estate as Will, had popped by after he'd moved in just over eight months ago with a box of chocolates and a bunch of flowers. She was friendly and kind and had made him feel welcome. Her husband, Bryn, seemed all right too.

'Yes, thanks. I always feel good after a run although I'm sure the shower will soon be calling.'

'I know what you mean.' Mari lifted one arm slightly and waved a hand in front of her nose. 'But there's nothing like a good sweat for clearing out the pores. You happy term's finished?'

'Very. You?'

'Delighted. Even with working part-time now, I'm still glad when the holidays roll around, although how much of a holiday I'll get with my two... who knows?'

Will laughed. Mari's girls were a handful. Anwen was in Beti's class at school and Seren was just two. The younger child seemed to be going through the terrible toddler stage if the fuss she made when Mari or Bryn were trying to get her in the car in the mornings was anything to go by. Beti had gone through this stage too, but Will had been so busy trying to care for her alone that he'd barely noticed he was in the midst of it until it had passed. Or perhaps he'd been too heartbroken in the year after Kayla left him to be affected by his daughter's mood swings. What did a toddler tantrum matter in comparison to his partner running off with another man?

'I was thinking, actually,' Mari said, 'with Anwen and Beti having birthdays within days of each other, why don't we have a joint party?'

'Oh, that would be great.' He swallowed his surprise.

'We could have it at our house or I could see if Mam and Dad would let us have the marquee.' She pointed at the large white marquee that sat in the hotel grounds overlooking the sea.

Will's heart sank; something like that would be expensive and while he managed on one wage, he didn't have money to splash around.

'Don't worry, love,' Mari said, touching his arm. 'They won't charge us for it.'

He blinked, feeling embarrassed that she'd read his expression. 'It wasn't that.' He cleared his throat, aware that Ffion and Hannah were now listening. 'I just… uh… thought it sounded exciting.' He grinned, suspecting he probably looked like a ventriloquist's dummy and that Hannah was probably thinking that he was the village weirdo.

'I'll speak to my parents and let you know, though I'm sure it won't be a problem.'

'Thanks.' Will smiled at Mari then found his gaze straying to Hannah again, wanting one more look at her pretty face and to check if what he'd thought he'd seen in her eyes was still there.

'You'll have to join us on a run one day while you're here,' Ffion said to Hannah. 'It's a great way to see the coast.'

Hannah's cheeks flushed, surprising Will. He thought he was the only one around here who blushed easily.

'I haven't run in years,' Hannah said, pushing a strand of hair behind her ear. Will noted the small freshwater pearl in her lobe, the curve of her neck as she leant her head to one side. 'But I'd like to have a go. I think. At some point...'

'I'm sure we'll persuade you,' Ffion said. 'And if you don't want to run you can always sit on the beach and watch as we suffer.'

Hannah laughed then and it was like the sun had come out from behind a cloud. Will had to clamp his jaw shut. This was ridiculous, he hadn't looked at anyone like this since Kayla and he didn't know Hannah at all. She was just a writer passing through and, like the summer heat, she'd soon be gone and Will would be returning to school for the autumn term.

'We'd all support you along the way.' Will felt his eyes widen. Had he really just said that? He'd thought it but it seemed that the words had escaped from between his lips. Now it was his turn to blush.

Hannah looked at him and this time, when she smiled, it did reach her eyes. 'That's very kind of you.'

Blood raced through Will's body and his heartbeat pulsed through his ears. What the hell was happening?

'Right, let's go and get some refreshments,' Ffion said, leading the way.

Hannah and Mari followed Ffion inside and Will was left alone, his pulse rate slowing gradually, his blush fading, and the strange tension in his body trickling away. But the one thing that remained as if it had been burnt upon his brain was the image of Hannah's lovely smile.

A smile like that could start a thousand races or reward the winner at the finish line.

Chapter 7

Hannah got out of the car and looked around. Yesterday, Mari had invited her for Sunday lunch and she'd been delighted to accept. Ffion had offered Hannah a lift with her and Joe and they'd arrived at the hotel at noon as promised to pick her up. The drive had taken about half an hour and Hannah had watched as the coast had spread out to the right of the road while fields and houses lay to the left.

When they'd reached Swansea city, Joe had driven the car up a few steep roads to take them to the housing estate where Mari and Bryn lived with their daughters. Ffion had insisted that Hannah take the front passenger seat and she'd sat in the back while Joe's giant dog, Odin, sat in the boot and peered over the back seat breathing heavily, making Ffion squeal whenever drool landed on her.

During the drive, Hannah's thoughts had drifted to Will more than once. The handsome man had just finished a run when she'd first seen him, but rather than looking sweaty and dishevelled he'd made her think of dark-eyed, brooding heroes from romance novel covers. She'd been surprised when he'd come over to them and done her best not to stare at his broad shoulders and muscular chest under the tight running top, but her body had betrayed her when her heartbeat had sped up and she'd wondered what it would be like to be held against a chest like that. After they'd left him, Mari and Ffion had told her how nice Will was and that had made things worse in a way, because if they'd said he was a lothario who left a string of broken hearts in his wake, then she could have forgotten about him completely. But they'd sung his praises and so Hannah had found herself wanting to know more about him and to meet him again.

Mari and Bryn's house had a lovely view of Swansea. Hannah took a moment to appreciate it, her eyes scanning from the city off to the left then the beach, the seemingly endless horizon ahead and the Mumbles and curving coastline off to the right. In the sunlight, the sea was almost too bright to look at, its surface shining like a mirror that reflected the sky.

'Gorgeous view, isn't it?' Ffion had come to Hannah's side.

'Incredible. And you said that the old university campus used to be here?'

'One of them, yes. I think they offered subjects like English, Drama, Media and so on here.'

'It must have been an amazing place to study.' Hannah could picture a campus on the site: old formal buildings with high ceilings and echoing corridors, a busy canteen where students gathered between lectures and seminars, gardens abundant with trees and flowers. Some of the trees that would have been here when the university buildings were still grew strong and tall and she wondered how many students had sat under their branches, shading from the afternoon sun as they chatted with friends, read books for their courses or made notes in planners. She could almost feel the history of the location as if the ground had absorbed all the learning that had occurred there. And now, houses stood in the place of the university, homes for people who might never think about what had been there before. But for Hannah, she'd always been aware of the history of places, perhaps because her own history was so fragmented, with her paternal family a complete mystery. That sense of not fully knowing who she was because she hadn't known her father's identity, as well as not knowing her mum for long because of her early death, had left her feeling incomplete, rootless, uncertain. While those around her growing up had yearned for money, glittering careers and success, Hannah had yearned for a home, a family and a sense of belonging. As she'd got older, she'd told herself she didn't need those things, but at times like this, when thoughts of people and places, of how the past and the present combined, she felt the old longings resurfacing. Her desire to find a place to call home, somewhere she could feel safe and secure, could trust and love, would, it seemed, always be there, however hard she tried to push it away, however hard she tried to run from it.

'Hello you lot! What're you doing standing out here. Come on in.' Mari had appeared on her front step wearing a bright red apron, her cheeks glowing, her short brown hair shining in the sun. 'I'm cooking up a feast inside and could do with a cold glass of wine. How about you?'

She ushered them all inside and through to a large kitchen diner. A balding man stood at the stove stirring something. When he turned to greet them, Hannah saw that he had sweat on his brow and a substantial belly under his pale blue shirt.

'Hannah, this is my husband, Bryn.'

'Hello there!' He raised a whisk. 'Just making the gravy so I can't shake your hand but welcome to our home.'

'Thanks for having me.' Hannah held up the bottle of wine she'd brought. 'Sorry this isn't cold but I picked it up from a shop on the way here.'

'No problem at all.' Mari accepted the wine. 'I have several bottles chilling as we speak. Right, seeing as how it's so warm, why don't you go out into the garden, and Bryn and I will join you shortly?'

'I'll take Odin straight out,' Joe said, his hand gripping the dog's lead. 'Let him run off some steam before he sees the girls.'

'Good idea, Joe.' Mari smiled her approval.

'You don't need a hand with anything?' Ffion asked her sister.

'Everything's under control.' Mari winked twice at Ffion. 'Bryn is becoming quite the master of the Yorkshire pud.'

'Good to hear!' Ffion giggled and Hannah caught the glance that passed between the two sisters as if they were sharing a secret. Perhaps Bryn hadn't always been so talented in the kitchen, she thought. 'Come on, Hannah.'

Outside was a decked area with a patio table, chairs and a rectangle of grass surrounded by flower borders and a six-foot wooden fence. Trees lined the rear fence and Hannah could see bird feeders hanging from some of the branches as well as bird boxes fixed high up on the trunks. The air was filled with birdsong and she could imagine how pleasant it would be sitting out here on a warm day in this green and private space. It would be the perfect spot to sit with her laptop and write, especially if someone was inside cooking her a delicious dinner.

'Take a seat.' Ffion gestured at the chairs. 'I'll go and get some wine.'

Hannah sat down, watching as Joe followed Odin around the garden. He was a handsome man with short blond hair, piercing blue eyes and rugby player build. Joe and Ffion made an attractive couple and the spark between them was evident, the way they gazed at each other and their hands met regularly as if they couldn't bear not to be touching.

Joe looked up and caught her watching him. 'He's going to do a poo. I just know it.' He rolled his eyes. 'He loves to poo on someone else's garden. It's why I always come prepared.'

Joe waved a bright green poo bag in the air and Hannah laughed. 'Rather you than me. What breed is he?'

Joe frowned. 'A cross between a Doberman and a spaniel I think.'

Hannah looked at the dog's square head with fluffy ears and amber eyes and nodded. 'I can see that. But I always thought of Dobermans as being fierce and intimidating.'

'Odin's not at all. He's as soft as they come. Big, yes. Clumsy, yes. But the spaniel in him makes him incredibly energetic and a bit mad at times.'

'He's lovely.' Hannah had never had a dog or a pet of her own. Having to leave the home she'd shared with her mum after she'd become ill then moving between foster homes had meant that she'd never had the luxury of being able to ask for a pet. It would have made moving on even harder anyway, created a heartbreak she might never have recovered from. She'd kept her distance from people – even the nice foster parents, because after she'd had to leave the first foster home when the father there had lost his job and they'd decided to move, she'd been devastated. They'd told her it wasn't her, that they had no choice for financial reasons, but it had hurt Hannah to know she could be so readily returned, like a mistaken purchase from a shop, and she'd vowed never to let herself care about people again. And now, looking back, she knew that had been an enormous decision for such a young child to make. After losing her mum, she'd needed love and stability, understanding and consistency. It hadn't been the fault of the foster carers, but the system had seemed unable to cope with her needs, failing to provide the safety net she'd needed, and so she'd come to accept that the only person she could rely on was herself.

'Odin!' Joe's shout broke her train of thought and she shook herself and sat up straight. She'd done all right by herself. She had a good career and was independent. That was all she needed in life and attachment was for those who were used to being loved and feeling safe. People who needed that stuff. 'I don't believe you just did that right by the flower bed.'

Joe crouched down and the dog ran off, heading straight for Hannah. She flinched, holding her hands up as he sniffed at her legs, her waist, her face. Joe had said Odin was soft but this close, he seemed enormous, and when he placed a large heavy paw in her lap she almost screamed.

'You OK?' Joe rushed over, a full poo bag dangling from his hand. 'Sorry about this. He doesn't realise how big he is and he often charges at people, expecting everyone to like him.'

Hannah was leaning as far back in her chair as she could, the dog's meaty breath making her grimace.

'He won't hurt you, I promise.' Joe's voice was filled with concern now. 'Odin, come here.' He reached for the dog's collar and gently pulled him backwards so he was sitting on the decking next to Hannah's chair. His paw slid from her lap and Odin gave a low whine as if disappointed. Hannah released the breath she'd been holding and lowered her hands. When she looked at Odin he actually looked sad, as if he'd been keen to make friends and Hannah had rejected him.

'I don't know what happened then. I just panicked.' In spite of the fact that she was wearing a vest top, her armpits were warm and a bead of sweat trickled down her back and soaked into the waistband of her shorts.

'I can understand that. But I promise he's harmless. I'll keep him away from you though, if you like.'

'What's all this?' Ffion appeared with a tray of glasses of wine, looking from Hannah to Joe. A tiny line appeared between her brows. 'Has Odin done something?'

'He did a huge poo,' Joe held up the bag, 'then while I was picking it up he charged at Hannah.'

'You OK, Hannah?'

'I'm fine.' Hannah rubbed her forehead. 'I just... I'm not sure why I reacted like that.'

'He's a bloody massive dog, that's why. The first time I encountered him he knocked me right over, didn't he Joe?'

'He did. But accidentally.' Joe's eyes were wide.

'I know it was an accident.' Ffion set the tray down on the table and two glasses of wine clinked together. 'Odin is a big softy.' She rubbed his head and kissed the tip of his nose. 'Honestly, you couldn't find a nicer dog.'

Hannah sagged in her seat. 'I'm sorry.'

'Why're you sorry?' Ffion kissed the dog again then took a seat next to Hannah.

'I'm embarrassed about my reaction.'

'Well don't be. You're among friends and you have no need to be.' She handed Hannah a glass of wine. 'Have some of this. It's fresh and fruity and will hopefully help you feel a bit calmer.'

'Thanks.' Hannah took a sip and it was good so she took another.

'I'd better put this in the bin,' Joe said, holding the poo bag away from him. 'I think the bins are out the front of the house. You OK to have him?' he asked Ffion.

'Of course.' She took hold of the collar while Joe went to find the bin. 'You know… Odin had a rough start in life but he's OK now. In spite of all that happened to him, he's a very loving boy.'

Hannah set her glass down and shuffled forwards on her seat then held out a hand. Odin sniffed it then lifted a paw and placed it in Hannah's hand. She held it there, marvelling at the side of his pads, the thickness of his claws, the tufts of fur that poked out between the claws, soft and chocolate brown.

'Joe adopted him when he was a pup from the local animal sanctuary. Odin and his litter mates were found in a warehouse in Neath. They'd been left there to die.'

'That's awful!' Hannah shook her head, gazing into the dog's beautiful amber eyes. 'How could anyone do that?'

'I have no idea.' Ffion shook her head. 'And yet, that difficult start didn't leave Odin resenting people. He's sweet, funny and devoted to Joe. Dogs have an amazing capacity for healing. Whatever they go through, they emerge wanting to trust people again. I know it doesn't always work out for them, but with time, patience and lots of love, they can heal.' She met Hannah's gaze. 'A bit like people.'

Was Ffion reading her mind? Did she somehow know what Hannah had been through and she was trying to communicate it, or had she been through something herself? She lowered her eyes to Odin again and ran her free hand over his soft head, feeling tears prickling at her eyes. Odin had suffered, been abandoned, and now he was part of a loving family, even giving strangers like her a chance to befriend him. She was happy things had worked out for him and felt awful for being scared of him.

'Oh!' Ffion put her glass down on the table and poked out her tongue. 'I'm not sure about that wine. I've had it before but it tastes a bit strange.'

'Does it?' Hannah sat up and discreetly wiped at her eyes with the back of her hand. 'I thought it was lovely.'

'Perhaps there was washing up liquid in my glass or something.' Ffion shrugged. 'I know that Mari doesn't like to put her good glasses in the dishwasher. That's put me right off though so I think I'll go and get some water instead.' She stood up. 'You want me to take Odin inside?'

Hannah looked down at the dog and he cocked his head on one side as if asking her too.

'We'll be fine.' She took another sip of wine and smiled. 'Just fine.'

'You be a good boy, Odin. Back in a moment.'

Odin lay down on the decking next to Hannah's chair and they both gazed at the garden. She took a few deep breaths and a calm settled over her. If a dog could learn to trust again, then perhaps she could too. It would take time, good people and patience with herself, but the more she saw of Ffion, the more she liked her, and the more she could feel herself wanting to open up to friendship. Something tickled her toes and she looked down, expecting to see a fly or wasp, prepared to bat it away, but Odin had shuffled forwards so that his muzzle now rested on her foot.

She sat back slowly, not wanting to disturb him, privileged that he felt safe enough with her to make contact like that. His chin was warm and soft against her skin, his large presence reassuring and comforting. He had chosen to sit with her as if he understood her earlier reaction had been temporary and that she did want to be his friend. There were ways to communicate that didn't require words, and right now, Hannah felt peace and acceptance in that.

Pulling her sunglasses down from her head, she blinked hard, telling herself that her eyes were watering because it was so bright and that she was not becoming emotional. Hannah was tough, not prone to displays of emotion, whatever her blurred vision right now might suggest.

Wasn't she?

Chapter 8

Will knocked on the front door and waited. Next to him, Beti was hopping from foot to foot as if her excitement was too much to contain. She had a bag with her stuffed with toys that she said she might need when she played with Anwen and Seren.

'Best behaviour today, Beti.' He winced inwardly at the words. He sounded like his mum.

Beti peered up at him then stopped hopping and took his hand. 'I would never embarrass you, Daddy. I always try to be good.'

He swallowed hard. 'I know that, my angel, I just… I don't know why I reminded you, actually. You don't need reminding.'

Best behaviour… was like the other phrases he heard himself uttering regularly: *be careful on the slide, don't forget to wear your coat at breaktime, don't run when you're eating, don't put coins in your mouth, hold the banister when you descend the stairs…* What was it about parenting that made you repeat yourself constantly? He knew what. Beti was his world and he wanted to protect her, for her to grow up safe and healthy, for nothing bad to ever happen to her. Losing her mum as she had was enough for one lifetime. Nothing should ever hurt his little girl again. Of course, at night when Beti slept soundly and he lay awake, thoughts of how hard life could be and how one day, something, somewhere, would hurt Beti raced through his mind. He'd run through scenarios of what it might be, his stomach curdling with fear and horror, his heart hammering as he tried to think about how he could protect her. *From everything!* It could be a friend at school, a boyfriend, a co-worker, a car accident, a fall, an illness... anyone or anything, really. People got hurt, emotionally and physically, it was a fact. Unescapable. And he only had so much power to protect her though he'd give everything to keep her safe.

'Don't look so sad, Daddy.' Beti squeezed his hand. 'We're going to have a yummy lunch and spend time with nice people. It's a good thing.'

He laughed softly and squeezed her hand in return. 'Yes, we are. I'm not sad. I was just thinking about things.'

'Well, think about happy things or Mari will think you don't want to be here.'

'OK,' he said softly. 'Here's my smile.'

He curved his lips upwards and Beti gave him a nod of approval. 'That's better, Daddy. You look much more handsomer when you smile. If I'm not happy in school, my teacher says, "turn that frown upside down".'

'She's very wise.'

The door opened and Mari stood there. She looked hot and bothered, as if cooking a Sunday dinner in this heat was a bit much.

'For you.' He held out a bag with a tub of homemade chocolate chip ice cream, a bottle of chilled rosé and a small bag of sweets.

Mari peered inside the bag. 'Thank you, Will, that's so kind. You didn't have to do this, you know.'

'Thanks for asking us over. You didn't have to do that.'
He winked. 'Beti is beyond excited about playing with
the girls and I'm very much looking forward to lunch.
I've starved myself all day, haven't I Beti?'

His daughter tutted loudly. 'Don't fib, Daddy, you had a
bacon sandwich for breakfast then you had a banana before
we left because you said your tummy was rumbling.' She
laughed and held her belly as if he was the funniest man on
earth. 'You're such a fibber.' Then her expression turned
serious. 'My teacher says you shouldn't tell fibs because
people won't trust you.'

'That told me,' Will said, swallowing his laughter while
looking at Mari who was also clearly trying not to laugh.

'Come on in.' She stepped back then gestured at the
stairs. 'Anwen and Seren are upstairs in Anwen's room,
Beti.'

Beti looked at Will, a question in her eyes.

'Yes, go on.' He smiled and she kicked off her shoes
then climbed the stairs quickly.

Will bent over and picked up her shoes then looked
around.

'Just leave them there.' Mari pointed at a shoe rack to
the side of the door.

'Thanks.'

'You look like you need a glass of wine,' Mari said.
'And I know I do. I poured one and haven't had a chance
to take a sip yet.'

In the kitchen, Bryn was setting the table while Joe
helped. Ffion was standing with her back to the room,
gazing out the window. 'It's just the cutest thing ever, I...'
She trailed off as she turned around. 'Oh hello, Will.'

'Hi.' He gave a small wave. 'What's cute?' he asked, expecting her to say there was a baby bird being fed by its mother or a squirrel jumping from tree to tree.

'Come and see.' She waved him over and he went, tucking his hands in his shorts pockets. Ffion placed a finger over her lips and Will nodded his understanding.

He looked out of the window to the trees at the end of the garden but couldn't see anything, then movement on the decking right outside the window caught his eye. His breath caught in his throat at what he saw and he coughed to clear it.

Hannah was sitting on the decking, cross-legged, with Odin next to her. She had an arm around him and he was leaning into her, apparently listening as she spoke quietly to him. Even though the window was open, Will couldn't hear what she was saying, but Odin seemed to be completely absorbed.

'You know what they say about dogs, right?' Ffion whispered as she stepped away from the window and Will followed suit, albeit reluctantly.

'What's that?' he asked, thinking of the million things his mother told him about dogs every day.

'They know good people. Odin likes Hannah so she's clearly a good person.'

Will raised his eyebrows slightly then gave a small nod. 'My mother says that. She also says it works the other way round too. If a dog doesn't like someone, there's a reason.'

'I believe that,' Joe said, coming to Ffion's side. 'Odin loved Ffion immediately, and so did I.'

Ffion's cheeks coloured and Joe wrapped an arm around her shoulders and kissed her head.

'Cut it out, love's young dream!' Mari bustled over to them, a glass of wine in her hand. 'Here you are, Will. Now, Ffion I need you to help me with something upstairs before dinner's ready.'

'With what?' Ffion frowned.

'I'll tell you in a minute.' Mari shook her head. 'Will, why don't you go and sit in the garden? It's a bit cooler out there. The oven is making the kitchen hot enough to roast us all.'

'Joe, there's a fan in the garage if you fancy getting it.' Bryn was draining vegetables over the sink now. 'It's quite heavy, mind, it's one of those tower ones.'

'No problem.'

The women left the kitchen closely followed by Joe so Will went outside through the French doors, suddenly nervous at the thought of being out there alone with Hannah.

'Hi,' he said as he approached the patio table.

She looked up and recognition crossed her face. 'Oh, hello.'

Odin wagged his tail then got up and came to greet Will. 'Hey boy, how're you today? Finding it a bit warm?'

'He is warm but there's a breeze out here.' Hannah got up off the decking and went to sit at the table. 'You here for lunch?'

'I am. You?'

'Yes.' She picked up a glass of wine. 'I feel very lucky to have been invited.'

'Mari and Bryn are great. Since we moved to the estate, they've been really friendly. My daughter, Beti, loves their girls.'

Hannah gave a small smile. 'How old is Beti?'

'Six. Nearly seven, actually. That difference is very important to Beti.' He grinned then sipped his wine, gazing out at the garden. He felt stiff with tension, wondered if Hannah was feeling the same. 'You?'

'Me what?'

'You have any children?'

He saw her swallow. 'No.'

He smacked his forehead. 'I'm sorry. That was wrong of me to ask. I know that just because you're a woman of a certain age you don't have to be married or have children. I only asked because you asked about Beti and… and…' His cheeks burned and his palms felt sweaty.

Hannah was laughing as she met his eyes. 'It's fine. I'm not offended. I know some might be but it's fine. I'm a journalist so I'm used to asking lots of questions anyway.'

'Not like one of those paparazzi types?'

'Not at all.' She visibly shuddered. 'I write travel articles.'

'Of course. I knew you were here to write about Cariad Cove and the festival. Sorry.'

'It's fine, honestly. Most of my… uh… friends and acquaintances are married, getting married, planning a family and all that… just not me.'

He noted that sometimes when she smiled, a dimple appeared in her right cheek. It was a small one but cute. Perhaps it only appeared when she smiled properly, when she was relaxed.

'So what does your job entail? Where have you been over the years?' he asked.

She sipped her wine then set the glass down on the table. 'You want a list?'

'Please.' He sat back and waited.

Hannah described a variety of locations she'd visited and Will listened attentively, admiring how her face lit up as she described golden sands and crystal-clear seas, craggy mountains and waterfalls, luxury hotels and two-man tents. She was a good storyteller and he could see how she'd be a good writer. He made a mental note to look her up when he went home so he could read some of her work and see some of the photos she'd taken. She intrigued him and he wanted to know more; she seemed so brave and strong, so independent and adventurous. Beti would be entranced by her stories, he felt sure, and he hoped he could persuade her to tell some of them over dinner.

When Mari came outside to tell them that food was ready, he almost groaned with disappointment. He could have sat and listened to Hannah all afternoon; she was the most interesting person he'd met in a long time and, though he didn't want to admit it to himself, she was also the most beautiful. She had an inner radiance that shone from her eyes and it might have been the wine but he found himself wishing, just for a moment, that he could bask a little longer in her glow.

Chapter 9

'Cherry pie?' Mari asked as she cut into golden pastry exposing bright red cherries in a shiny red sauce. 'We have cream or custard to go with it.'

Hannah discreetly undid the top button of her shorts then held out her hands for the plate. 'Yes please!'

Dinner had been delightful and she'd eaten her fill and more. Her belly was straining against her shorts but the Sunday dinner had been too good to waste and when Bryn had offered her seconds, she'd been unable to refuse. She'd seen that Will had accepted more too and it made her feel better about her own lack of restraint.

While the adults sat at the kitchen table, the children had been seated at a smaller table on the decking just outside the French doors. Hannah had been aware of Mari and Will watching them like hawks might watch their chicks, keen to ensure that they were safe and eating their food, not being distracted by one another or by anything else. Mari had got up a few times to see to Seren, who was little more than a toddler and who, at one point, had managed to get an impressive amount of gravy in her mop of ginger curls. Meanwhile, Bryn had been the happy host, bringing more Yorkshire puddings to the table along with extra slices of tender beef and thick, rich brown gravy.

'Daddy!' Beti had come inside and was tugging at Will's hand. 'Come and sit outside.'

'I will do once we've finished dinner.' He reached out and tucked a strand of hair behind Beti's ear. It was a tender gesture and Hannah found herself watching them together, fascinated by their interaction. She had no point of reference to understand if all dads were like this, and she suddenly yearned for a close friend she could ring up to ask so she could share some of the burden of these new thoughts and feelings. Bryn spoke gently to his daughters and had picked Seren up when she'd come into the kitchen earlier, but there seemed to be a very close bond between Will and his daughter. She wondered where his wife or partner was and why she was missing this wonderful dinner.

'Will you play football with us?' Beti asked.

'Of course I will.'

'Will that lady play?' Beti peered around Will at Hannah, her amber eyes surrounded by dark lashes like Will's, a finger in the corner of her mouth showing her uncertainty about Hannah.

'Uhhhh…' Will glanced at Hannah so she smiled.

'I'll play. I love a game of football.'

Beti blinked at her and Hannah felt as if the little girl was sussing her out. 'Are you any good?'

Hannah paused as if mulling it over before giving a quick wink. 'I've been known to score a goal or two.'

'You can be on my team then,' Beti replied firmly.

'*Please*,' Will said making Beti turn her gaze on him.

'Pardon, Daddy?'

'You didn't say please when you asked Hannah to be on your team.'

'I thought she'd feel lucky, Daddy.'

Will sighed so Hannah leant closer to him. 'It's fine, honestly.' Then louder, she said, 'I'd love to be on your team, Beti.'

'Yay!' Beti grinned then skipped back outdoors, her curls bouncing.

'Thanks for that,' Will said, his brown eyes meeting Hannah's. She found herself wondering if the shadow of dark stubble on his jawline would rasp against her palm if she touched it.

'No problem.' Her voice wavered as she replied, and she had to make an effort to push her wayward thought from her mind.

'Beti is well mannered usually, but sometimes, when she's excited, she forgets to say please.'

'She's very young.' Hannah waved a hand. 'Honestly, it's fine.'

'Cherry pie, Will?' Mari held the spatula and knife aloft and he turned his attention to her.

'Yes, please.'

Hannah returned her attention to her dessert and poured some thick cream over the very tasty-looking pie. She ate slowly, savouring every mouthful, and let the conversation at the table wind around her like a hug. There was something so comforting about having dinner with other people, about being welcomed into their home and treated like one of the group. It didn't happen often for Hannah, very rarely in fact, and so she intended on making the most of the afternoon.

–

'Goal!' Beti shouted then ran in a circle around the garden. 'Hannah, you're amazing! You should always be on my team because you're much better than Daddy.'

Hannah smiled at the praise and at the comment about Will and gave a small bow.

'She's right,' Will said. 'You are good. I'm not sure you're better than me, of course, but time will tell.' There was laughter in his eyes and it made him look even more attractive.

'It's a relaxed game in a back garden. I'm hardly kicking it from one end of the pitch to another and I've never played professionally so I'm sure you are better than me.' Hannah laughed then wiped a hand over her brow. The late afternoon was warm, and after helping to tidy everything away following dinner, they'd been playing football for at least an hour. Beti was a serious organiser, putting the adults into two teams and telling everyone what their roles would be.

'I'd have you on my team any day,' Will said. 'Professional or not.'

Hannah stared at him and his face reddened, the flush spreading from spots on his cheeks to flood his face. 'I mean... You... Uh...'

Hannah smiled then looked away, not wanting to increase his embarrassment. People said things sometimes without thinking them through and Will's comment was innocent enough. Why he was blushing though, she wasn't sure, although from what she'd seen of him already, he did seem to be quite sensitive. She found it endearing, especially in light of the fact that a lot of men she'd encountered over the years were uber confident and self-assured. When she went abroad and worked out in the hotel gyms, she'd been approached many times by confident men with rippling muscles who walked as if they carried rolls of carpet under their arms. Those men liked themselves – a lot – and assumed Hannah would like them too. Sure, she'd had drinks with some of them, even spent the night with one or two of them if she was in the mood for company, but that was where it ended. There was no lasting attraction, no bond that made her want to take their number, nothing that endeared them to her. Perhaps it had nothing to do with how they looked and more to do with her. She'd never been in the market for more, had never sought out a man to fall for, never wanted to know more about a man.

Until now…

What?

Where had that voice come from? She'd clearly had too much wine and too much sun.

'I'm going to go and wash my hands,' she said to no one in particular then hurried inside. In the small toilet off the kitchen, she ran the cold tap and put her wrists under the flow. It was a trick she'd used before to cool down and when it failed to work quickly this time, she leant over the sink and scooped up handfuls of water then splashed it over her face.

Meeting her eyes in the mirror, she stared hard at her reflection. Her hair was sticking out like a frizzy halo, so she smoothed her damp hands over it then wet them again. Why she had to have hair that went from wavy to frizz instead of gorgeous soft curls like Beti, she had no idea. She suspected that Will had those same curls but his hair was short enough that they didn't get a chance to fully develop. Did Beti get her curls from his side of the family or from her mum's or from both parents? Hannah's mum had straight hair so hers must come from a different generation on her mum's side or from her father. The old longing to know more about her family history welled inside her and she sighed. Spending time with other people's families was heart-warming but it also brought things to the surface that she was usually so good at squashing.

A loud banging on the door made her jump.

'Let me in!' It was Beti. 'Please… I'm bursting big time.'

Hannah opened the door to find Beti jigging up and down.

'Ooh! It's coming.' Beti hobbled inside and before Hannah could turn away, she was on the toilet seat, legs swinging as she sighed with relief.

'I'll just… leave you to it.' Hannah averted her eyes, pulling the door closed behind her.

'No! It's OK,' Beti said. 'I'm nearly done.'

'I was just going, anyway.' Hannah kept her eyes on the kitchen units ahead of her.

'Don't close the door,' Beti said. 'I might get stuck.'

'Really?' Hannah said, the urge to flee welling inside her now. She didn't do children; didn't know what was expected of her in situations like this.

'I'm done!' Beti flushed the toilet then Hannah heard the taps go on. 'Dammit to bloody hell! I can't reach the soap.'

'Oh…' Hannah turned around, suppressing her laughter, and picked up the liquid soap bottle then squeezed some onto Beti's hands. The little girl washed them thoroughly then dried them on the hand towel.

'Thank you for helping,' Beti said, smiling up at Hannah. 'You're very good at football.'

'Thanks.'

A tiny frown marred the flawless skin of Beti's brow. 'You're very pretty too... but not as pretty as Miss Dix, my teacher in school. She's got longer hair.'

'Uhhh... thanks.' Hannah bit the inside of her cheek as she tried not to laugh. 'That's a very nice compliment.'

'What's a compliment?' Beti's frown deepened.

'When you say something nice to someone.'

'Do me a compliment.' Beti's amber gaze bored into Hannah while she tried to think of what to say.

'You... are...' *Think of something that's not connected to appearance!* 'You... are... clearly a very intelligent young lady.'

Beti pursed her lips then exhaled loudly. 'I guess that'll do. My teacher says that intelligence and hard work matter more than looks.'

'And she's right.' Hannah was impressed.

'Is that why you have hairy knees?'

'What?' Hannah looked down and sure enough, she'd missed her knees with the razor in the shower that morning and must have been walking around like this all day. Something bubbled in her chest and then laughter burst from her and she leant over, hands on her hairy knees.

Mari appeared in the kitchen with Seren on her hip. 'What's funny?'

'Hairy... knees.' Hannah gasped as she stood up and when she saw the confused expression on Beti's face, she laughed even harder.

'Hairy knees?' Mari asked.

Beti walked away shaking her head. 'I'll never under-stand grown-ups.'

Hannah met Mari's gaze and the two of them started laughing. Hannah laughed so hard her stomach and her cheeks began to ache and just when she'd begun to calm down, Will came inside and asked why she and Mari were so red, which set them off again.

When Hannah finally regained her composure, she was hot and sweaty again so she went back to the toilet to wash her face, and couldn't help smiling at her reflection even though her face was aching now. She felt like she'd just released something that she'd been holding inside for some time and it was all thanks to a six-year-old girl named Beti.

Chapter 10

'What's new with you?' Will's sister, Alice, picked a breadstick from the glass on the table then munched on the end.

'What's new with me?' Will shifted in his seat. 'Nothing, I guess.'

'Nothing? Oh come on, William, I can see it from here.' Alice pushed her long brown hair back behind her ears. She usually wore it in a neat bun or chignon so he was surprised to see it down today.

'See what?'

'Something's happened.' Alice ate while keeping her dark brown gaze fixed on Will. Her eyes gave nothing away; her face was a flawless pale mask that hid her emotions unless she wanted to reveal them. She was a criminal lawyer and practised at concealing her thoughts and feelings; it was part of her job to appear to be shocked by nothing, to be in complete control of her expressions so as not to reveal any weaknesses to the opposing side in a courtroom. Knowing her as he did, Will was aware that Alice felt things deeply, that she worried and was unnerved by things but that she was good at hiding her innermost reactions. She also had a way of eliciting the truth that was part training and part instinct.

'Why do you say that?' Will picked up a breadstick and popped the end in his mouth, not because he wanted it but because he wanted to buy himself some time. It seemed that this evening's visit to the cosy Italian restaurant in the Mumbles was not going to be as relaxing as he had hoped.

'I can see something in your eyes that's not usually there. Has Kayla been in touch?'

Will avoided the question, turned his phone over and glanced at the screen. Nothing. No messages or missed calls.

'Beti will be fine, Will. She's with Mam and Dad, so she'll be having a great time.'

'Just checking. I have to make sure that I haven't missed any texts or calls. It's part of being a parent.'

'And I wouldn't understand that, right?' Alice's face was still expressionless but her tone was different, laced with an edge.

'I didn't say that, Alice.'

'No but everybody else thinks it. Alice the "spinster career woman" doesn't have a clue what it's like to be a parent. Poor Alice. Awww, bless her. No man will gift her his seed for her empty womb so she can't have a baby and live happily ever after.'

Will snorted. 'Not this again.'

Now Alice cocked an eyebrow then her lips curved upwards. 'Well, it's what some people think. Why don't they understand that not every woman has to have a husband and a family? I am perfectly happy with my life exactly as it is and have no desire to settle down or procreate. I'm not judging anyone who does but I wish they'd stop judging me.'

'I'm sure your partners in the law firm don't feel that way.'

'That's true.' She finished her breadstick then sipped her water. 'I think old Jonty would have a fit if he got a whiff of my ovaries revving up.'

'I'm sure he would.' Jonty was one of the four partners in the law firm where Alice had started as an intern and worked her way to the top. She had become a force to be reckoned with over the years and Will was very proud of her. If ever he knew of anyone in trouble or need of legal advice, he recommended his sister and her partners every time. Even if it wasn't the type of case she dealt with she would refer them to someone who could help, so extensive was her contact list now. Several times, other firms had tried to poach her but Alice was loyal and refused to be wooed.

'Anyway, we digressed slightly there, Will. What I was asking, rather indirectly perhaps, was if there is a new love interest in your life.'

'A love interest?' Will said rather loudly which he regretted instantly because a waiter had appeared at his elbow. They ordered their meals and a bottle of red wine and he took a deep breath, preparing to answer Alice's questions. He wasn't quite sure what she wanted to know but experience told him that she often knew something about him before he was even aware of it himself.

Wine sampled and poured, Will and Alice were left alone again. The restaurant was one Will had been to several times over the years, owned by the same couple for as long as he could remember. They always made an effort to greet returning customers warmly, asking about their families. Years ago, Will had come here with Kayla and his parents. Then, when Will had gone back there after Kayla had left, he'd been asked about Kayla, if she was well, where she was that evening. Luckily, he'd been with Alice and she'd answered for him, clear and brief, before settling Will at a table and heading for the bathroom. During that absence from the table Will suspected she'd gone to find the owners to let them know the basics of his situation so they didn't enquire after Kayla again. Of course, they didn't go around telling everyone their business but it would also spare the blushes of the restaurant owners when Will next came for a meal.

'Back to my question, Will.' Alice raised her wine glass. 'Has someone caught your eye?'

'It's the holidays,' he said.

'Evasive.' She frowned, the wine relaxing her and revealing Alice-the-sister with expressions aplenty as Alice-the-lawyer stepped aside.

'I haven't been anywhere, really.'

'You broke up last week.' It was a statement but Will felt its weight as a question.

'I did.'

'And you've been nowhere in the meantime?'

He picked up his wine and gazed into the ruby liquid. 'I went for a run with the club and I went to a friend's for Sunday lunch.'

'Your neighbours' house?'

'That's right.'

'Aha!' She wagged a finger at him. 'There was someone else there. Someone who's not usually there. Someone you like…'

Will rolled his eyes dramatically in the way he used to do as a teenager. It had always got to Alice then but now it had no effect at all.

'There was a woman there and you found her attractive. That's what it is. After all those years alone, not seeing anyone at all, you've met someone who makes your heart lift.'

'All right, Poirot.' Will laughed. 'But you're seeing more in it than there actually is.'

'Will... I have known you all your life. I'm used to working people out, to assessing whether they're telling the truth – to me and to themselves – and you look different. I hate to admit this, baby brother, but you've seemed so switched off since Kayla left. You're an amazing dad and Beti adores you but you don't seem... lit up by anything anymore. When we were kids you always had this happy glow about you then you fell in love with Kayla and that glow intensified to the point that I was worried you'd spontaneously combust. But when she left... It was heartbreaking. Mam and Dad were so worried about you. I was worried about you.'

Will put his glass down and adjusted the cutlery on the table in front of him. He loved Alice but sometimes her frankness was hard to handle, the things she said often difficult to hear.

'I'm doing OK,' he said. 'I have Beti, you, Mam, Dad and a job I love.'

'And you have friends too, I know that, but you're a young man and you are entitled to have someone special in your life.' She held up a hand. 'I mean apart from Beti. You should have a woman to love who loves you.'

'Pot and kettle?' He tilted his head on one side.

'We're different, Will. I'm fulfilled. Independent. I don't need someone in my life.'

Will pushed his hands through his hair. 'I don't need someone.'

'Maybe not… but you can't deny that if you had someone, you'd be happy about it.'

He cleared his throat, lowered his eyes to the table. Alice wasn't entirely wrong. He had thought about how it would be if he had a partner, someone to love who loved him and Beti, but it was all so complicated.

'I know what you're thinking now.' Alice took another breadstick. 'That you can't possibly risk a relationship because of Beti.'

'I can't let her get hurt. She's far too precious and she's been through enough.'

'What makes you think that a new relationship would go wrong?'

'I've hardly been successful thus far, have I?'

'You had *one* relationship.' Alice held the breadstick up to make her point. 'One. How does that prove anything? Kayla was wrong for you from the start. We could all see it but Mam and Dad said you had to make your own choices, that we had to let you make your own mistakes even if we did all want to stop you falling for her.'

It wasn't the first time Will had heard these arguments but they still smarted.

'Maybe that's all true. I don't know. It's difficult because of Beti and sometimes I can't remember how I felt about Kayla because whatever happened, I have Beti because of her. But… I think I loved her.'

'And she's gone. With someone else. You can give yourself permission to move on. And stop using Beti as an excuse to stay single.'

'That's an awful thing to say. Beti isn't an excuse for anything.'

'It's true though, Will. Beti will grow up and move out and you'll be left alone, an ageing teacher wearing patterned cardigans and Sta-Prest trousers, going to bed at nine and hobbling around because your knees are shot after all that running.'

Will laughed although the image was not pleasant. He knew that Alice was teasing him but of course he'd thought about what would happen when Beti grew up and left home. Not often, because she was still just a little girl and he wanted to treasure every moment and to be present for it, but now and then, thoughts of the future crept in and he did struggle to imagine what lay ahead for him.

'OK… you're right. There was a woman at Mari and Bryn's and she is… quite lovely.'

'Quite lovely? That's so sweet.' Alice's eyes lit up, she was clearly satisfied now she'd got to the bottom of things. 'Tell me more.'

'I don't know much more. She's a journalist… staying in Cariad Cove. She's here to write about the Summer Festival. She's quite successful in her field… according to the articles I've read.'

'You've checked her out!' Alice clapped her hands. 'You must really like her.'

Will gave a small shrug, irritated by the heat crawling up his neck. Why was it that even now his sister could make him blush?

'I was interested in finding out what she'd written, that's all.'

'Is she pretty?'

There was a beat of silence. Will touched the stem of his wine glass, gazing at his distorted reflection in the side of the glass.

'Yes.' He looked up and Alice was nodding her approval. 'Very. But it's more than that… she's interesting and intelligent and Beti really seems to like her. Beti made her play football and asked her lots of questions and… well… she told me when we were back at home that she likes Hannah and wants her as a friend.'

'Hannah. Nice name.' Alice raised her eyebrows. 'And is that all Beti said?'

Will swallowed hard. Beti had also asked Will why she couldn't have a mummy like Hannah who'd play football and have Sunday dinner with them and help her wash her hands. Will had been gobsmacked, struggled to answer the questions because deep inside he'd been asking the same things too.

'Be kind to yourself, Will. Give this one a chance and see where it goes.'

'You're completely jumping the gun here, Alice. Nothing happened between me and Hannah. Nothing at all.'

Their food arrived and Will and Alice tucked in. He held his sister's words in his head, turning them round and round, trying to decide if her advice was right or if it would just lead him along a path to heartbreak once more.

He had two hearts to consider now, two hearts to protect, but he was also starting to wonder if by being so protective he was also robbing those two hearts of the potential happiness of bringing someone else into their lives.

Chapter 11

The last Saturday of July arrived, bringing with it the start of the Cariad Cove Summer Festival. When Hannah went down for breakfast, the hotel was busy despite it being just after eight. She helped herself to coffee, poached eggs and toast from the buffet then sat outside in the garden to eat, observing the hotel staff as they scurried about. Other guests brought their breakfasts outside, some of them saying good morning to Hannah, now recognising her as a guest too.

All week, since dinner at Mari's on the Sunday, there had been one thing or another happening in and around the hotel, along the beach and in the beach car park as people prepared for the festival. Bunting had been hung from lampposts and trees, colourful signs directing visitors to the beach and the stalls at the village had been set up along the roads and junctions, and cones had been used to reserve spaces in the hotel car park for special guests.

The previous evening, as dusk fell, Hannah had strolled down to the beach after dinner to find a local band consisting of two female singers, two men playing acoustic guitars and a third on a harmonica sitting around a fire. They'd covered songs from bands including The Beatles, The Eagles and Neil Diamond, all songs that made her think of her mum, and Hannah had been drawn to their periphery. She'd sat on the sand near them, enjoying the music and the way that they encouraged their audience to sing too. Soon, there had been around fifty people gathered and although Hannah had been self-conscious about singing at first, she soon forgot her anxiety and joined them. When someone had handed her a beer too, she felt like a part of the group and her inhibitions fell away like the sand that dropped from her trousers when she stood up to dance.

It had been an enjoyable few hours, drinking beer from a bottle, her bare feet in the sand, while music filled her heart and moved her body. She'd felt as if her mum was with her, smiling her approval, singing along with them all.

Walking back to the hotel, she'd felt there was something magical about Cariad Cove in the way it could get inside you and release things you'd long since buried. It was uplifting and also terrifying because Hannah had worked hard to push certain memories away, but she could see how being in Cariad Cove might work them loose. However, the joy she'd experienced at the beach and the sense she'd had of her mum being near, even if only in her heart and mind, led her to decide to relax and see what happened during her stay. Remembering might not be easy but sometimes forgetting was just as hard to do.

Last night, Gwen Evans had told Hannah that it would be a busy weekend as stall holders arrived for the festival, and that if Hannah had any intention of leaving the cove, she'd find it difficult because of the sheer volume of traffic expected. Luckily the walk from the hotel to the village was a short one and Hannah knew that if she needed anything she could get it at the village shop although, right now, everything she needed was right there in the cove.

When she'd finished her breakfast, she took the plate and mug inside then went back up to her room to grab her camera, bag and sunhat then she went back down and headed for the beach. She felt a flutter of excitement inside at the prospect of the days ahead. Coming to the hotel early had been a good plan because it had helped her get a sense of the village and the cove before the festival, as it would be during the holiday season. The magazines she was writing for wanted details about the location and the build-up to the festival as well as its duration, but Hannah knew she could use the knowledge she'd gained to write about Cariad Cove for other articles if she wanted to do so. She was already wondering what it was like there through the seasons, especially in the autumn when the leaves on the trees would change colour and make for fantastic photographs and then in winter when the sea grew choppy and the sky turned slate grey.

But for now, she needed to focus on the festival and anything else could be considered once the season was done.

–

Will parked his car in the village at Cariad Cove, knowing that if he drove it down to the beach, he'd probably have trouble getting out at the end of the day. He'd smothered Beti in sunblock that morning, so much that she looked paler than usual, then taken deep breaths as she'd told him what she wanted to wear – a mermaid outfit complete with tail and long pink wig. Then he'd used reverse psychology to convince her to wear something sensible.

He knew that she'd want to go in the water at some point, so had packed towels, her costume and spare shorts for himself – but also wanted her to be cool enough while they walked around, so a white T-shirt and shorts seemed the most sensible option. Beti wrinkled her nose at his suggestion but when he told her that most people would wear shorts as it was going to be hot, Beti had asked if Hannah would be wearing them too and he'd told her that he expected she would. Beti had begged him to text Hannah and ask, which he'd made all manner of excuses to avoid doing, but thankfully Beti had seemed to come to her own conclusion in the end and dressed in the shorts and T-shirt. Although when she'd asked him to shave her knees so they'd look good in her shorts, he'd had to fake a desperate urge to use the bathroom to avoid having a long conversation about why it was fine that she had tiny blonde hairs on her legs. That would keep for another day…

While Will had prepared a packed lunch, Beti had gone to brush her teeth and find her sunhat. As he chopped tomatoes, he thought about how much easier it would be if Beti had a mother to ask about outfits and hairy knees. Didn't little girls emulate their mums? Alice had when they'd been young, often wanting her hair done like their mam's or to borrow her jewellery, to have a squirt of her perfume. It had changed when Alice had become a teenager though, all scowls, black lipstick and loud music, but that had been a phase and soon she'd emerged as a sophisticated young woman, her respect for their mam restored. Dorothy had been patient with Alice, seeming to let Alice's jibes roll off her back like water off a duck's feathers. But then she'd had the support of her husband

and her experience as a teacher to fall back on, and surely two parents were stronger than one?

Will wondered how he'd manage when Beti became a teenager. Would he remain calm and collected or become a jabbering wreck? Beti already tested him with her formidable will and feisty personality, but he was able to speak to her calmly and to reason with her – most of the time. As she aged though, would this get harder to do and would she lash out at him, her only parent? The thought made his chest tighten because he loved her with everything that he had and couldn't bear the thought of her ever being angry with him or even hating him. And yet, he would be the only person she could rebel against and so he knew that it was a possibility. He'd spoken to enough parents at school to know that teenagers often turned against their parents because they were the safe harbour, the only people they could turn their frustration on, knowing that they wouldn't be abandoned.

'I'm ready, Daddy!'

He turned to find Beti grinning at him. 'Yes you are. I won't be long.'

He turned back to the counter, love flooding through him. Beti was still wearing the shorts and T-shirt but she'd somehow managed to tuck the mermaid tail in the back of her shorts and it now floated behind her like a train on a princess gown. And that was fine by him because Beti was, and always would be, his little princess.

–

Shouts and laughter reached her ears and Hannah raised a hand to shade her eyes as she peered up the beach. Not far from the Cariad Cove Hotel was a car park where stalls had been set up. Colourful bunting flapped in the breeze and the awnings of stalls fluttered around their stands like giant white butterflies trying to take off. Aromas of hot dogs and onions, donuts and candyfloss filled the air, tempting people to eat alfresco.

Hannah raised her camera and snapped some photos of the scene, admiring the contrast of the sand dunes and the stalls, the trees and the hotel, with its black roof tiles, arched windows on the first floor and French doors that opened out to the lush and resplendent grounds. With the sun glinting on its windows, the different shades of green in the surrounding trees and bushes and the pots and hanging baskets filled with colourful flowers in full bloom, it looked like a glorious place to stay. The kind of hotel that would win awards, the kind of hotel she realised she wanted to tell the world about.

Ffion had told Hannah about how Gwen and Aled Evans had worked hard to build their business and to adapt to changes over the years, and they'd done well. They were also delightful people and Hannah felt that Ffion and Mari were lucky to have them as parents, knew that she'd have treasured them had they been her own. But then, she wondered, did people ever really know how lucky they were? Was it only when you lacked something that you could actually appreciate its worth?

She turned back to the sea, breathing in the clean air that was laced with the tang of seaweed and salt. She'd worn her flip-flops down to the beach but had tucked them into her small rucksack so she could walk in the water and now the sea lapped at her white shins, cool and so clean she could see the dark green seaweed floating nearby, the shells on the seabed, the tiny translucent fish that darted nervously around.

The beach was already starting to get busy and she suspected that by noon, there would be hordes of people vying for space on the sand, purchasing food and drinks from the stalls and browsing the wares on offer from local businesses. She'd head up to the stalls now and interview some of the visitors there to find out what had drawn them to the location, as well as some of the stallholders to ask what they expected of the festival while they still had time to talk.

—

'What about here as a base?' Will asked as he gestured at a space on the sand near the dunes. They could set up their picnic blanket, windbreaker and cooler and be free to swim, build sandcastles or browse the stalls in the nearby car park.

Beti shrugged. 'I guess it's all right, Daddy.'

'Just all right?'

She giggled. 'I was teasing you, silly sausage! It's fabulous and will be a good base, Daddy.'

Will put the cooler down then slid the rucksack off his back, laughing softly. It always amused him when Beti repeated words and phrases he'd used. She was like a mini version of him and he knew it was because they spent so much time together. Of course, she also repeated things his mam and dad said too, and sometimes she said things she'd heard Alice say – but the latter wasn't always a good thing, especially if she was using Alice's occasional explet-ives. Alice wasn't always PG-friendly when she talked and Beti was always hungry to develop her vocabulary, so when aunt and niece got together, Will often found himself on tenterhooks wondering what Alice would say next.

Once Will had created a cosy area for them, he stood up and looked around. 'What would you like to do first, Beti?'

'Swim!' She waved her mermaid tail around.

'That tail's not made for going in the sea though. You know that, right?'

'Mermaid tails are made for the water.' She pouted. 'You know that, right?'

'Beti... that tail is part of a dressing-up costume so wearing it in the water will probably ruin it. Come here.' He knelt down and took hold of the tail then read the label on the underside. 'See... it says *wipe clean only*.'

'But I want to swim like a mermaid.' She undulated her body to demonstrate what she meant.

'Then we'll have to look for a tail that you can wear in the water. OK?'

Beti peered up at him then her shoulders relaxed. 'OK. Promise we can find a real one.'

'I'm not sure that it will be a real one as mermaids aren't real...' He bit his lip, experiencing that feeling that stopped him in his tracks when he'd slipped up and said something he shouldn't. But it was OK... this wasn't about Santa or the tooth fairy. 'Anyway... I'm sure we can find one that you can wear in the water.'

'Yay!' Beti tugged the tail out of her shorts then lay it down on top of the cooler. 'Let's get changed quickly. Oh, and Daddy?'

'Yes?'

'Mermaids are so real! I watched a docermentry about a man who found one in a swamp.'

'Oh… OK.' Will decided to let the subject drop for now whilst making a mental note to ask his mam and dad if they'd been letting Beti watch the Discovery Channel again.

Will held a towel up so Beti could put her swimming costume on then he undressed, glad that he'd had the foresight to put his board shorts underneath his clothes just before they left home.

'You're ready already!' Beti clapped her hands. 'Clever Daddy.'

'So I am.' Will placed his hands on his hips and looked down at himself before reaching into his bag. 'Here, put your armbands on.' He blew one up and gave it to her then did the other one.

'Come on then.' Beti took his hand and they jogged down to the water, passing families on towels and picnic blankets, in deckchairs and with colourful umbrellas and windbreakers. Dogs barked, children laughed and screamed, and the smell of coconut sun cream filled the air. Summer had come to Cariad Cove and it was glorious.

When they reached the water, Will slowed down, keen to acclimatise gradually to the cold. Beti gasped as the water lapped at her toes, legs and belly, still holding tight to Will's hand.

'You OK?' he asked.

'It's chilly.' She nodded, her teeth chattering. 'Makes me want to do a wee.'

He chuckled. 'You'll get used to it soon.'

When the water was up to Beti's chest, Will lowered himself into the water so just his shoulders were still out, unconsciously tensing as the water caressed his skin. He took both of Beti's hands and they rode the gentle waves, bobbing along on them. Will walked out a bit further so he could lift his feet from the seabed too.

'Don't let go of me, Daddy.'

'I won't. I promise.'

'Look at that!' Will followed the direction of Beti's gaze. Two teenaged boys were floating around on inflatable dolphins, using their hands to paddle along, laughing as if they hadn't a care in the world.

'Pretty cool, huh?'

'I wish I had one.' Beti watched the boys as they moved away. 'They are the most beautifulest things in the world.'

'We can get you an inflatable.'

'Can we? But only if you stay with me, Daddy, because otherwise I could float away and get caught on the tide and then you'd have to call out the lifeboat and I'd be on the news and everybody would be worried and Mummy would be cross and...' Beti frowned. 'Would she be cross, Daddy?'

Will's mouth was dry because of the picture Beti had just painted. The idea of her drifting away and being in danger had roused his biggest fears. 'Sorry?'

'I said would Mummy be cross if I floated away?'

He felt Beti's amber eyes roaming over his face, sensed her desperation to hear that Kayla cared about her enough to worry if she was swept away on an inflatable. There was a heaviness in his chest as he opened his mouth to reply.

'I don't think she would be cross... but she would most definitely be worried. She might be a bit cross with me, actually, if I was irresponsible enough to allow you to get into danger, but she wouldn't be cross with you. Not at all.'

'Would she be worried enough to come home to see me?'

Will closed his eyes for a moment, telling himself that his vision had blurred because of the salt water. When he opened them again, he blinked a few times. 'Mummy would be worried, Beti, but it's not going to happen because I'm here and I'll never let anything hurt you.'

Avoidance tactics, that was what his mother called it when he didn't give Beti a direct answer. She understood why, she had told him, and in some circumstances, it was wise to avoid giving Beti an answer that would hurt her and to avoid telling an outright lie. But, she had also said, at some point in time Will would have to be completely honest with Beti and tell her that Kayla was not coming home and that she had built herself a new life without them. For Will, the thought of Beti being hurt by the truth was heartbreaking, and it drove him to be the best possible dad he could be for his daughter. If only things had worked out differently and Kayla had been happy with her life in Wales then Beti would have a mum and dad together and all would be well.

But would it? Really?

Being a teacher, he'd had training about how to help children with all sorts of backgrounds and emotional diffi-culties, and that had informed him that sometimes it was better for people to separate than to stay together just because of the children. If two adults were unhappy in their relationship then that could be detrimental for the children and separating might well be the best move for all concerned. Kayla would have been unhappy if she'd stayed with him and that would have made him and Beti unhappy. As it was, they enjoyed their time together and with Will's parents and Alice, and Kayla stayed in touch with Beti via video call – even if it wasn't as often as Will would have liked for Beti's sake.

'Don't be sad, Daddy.' Beti squeezed his hands. 'I love you.'

He tried to swallow the lump in his throat. 'I love you too.'

'Shall we go back and have something to eat. I'm starving now and I've just done a wee.'

Will bit his lip and looked at the sky as he tried not to laugh. 'I don't think it's quite lunch time.'

'That doesn't matter. It's the summer holidays. We can eat whenever we want to, remember?' Beti grinned at him.

'You're right. It doesn't matter at all. And if we eat all our packed lunch now, we can have something from the stalls later on.'

'Ice cream?'

'Yes.'

'Hot dogs?'

'If you like.'

'Popcorn?'

'Are you *that* hungry?' he asked, laughing.

'Daddy, you have no idea.'

He guided them towards the shore until Beti could reach the seabed again then they waded back to the sand. As they walked up the beach, he spotted a familiar face and his stomach fluttered. The woman glanced away as if embarrassed but when she looked at him again, he hesitated for a fraction of a second before raising his hand in greeting and pointing to the base he'd set up near the dunes. When Hannah gave him a thumbs up, the fluttering in his stomach increased.

She was coming over…

Chapter 12

Hannah weaved her way around couples and families, avoiding excited dogs and toddlers, looking up every so often to check she was heading in the right direction.

After spending some time interviewing tourists and stall holders, she'd gone back down to the beach to get some photos and she'd caught sight of two familiar figures emerging from the sea. Will had come from the shallows holding Beti's hand, the water running from his skin making it glisten in the sunlight. Hannah had tried not to stare at him but she couldn't fully ignore his attractive muscular physique, the fact that he was strong and toned, and the sight of him made her knees weaken as some primitive part of her responded to him. And then there was Beti: small, happy, sweet, chatty. Beti didn't seem to pause for breath as they walked up the beach while Will smiled and bobbed his head indulgently. He seemed to be a good person, a good father and also… he was simply gorgeous.

And then he'd looked up and caught Hannah staring at him. She'd dragged her gaze away, her cheeks flaming in mortification. She wished the beach would open up and swallow her whole, suck her down like quicksand. But of course it didn't, and so when she'd allowed herself to look at him again and he'd waved at her, she'd waved back. He appeared to gesture at an area near the dunes so she'd given him a thumbs up and was now heading over there, hoping with all her heart that he'd be dressed again by the time she reached them. The last thing she wanted was to feel the awkwardness of speaking to him while trying not to stare at his broad shoulders, defined pecs or those carved abs.

What are you, Hannah, a teenager with no self-control?

She shook the voice away. It was fine to find someone attractive. Absolutely fine. And yet with Will, it was more than the fact that he had a good body, a handsome face and eyes like melted chocolate. It was the fact that he seemed so genuine, to be such a good father and also, perhaps, because she'd seen a fleeting sadness in his eyes that made her wonder where Beti's mum was. So far, she'd only seen him alone or with Beti. Could he be separated or divorced, possibly even widowed? Hannah had never felt an urge to look after a man, to care for one, but when she was around Will she had found herself wondering – while he was looking after Beti, who was looking after him?

When she reached the spot near the dunes, she cleared her throat to announce her arrival and Will appeared from behind a windbreaker.

'Hello.' He smiled shyly.

Hannah was relieved to see that he was wearing a T-shirt with his board shorts.

'Hi.' She tucked her hands in her pockets. 'Did you have a nice swim?'

'The water's lovely.'

'What about you, Beti?'

The little girl stuck her head around the windbreaker. 'It was good but now I can't get my T-shirt back on.' Beti had managed to get her T-shirt caught so that one arm was through the neck hole and the rest of it was twisted. 'I didn't dry properly.'

'Come here.' Will reached for Beti and she allowed him to take the T-shirt and shake it out then put it over her head. 'Better?'

'Much better, Daddy.'

'Let's get some more sunblock on you then we can eat.'

Beti groaned and rolled her eyes dramatically. 'I hate having sunblock on. It's yucky and all the sand will stick to my skin.'

'But that's a lot better than sunburn.' Will shook the bottle of sunblock and Beti pulled a sunhat on then stood in front of Will while he rubbed the viscous white fluid over her hands and arms, legs and feet and the back of her neck.

'Now I'll do you.' Beti took the sunblock and Will crouched down while she smeared sunblock over his neck and ears then over his arms. While she slathered him with the sticky white cream, he glanced up occasionally at Hannah. 'Ha ha, Daddy, you look like a snowman.'

Will patted his cheeks then rolled his eyes. 'How much did you use, Beti?'

'Enough to stop you burning.' Beti wiped her hands on a towel while Will tried to rub the cream in, taking some of it from his cheeks then using it on his legs. 'I'll get our picnic out now.'

'Would you like to join us?' Will asked.

Hannah looked at Beti then back at Will. 'I was just… working actually. I won't take your lunch.'

'Don't worry about that, Hannah, Daddy packed enough to feed five families.' Beti pointed at the piles of foil-wrapped food on the blanket in front of her. 'We have crisps and carrot sticks and muffins too.'

'Wow! That all sounds lovely.' Hannah appraised the spread as Beti started to unwrap it. She was, she realised, actually quite hungry now.

'Join us then. We have plenty.' Will had picked up a towel and he was cleaning some of the sunblock out of his ears. When he put the towel down, Hannah spotted a blob of cream on his earlobe. Before she realised what she was doing, she reached out and wiped it away. Their eyes met, his lips parted and Hannah's heart raced.

What was happening?

She held up her hand to show him the cream on her thumb and he glanced at it, then handed her the towel and she wiped the cream off. When she looked up again, Will was taking a seat on the blanket and she watched, feeling lightheaded after the intensity of the moment when their eyes had met, as he helped Beti get the rest of the picnic out of the cooler including some glass bottles of fizzy orange. He opened one then handed it to her.

'Thanks.' Hannah sat down and Beti shuffled around so that the three of them made a triangle around the food, like any other family on the sun-drenched beach.

She sipped the drink and the bubbles fizzed on her tongue while the sweet orange teased her tastebuds. It had been ages since she'd had fizzy orange and it was really nice.

'Help yourself,' Will said, handing her a plastic picnic plate with a mermaid print.

'Thank you.'

She placed some sandwiches and carrot sticks on the plate then added some plain crisps and the three of them ate, listening to the sounds of the summer beach. The food was simple but delicious and she knew it had something to do with the company and the fact that she felt privileged to share lunch with this lovely man and his daughter.

–

Will folded the foil he'd used to pack the sandwiches then placed it back in the cooler intending to recycle it at home later. He held out a plate with three muffins left on it to Hannah and she took one, while Beti helped herself and then Will had the last one. They were chocolate chip, moist and scrumptious, made from a recipe his mam had given him. He polished his off quickly then finished his fizzy orange and set the bottle in the cooler too.

'You recycle everything?' Hannah asked.

'He does.' Beti's expression was serious. 'Absolutely everything. Daddy is very passionert about recycling.'

Will shifted his position. 'I do it because I'm trying to help make the world a good place for you and your children, Beti, even for your children's children.'

Beti frowned. 'What if I don't have children?'

Hannah ducked her head, trying, Will suspected, to hide a smile.

'Beti has an answer for everything,' Will said. 'Don't you, my princess?'

'Not everything, Daddy, like I still don't know if Santa Claus visits all the children in the world.' She fixed her precocious amber gaze on Hannah. 'I find it hard to believe that he can travel around the whole world in one night. I mean… even with magical reindeer, it's got to be tough.'

'I'm sure it is a… challenge,' Hannah said, briefly catching Will's eye.

'Daddy says that it's all to do with magic and the fact that the times around the world are different, so Santa doesn't have to do it all at once, but… well… he'd be exhosted.'

'Exhosted?' Hannah raised her eyebrows.

'Terribly exhosted. No wonder he sleeps all damned year after that.' Beti looked at her muffin and picked a chocolate chip out of it then placed it on her tongue. 'Would you like to come to the stalls with us now?' she asked Hannah.

'Beti…' Will shook his head. 'Perhaps Hannah has plans.'

'Do you?' Beti asked.

'I don't, actually. I'm going to take some more photos but I have all week to interview people and to get what I need for the articles. The advantage of being self-employed is that as long as I get my work done, I can do it anytime, anywhere.'

'What's self-employed?' Beti screwed up the paper casing from her muffin and Will took it from her and put it in the cooler.

'When you work for yourself.' Hannah tucked her legs to one side and stretched her back. 'I work for myself by writing articles about places I visit then I sell them to magazines and newspapers.'

'Wow!' Beti's eyes were round. 'You're a writer?'

'I am.'

'Will you come and speak to my class about it?'

'Uh…' Hannah paused. 'When would this be?'

'When we go back to school, of course. Miss Dix says writers are very clever and I bet she'd love to speak to you.'

'Don't forget that you'll be in different class next year, Beti,' Will said, knowing that this was something Beti was not happy about because she had adored her teacher.

'Bum! I did forget. But if you came to assembly you could tell all the children then.'

'I'm not sure that I'll be here in September.' Hannah put her muffin down and rested it on her knee. 'Actually, I know I won't be.'

'Why not?' Beti placed a hand on top of Hannah's and leant forwards, as Will had seen her do with her friends when she was particularly interested in what they had to say.

'I… I came here for the festival and after it's finished, I'll be moving on.'

'Hannah will have other jobs elsewhere.' Will could see the disappointment on Beti's face and he understood how she felt. He'd known Hannah was only here for the festival but somehow, he'd managed to put it from his mind.

'Not yet,' Hannah said, looking from Will to Beti, 'But at some point soon.'

'Where is your home?' Beti asked.

'I live in Watford.'

'Do you have a big house?'

'Beti…' Will held up a hand. 'That's enough questions.'

'It's OK.' Hannah said. 'I don't have my own house. I live in houses that I rent from other people. I travel so much that there's no point buying a house of my own. I'd rarely be there and it would be a waste when so many people desperately need somewhere to live.'

Beti looked shocked. 'That's very sad. I wouldn't like not to have a home. Nanny says home is where the heart is and if you don't have a home... then where's your heart?'

The colour seeped from Hannah's cheeks and she seemed lost for words.

'I... Uh... That's a very good question.'

'Oh look!' Will pointed over at the stalls. 'I think I can see a stall selling inflatables.'

Beti shot up like a meerkat, her question forgotten. 'Blinking heck, Daddy, we can buy one! Will you come and look with us?' She patted Hannah's shoulder excitedly.

'Sure.' Hannah sighed and Will realised that she was relieved to have had the subject changed.

'Shall we go and have a look while Daddy tidies up?'

Hannah looked at Will to check if this was all right.

'Go on and I'll catch up with you. But Hannah...'

'Yes?' She stood up and slid her feet into her flip-flops.

'Don't let her persuade you to buy anything. I'll get her one when I join you.'

'OK.' She took Beti's hand and they strolled down to the shore then along the sand, the easiest route to take now that the beach was so busy.

Will watched them for a moment, enjoying how they looked together, as if they did this all the time. *But Beti and her questions...* He knew it showed that she was bright and interested but sometimes she put people on the spot. And that last question about home and the heart. It was something his mother said all the time and Beti often told him she loved their new home, but then she'd loved the last one too. For Will, home was wherever Beti was, where his parents and sister were, along the Gower Peninsula where the sea met the sand, where the cliffs met the coastal path, where he could enjoy the city but be at the beach in minutes. He loved where he lived and never wanted to live anywhere else. How must Hannah feel then, not having a house of her own, not even having more than a place she rented for a brief time? That sense of not having a home must be hard. Then again, if she loved to travel so much, perhaps she was a free spirit who didn't want to be tied down to a property. And yet… he'd seen the expression on her face when she'd answered Beti, one of uncertainty, of flailing, as if Beti had hit a nerve. A very raw nerve.

He'd enjoyed sharing lunch with Beti and Hannah, had felt relaxed in Hannah's company and knew that Beti did too. It felt like they'd known her for a long time and not like she'd only recently entered their social sphere. It was a shame that she'd be leaving at the end of the festival because he had a feeling that she'd fit right in around Cariad Cove if she wanted to stay.

He stood up and dusted off his board shorts then quickly changed underneath the cover of a towel into his dry shorts. He'd better go and catch up with Beti and Hannah before Hannah had her arm twisted and Beti ended up with a full-sized dinghy. Stranger things had happened when she'd gone shopping with Alice, like the time she'd come home with an artist's easel and a set of watercolours (that she'd used once) and the other time when she'd convinced Alice to let her have her make-up done at the Boots' counter. She'd rocked up looking like one of those children involved in beauty pageants and Will shivered at the memory; he hadn't liked seeing his baby girl wearing bright lipstick, thick mascara and foundation. Not at all.

He set off down to the shore, trying to shake off the sense that he liked Hannah more than he'd liked any woman for quite some time, while also wondering if it was because he knew she wasn't sticking around. Perhaps his heart's way of protecting itself was to find only women he couldn't be with attractive, because then there was no chance at all of getting hurt.

Perhaps it was something different altogether and he was feeling drawn to Hannah because she was different, because something in him recognised something in her.

Perhaps…

Chapter 13

'Wow!' Beti exclaimed and pressed her little hands together. 'I just love this one.'

The look of awe on the little girl's face made Hannah yearn to take a photo but she suppressed the urge, not wanting to ruin the moment. Instead, Hannah turned her attention to the stall of inflatables. The one Beti had chosen was a large pink dolphin wearing a sunflower on the side of its head. The dolphin had green eyes with black eyelashes drawn around them and appeared to be wearing lipstick.

'That's something all right,' Hannah said.

'Can I get it?' Beti gazed up at Hannah, her amber eyes filled with awe.

'Well… your daddy said to wait until he got here.'

'What if someone else buys it?'

'I'm sure they won't.'

'But I don't like any of the others as much as this one and if it goes then I'll be very sad and disappointed and… and…'

Hannah was already opening her bag for her purse. The thought that Beti would miss out on the dolphin and be disappointed was more than she could bear. The adorable little girl and her charming dad had just shared their picnic with her so buying this for Beti was the least she could do.

'Hello.' She waved at the man behind the table. 'Could we have the pink dolphin, please?'

'Of course you can.' He used a pole with a hook at the end to lift the inflatable from the rail it was hanging on then placed it on the table. 'That'll be twelve pounds, please.'

Hannah got the cash out of her purse and handed it to him while Beti ran a hand along the dolphin's side. 'She's just beautiful.'

'And now she's yours,' Hannah said as she picked the dolphin up and went to hand it to Beti but Beti could barely see over the top of it. 'Would you like me to carry her?'

'Yes please, but I can hold on here.' Beti showed Hannah the flipper she'd was already holding and Hannah thought it was the cutest thing she'd ever seen.

'What's going on?' Will had arrived and he cocked an eyebrow as he looked at the dolphin.

'Hannah bought her for me and isn't she just the prettiest thing in the world, Daddy?' Beti spoke to Will but kept her eyes on the dolphin as if she couldn't bear to look away.

'She is rather lovely. How much do I owe you, Hannah?'

'It's fine.' Hannah shook her head over the dolphin. 'My treat.'

'No, no, I'll pay you back.'

'Please… I'd like to get her for Beti.'

'Will you come in the sea with me and have a go on her?' Beti peered around the side of the dolphin at Hannah but her stomach sank to her flip-flops.

Swim? Her? She just couldn't.

'Oh… I… uh… don't have my costume.'

'Well go and get it.' Beti grinned, showing off a gap where her bottom teeth should be. Beti smiled a lot but Hannah hadn't noticed the gap before and it endeared Beti to her even more.

'Uhh… I don't think so.' Hannah gave a brief shake of her head.

'It's not far to the hotel so you can go and get it then come swimming.'

Hannah opened and closed her mouth like a fish out of water.

'Perhaps Hannah doesn't like to swim, Beti.' Will placed a hand on Beti's shoulder.

'Why not?' Beti's eyes widened. 'Is it because you watched that film about the big shark and he ate all the people and one had blood coming out of his mouth and Daddy said I shouldn't know about it but I wanted to know what happened because then a little boy went in the water and then… and then…' She knitted her brows. 'I forgot what happened next.'

'I didn't let her watch it, of course I didn't, but a boy she's at school with watched it one bank holiday and told her and she was fascinated.' Will shook his head. 'I think it's a bit scary for someone so young but some parents don't, apparently.'

'Oh I agree. Best wait until you're older to watch that one,' Hannah said, hoping the subject of her swimming costume would be forgotten about.

'How old? Your age?' Beti asked.

'Yes. My age.'

'How old are you?' Beti stroked the dolphin's head. 'I think you're about fifty-seven.'

Hannah grimaced. 'Really?'

'Noooo.' Beti giggled. 'Fooled you. I think you're eighteen.'

'I wish.' Hannah gave a wry laugh. 'Bit older than that.'

'Are you daddy's age? He's thirty-three.'

'A tiny bit younger. I'm thirty.'

'That's older than my teacher.'

'Everyone is judged or compared with Beti's teacher. It seems to be a little girl thing,' Will explained, pushing a hand through his hair. 'Sorry.'

'It's fine. I don't think I'm over the hill yet,' Hannah said, flashing him a smile. 'And neither are you.'

Colour filled his cheeks and she realised he might have thought she was flirting. Which she wasn't.

Not. At. All.

Was she?

'And you didn't answer my question.' Beti tapped Hannah's hand where it rested underneath the dolphin.

'Which was?' Hannah wasn't sure which one Beti was referring to now as she'd asked so many.

'About swimming and the shark. Are you afraid it will come along and bite your legs off?'

'Goodness, no! Not in these waters anyway.' Hannah laughed then the smile fell from her lips. 'I just… I'm not a good swimmer.'

'You should learn then.' Beti held her gaze, her amber eyes assured. 'Everyone should be able to swim because you never know when you'll fall off your boat or get swept off the beach by a wave and then you'll be sorry if you didn't learn how to swim because you'll drownded and have to be buried in the ground or burned in a fire and have your ashes sprinkled on the wind.'

Will was mouthing *sorry* at Hannah over Beti's head.

'I know. You're right, Beti, I should learn.' Hannah nodded.

If only it was a simple as not being a good swimmer, she thought. If only everything was as simple as Beti seemed to believe it was.

'Well, why don't you paddle while Beti and I take her dolphin in the water then we can get donuts and hot chocolates afterwards?' Will asked.

'I don't want to take up any more of your day.' Hannah didn't want to impose and for them to get sick of her but she was having a splendid time and wasn't ready to return to the hotel alone just yet.

'We'd like you to… If you'd like to, that is.' Will lowered his eyes to the dolphin and she saw a tiny muscle in the side of his jaw twitching. He was almost as cute as Beti.

'Only if you're sure.'

When he met her eyes again his easy smile reassured her that he meant it.

'Come along then, ladies. Let's get this dolphin in the sea where she belongs.' Will held out his hands and Hannah handed the inflatable to Will then he flashed her and Beti a wicked grin. 'Catch me if you can!'

He jogged away and Beti stared at his retreating figure. 'He took my damned dolphin. Bloody hell, Daddy!'

'Better go catch him then!' Hannah held out her hand and Beti grabbed it then they raced after Will, laughing all the way to the water's edge.

—

When Will reached the sea, he realised that he was still in his clothes so he turned and waited for Hannah and Beti. They were giggling as they ran, holding hands and trying to avoid people lying on towels, dogs that chased after balls and mounds of seaweed. They looked good together, Beti with her brown curls and Hannah with her shiny blonde hair that was working its way from her ponytail as she ran. He couldn't help noticing her shapely legs and her other curves, the type of curves that could make a man weak. It had been a long time since Will had held a woman and he was only human after all, so while he felt a bit guilty admiring Hannah, he didn't think it would hurt anyone. Besides which, it wasn't just her looks that he found attractive; he liked how she was with Beti and with him, how she could spend time with them without disturbing the equilibrium, how she could be around them and not feel awkward. Will felt comfortable with her and that surprised him because he wasn't used to feeling comfortable around many women other than his relations.

Finally, they reached him and Beti let go of Hannah's hand and flung herself at the dolphin. 'There you are, Digby.'

'Digby?' Will frowned. 'Isn't it a girl?'

'Digby's a good name.' Beti took it in her arms but she could barely reach around it. The name sounded familiar and then it dawned on Will; Digby had been the name of the cat that lived next door to his parents. Beti had loved the cat and always made a fuss of him when he appeared in the front garden or on the street. He never came into the back garden because of the dog but he was happy to frequent Will's parents' front garden and to use their borders as a toilet. Digby had passed away over a year ago but it seemed that Beti had not forgotten him.

'Well if we're going to go in the water, we'd better get our swimmers back on.'

'Do we have to?' Beti wrinkled her nose.

'Better had or our clothes will be wet.'

'OK, Daddy. Hannah, will you watch Digby while we change, please?'

'Of course I will.' Hannah accepted the dolphin.

'We'll be quick,' Will said.

'Don't let anyone take Digby.' Beti waved at the dolphin. 'Be right back.'

-

Hannah turned and gazed out at the water. The light was changing as the afternoon wore on and the sea that washed over her feet was warmer than earlier on. The urge to wade in and feel the sweet caress all over her body was suddenly overwhelming, but Hannah knew that it was something she just couldn't allow herself to do.

Not now. Not here. Not ever?

The shouts and laughter of people in the sea were so uplifting; they were clearly happy and having a good time. She'd denied herself that for so long and why?

You know why…

The same with running. She hadn't run for a long time either.

She had put a stopper in her emotions and for some reason, here in this Welsh cove, it was starting to move, making her wonder if it was going to pop like a cork from a shaken bottle of champagne and everything would come gushing out.

Things weren't straightforward, and at one point in time, Hannah had made a decision. She had felt that giving up on certain things was the only way she could cope. She knew that not everyone would understand her motivation, but she'd done what she could to survive. Being here today with Will and Bet was making her question whether things had changed, whether she could start to move on with her life and to forgive herself for the mistakes of her past or if she would be forever a hostage of them.

When Will and Beti joined her again and she watched them splash through the waves, hand in hand, with Digby between them, she had to root herself in the sand to prevent herself from chasing after them. She knew that if she did, long buried things could rise to the surface and that might be her undoing.

Chapter 14

From the beach, Hannah watched as Will and Beti cavorted in the sea. They were in the water up to Will's shoulders with Beti sitting on the pink dolphin's back, armbands on, her grin evident even from the shore. Every so often, Beti's shrieks of delight reached Hannah and brought a smile to her lips. Will and his daughter shared a special bond and clearly loved each other's company. Having never known her own father, Hannah had no idea whether he would have loved her, whether he'd have spent summer days teaching her to swim, sharing picnics with her on the beach or taking her to summer festivals. Her mum had done her best as single parent, had been loving and kind, fair and hard working. She had instilled morals in Hannah from an early age and Hannah knew that her mum had helped her to become the woman she was today. Not perfect, no. Not as 'together' as she'd like to be. But she did believe that she had a good heart and that she'd help others if she could. As for other things – love, romance, a family – those things had eluded her and she knew that was partly her fault. Hannah had erected a barrier around her heart in order to keep it safe from harm and by doing so, she had probably missed out on experiences that would have brought her joy.

She lifted her camera and snapped some pics of Will and Beti, thinking that they'd like to have them. She could send them to Will and he could print them out and frame them, see the evidence that he was a wonderful father to his very precious little girl.

As she zoomed in on Will and Beti, everything around her seemed to fade away. She no longer heard the seagulls fighting over scraps in the sand, no longer saw the other people on the beach and in the sea, no longer felt the sand between her toes. Two people could be everything to someone, could be a whole world, fill a heart, if that person was prepared to let them in. Her mum had told her to live for today, to grab it with both hands because nothing else was guaranteed – not tomorrow, not next week, next month or year. As a child, Hannah had secretly scoffed at the idea because she thought that she and her mum had forever. After she'd lost her mum, she hadn't wanted to care about anyone because the thought of losing someone else that she loved was far too awful.

Now though, she knew the truth and more than anything, here, today, she wanted to make the most of the gift that was the present.

Lowering her camera, her awareness of the world around her returned and she closed her eyes for a moment, breathing deeply, letting the air cleanse her from within. Sounds surrounded her, the breeze toyed with the tendrils of hair that had escaped her ponytail and she licked her lips, tasting salt and a hint of orange left over from the fizzy drink.

Emotion welled inside her. *Why now? Why here?* What exactly was she feeling?

As she puzzled over her inner sensations, something snatched her from her reverie and her eyes snapped open. Someone was in trouble.

Further along the beach, she could see an elderly woman standing alone in the shallows. The hem of her floral skirt was wet and her back hunched over as she wrung her hands together. She was reaching out to something but Hannah couldn't see what it was.

Something white rose above a small wave before disappearing again. The woman shouted again but her voice was so frail that it was swallowed by the noise on the beach.

Hannah glanced at Will and Beti. They were fine.

And then she ran…

Will peered up at the beach then rubbed at his eyes. It was bright out here, even with the sun lower in the sky, but he'd been aware of Hannah standing on the shore watching him and Beti play. It had been nice, comforting even, to have another person with them, like having a third member of the team. He'd seen Hannah raise her camera and take some photos and he was delighted because the thing about being a single parent was that he often took photos of Beti alone, unless his parents or Alice were around. And most of the time, on days like today, it was just him and Beti anyway, so these moments were never captured in photographs. He'd have to ask Hannah for copies.

Except that Hannah had disappeared. As he moved Digby around in the water, making Beti squeal, he scanned the beach to see if Hannah had gone up to their small camp by the dunes. It was too far to see clearly but there were so many people on the beach now that it would be hard to tell anyway.

'Daddy, look!' Will followed the direction of Beti's pointing finger and saw an elderly lady in the shallows, her face pale and her hands held out as if praying to the sky. Beyond her, a figure raced through the water then dived in. 'It's Hannah. She's… only blinking swimming.'

His heart skipped a beat as he watched. Hannah had said she couldn't swim well, so what the hell was she doing? She could be in danger.

He started to push Digby to the shore, aware that he had to get Beti out of the water before he could do anything to help. The water sucked at his shorts, clung to his legs and the sand slipped beneath his soles but he lifted Beti off her dolphin then jogged with her on his one hip, Digby on the other.

'What're you doing, Daddy?' Beti was half laughing, half crying as she bobbed up and down. 'I don't want to get out of the sea.'

'I have to help. Something's wrong.'

When he reached the spot behind the elderly lady, where Hannah's things – including her expensive-looking camera – had been abandoned on the sand, he set Beti down with Digby. He looked into her eyes, 'It's very important that you wait right here for me. OK?'

Beti nodded and her bottom lip wobbled.

'Don't worry. I'll be right back.'

'OK, Daddy.' She gave a sombre nod then he turned and ran into the water.

Hannah had reached the woman, thrown her things down, then waded into the sea before diving into the waves. All thoughts about anything other than whatever was in the water vanished and she was on autopilot, her old affinity with the water kicking in.

She came to the surface and looked around. Nothing. Took a breath and dived again. Through the grey light of the water, where sand and seaweed swirled, she could make out a small white shape writhing as bubbles escaped from its mouth. She swam towards it, reached out and grabbed it then pushed upwards.

They broke into the air together; Hannah and the small white dog.

It struggled in her arms so she held it against her chest. 'It's OK. I've got you. You're OK now, poppet.'

Lying on her back, she kept the dog's head out of the water then kicked her legs, heading for the shore and the elderly woman whose cries were turning to sobs of relief.

Strong hands took hold of Hannah's arms and she felt a body behind her. Cold skin against hers made goosebumps rise on her flesh.

'It's all right, Hannah. You can stand up now.'

She lowered her feet, still holding the squirming dog tight. Will's hands moved as he came around her and he cupped her face. There was something in his eyes that she couldn't fathom, his hands on her cheeks were trembling and she realised that she was trembling too.

'Let's get you both out of the water.'

With his arm around her shoulders, he led her to the waiting woman. The dog barked and she took it in her arms, laughing and smothering its damp head with kisses.

'Oh my god, thank you so much. Thank you for saving my baby.'

Hannah opened her mouth but nothing came out, shock had struck her dumb.

The woman patted Hannah's hand. 'He's all I've got in the world. I lost my husband last year and adopted Bennie and he's become my best friend. He loves chasing his ball… and it went into the water… and then I couldn't follow him in because of my hips. And… I thought I'd lost him when a wave swept him away.' Tears were running down her face and the dog licked them away.

'We should get you all seen by a first aider,' Will said.

'I've got your things here,' Beti said, holding up Hannah's camera and bag. 'I kept them safe.'

'Thank you so much.' Hannah's voice was little more than a whisper.

'Come on.' Will still had his one arm around Hannah's shoulders and she saw him go to take Beti's hand.

'It's OK, Daddy. You have Digby because he's too big for me to carry and I'll bring Hannah's things.'

'Thanks, Beti.'

They walked slowly across the beach with the elderly lady and her dog then up the concrete ramp to the first aid station. Hannah was grateful for Will's strong arm around her and for his reassuring presence beside her because she knew she was in shock. Not because she'd had to rescue the dog but because she'd been in the sea after such a long time. Years ago, she had vowed never to swim again in open water, never to allow herself to enjoy the rush as the waves swept her along, fearing that as the sea freed her body, it would release her pent-up emotions too.

Here, today, at Cariad Cove, she had broken that vow.

To save a dog.

For the elderly lady, it had been so much more than that. She had said that the dog was her world and so Hannah had rescued someone's reason for being.

If only she could find a way to do that for herself.

–

Bathed in the glow of the setting sun, the surface of the sea was burnt orange now. The atmosphere on the beach had changed as people packed up and left and the stalls in the car park shut down for the day. It was quieter than earlier but there were still small groups of people on the beach, sitting around campfires or barbecues and couples and individuals walking dogs along the sand. The breeze had died down, leaving the air pleasantly balmy, fragranced with cooking food and the tang of the warm sea. Even so, Will had got two blankets out of his backpack and wrapped one around Beti's shoulders then given the other one to Hannah.

After they'd been to the first aid station, and Hannah had been given the all-clear, they'd waited to see how the elderly lady got on. She'd been given a cup of hot sweet tea while her dog had been given a drink of water and a treat, then one of the first aiders had taken her back to her home in the village. She'd thanked Hannah effusively before leaving, and Hannah's eyes had glistened but she'd remained modest, refusing to accept praise or the monetary reward the woman had offered.

Will had then asked Hannah if she wanted to go back to the hotel, feeling sad that their day had come to an end but knowing that Hannah was soaked through and could get cold. She'd said that she would go back to her room to grab some dry clothes and then, if it was OK with him and Beti, she'd like to return to the beach with them.

And so they were sitting around a small fire that Will had built, with marshmallows on sticks and cups of hot chocolate that he'd purchased at the hotel.

'The sky is incredible,' Hannah said, and they all gazed at the peach and lavender hues, the slivers of blue-grey and the fluffy white trails left by planes that looked as though an artist had feathered them there with a small brush.

'It's beautiful,' Will agreed. Then he looked at her and the words *Just like you…* echoed through his mind. *Beautiful, brave and selfless.* So different from Kayla who had only ever seemed capable of thinking of herself. He couldn't imagine Kayla diving into the water to rescue someone's dog; she'd have worried about breaking a nail or ruining her make-up. Ironic that she'd got together with a surfer, but then he did the swimming and not her. He shook himself inwardly to get all thoughts of his ex out of his mind.

Beti yawned.

'Tired?' he asked.

'No, Daddy.' She yawned again and he laughed.

'Somehow I think you are.'

They fell silent as they sipped their hot chocolates. When Beti lowered her cup, she had a chocolate moustache that was so cute Will didn't have the heart to tell her it was there.

'Hannah?'

'Yes?'

'Why did you say you couldn't swim?'

Hannah opened her mouth then puffed out her cheeks. 'I think I said… that I can't swim very well.'

Beti stared at Hannah, waiting.

'I… See, I used to swim. I used to like to swim but then something happened and it changed my mind. I was quite a good swimmer and perhaps I should have said *that*… but I was worried that you'd try to persuade me to go in the water and… I didn't want to.'

Beti's eyes were like saucers and her mouth kept opening and closing, which looked comical with the chocolate moustache.

'That's enough questions for today, Beti,' Will said, reading the situation. 'Sometimes people don't want to tell you absolutely everything about themselves.' He looked at Hannah and she gave him a tight smile.

'I'm sorry. I just… your daddy's right, Beti. I have reasons for what I said and for why I don't swim any more but they're difficult to talk about.'

'Nanny says that you should always talk about your problems. She says that a problem shared is a problem halved.' The latter phrase emerged singsong as if Beti said it often.

Hannah put her cup down then pulled her knees up to her chin. 'Your nanny sounds very wise.'

'She is.' Beti nodded. 'Very clever too. But just so you know, Hannah, if you ever want to talk about it… you can talk to me. We're good friends now.'

Hannah smiled. 'Thank you, Beti, that's very kind.'

'Or my daddy because he's a good listener too.'

Will held up his hands. 'Good to know, I guess.'

'Thank you both.'

'Nanny also says that people need people and that Daddy has been on his own for far too long now and he should get out there and—'

'Beti!' Will scowled at his daughter, keen to convey that she'd said enough. 'Those are things that Nanny said to me when she thought you were in the garden with Indiana Bones.'

'I'd come in for a wee and I heard her and it makes sense. Mummy's been gone a looooong time.'

Will swallowed, staring into his empty cup. Young children often said what was on their minds and Beti meant no harm but sometimes her way of cutting right to the heart of matters was difficult to deal with.

'She has,' he said softly. 'But Nanny isn't always right. Mostly… but not always.' He didn't know why he was disagreeing because in this case; he did think his mam was speaking a lot of sense but he also didn't want Hannah thinking he was some kind of desperate weirdo looking for a wife replacement for him and a mother for Beti.

'Can I go and have one last paddle, Daddy, now that the tide is in?' Beti asked, already standing up. 'It's not far to walk.'

'Of course. But stay in the shallows. I'll be down in a bit. And don't take Digby because the temptation to put him in the sea will be too great and then a wave might carry her away.'

'Okaaaaayyyyyyy.' Beti trotted down to the sea, kicking up sand as she went.

'I'm so sorry about your wife.' Hannah placed a cool hand on his arm.

'Oh… It's OK. Thanks. But she was my partner… we weren't married.'

Hannah held his gaze, the red–gold horizon reflected in her pupils making it seem as though they were on fire. Her hair was down now, wavy from the sea, her skin glowing from a day in the fresh air. Her lips…

He looked away then pushed up to his feet. He had to focus on Beti. She was standing at the water's edge now, waiting for him.

Hannah stood up. 'Beti is amazing.'

'Thank you. I agree.'

'She's funny and wise, but she's also very sweet. You've done an amazing job, especially seeing as how you've done it alone.'

'Since Beti was a toddler.' He cleared his throat. 'I sometimes worry that I'm getting it wrong but I do my best.'

'It must be hard, at times, being a single parent.'

'It is, sometimes… when I doubt myself. But there are many positives. I mean, we get to spend a lot of quality time together and I've been very lucky with that. Beti is my reason for getting up in the mornings.'

He could feel Hannah's eyes on him, smell her bergamot and lime perfume, knew that if he moved his right hand a fraction it would brush against hers. He hadn't spent this much time with a woman he wasn't related to in years and old longings that he'd pushed away for so long were raising their heads. It was because of who Hannah was, because she had something in her eyes that he recognised, a secret vulnerability that he could identify with. She was strong but he sensed that she wished she didn't have to be, not all of the time anyway, that she would benefit from having someone in her life who understood her, who could be there for her.

And yet... he barely knew her. He couldn't get carried away with thinking he knew her when there was much he didn't know.

'Shall we join Beti? Just for five minutes.' He looked away from Hannah, not wanting to put pressure on her yet yearning for her to stay a little longer.

'I'd like that.'

They padded down to the shoreline together, so close that their arms brushed against each other a few times, but neither of them jumped away. There was something between them, something that had potential, but Will wasn't entirely sure yet what that something was.

Chapter 15

Two days later, Hannah walked up to the village to meet Ffion. The previous day she had slept in later than usual, had a late breakfast, and then gone back to bed. It was so unlike her but she'd felt exhausted and slept right through until dinner. When she'd woken, there had been a text message from Will asking if she was all right after Beti's question time and the dramatic dog rescue, and one from Ffion inviting her to the village for lunch.

During her walk, she thought about the day she'd spent at the beach with Will and Beti. It had been enjoyable, she liked their company and found being around them easy. Her heart ached for Will losing his partner but she didn't know the details and hadn't liked to pry. Will hadn't said much so she wasn't going to push him. However, he had told her that if she wanted to talk, he was there and she'd said the same to him later on as they'd strolled back to the hotel.

Before they'd parted, Beti had asked Will if Hannah could accompany them to the animal sanctuary one day and so they'd exchanged numbers, something that Hannah was happy about because she'd been trying to think of a way to ask. Had Will been a woman, then it would have seemed the natural thing to do, but because she liked him and found him attractive, she didn't want to seem like she was pushing for anything other than friendship. Of course, she wasn't. How could she be when her time in Cariad Cove was limited and soon she'd be just a memory for Will and Beti as they would be for her?

She placed a hand over her chest. Was that heartburn? Perhaps the two croissants she'd devoured for breakfast hadn't been a good idea. It had to be heartburn because the idea that the thought of not seeing Will and Beti again might be causing a burning in her gut was inconceivable. Ridiculous. Dramatic beyond comprehension.

Hannah reached the edge of the village and paused, taking in the view of pretty stone cottages, some newly built houses with first floor balconies, an old church complete with moss-covered lychgate, and the village green. In amongst the buildings, trees grew tall and hedges broad, flowers bloomed in borders, pots and window boxes and colourful bunting was tied to lampposts and signposts. Stalls were set up in a semi-circle on the green while others stood along the outside of the church walls. At the centre of the green were rows of tables where people could sit to rest, grab a coffee or eat the food they'd purchased at one of the catering stalls.

She'd walked the road way but knew that if she continued on through the village, she'd reach several fields and beyond them was the coastal path and the sea. The sky beyond the village had that openness to it that Hannah associated with beachside towns and villages, the sense that if you kept on going you would find an endless horizon, experience the sense of freedom that living near the sea offered.

Hannah had always craved that feeling of freedom, of knowing that she could keep on moving, ever since she'd lost her mum. But here, in Cariad Cove, she felt different. The village was pretty, it was near the beach, it wasn't far from the city of Swansea and other interesting places were within driving distance. Yet there was more to it than that. Cariad Cove had people she liked and could care about. It had a sense of community. It had Ffion, memories of time spent with Will and Beti. If she ever decided to settle somewhere, this was the type of place she pictured herself putting down roots.

She'd agreed to meet Ffion at an old bookshop in the village that had its own coffee shop. It sounded just perfect to her because coffee and books were two of her favourite things. Ffion had told her that it was just off the green along a side street, and so she crossed the road and headed in that direction.

On the side of a building, she spotted the sign Ffion had told her about of an owl sitting on a book pile and headed for the front door. Pushing it open, she experienced a flicker of childlike joy as an old-fashioned bell tinkled and the door closed slowly behind her. The smell inside was incredible and she paused for a moment to savour it: old paper, coffee and chocolate, laced with undertones of spice. She breathed it in, savouring the aromas of books and the coffee shop that was at the rear of the building.

'Hello.' A man behind the counter smiled at her over his halfmoon glasses.

'Hi.'

'If you're looking for anything in particular, let me know. If not, enjoy your time at Owlbert Einstein Books.'

'I will, thank you.' Hannah flashed him a smile then walked through the shop, browsing the signs on the shelves. There were hardback books from the current chart, tables of brightly coloured paperbacks set out in genres, shelves of leather-bound books and all kinds of reference books, and two large glass cases of rare and first edition books, some of which had labels beneath them stating that they were signed. It was a treasure trove for bibliophiles and Hannah suspected that book collectors would come from miles away to visit it, although they probably did a roaring trade online too. But to order from here online would be to miss out on the experience and she knew that she'd be back here to spend more time browsing the shelves while she was staying in Cariad Cove. She'd also ask permission to take some photographs so she could add the bookshop to her articles.

After she'd passed through two rooms of books, she found a short staircase that led down to a cafe area with a counter to the left, five round tables and French doors that stood open to a walled garden. She could see Ffion sitting in at a garden table so she made her way outside, savouring the intoxicating scent of roses that filled the air.

'This place is amazing,' she said as she sat opposite Ffion.

'It's pretty special, right?' Ffion smiled. 'I love coming here. It's good to see you.'

'Likewise.'

Hannah looked around the walled garden. There were trellises on each stone wall on which a rainbow of roses grew, including around the French doors that were painted bright green. In each corner of the garden was a basket chair suspended from beams and in two of the chairs people were reading.

'So how've you been?' Hannah asked, focusing her attention on Ffion now. She hoped that her alarm wasn't showing on her face because Ffion did not look well.

'I'm really tired, to be honest with you. I don't know what's wrong because I've been eating healthily, running and sleeping ten or twelve hours a night but I just can't seem to get enough rest.'

Hannah noted the purple hue beneath Ffion's eyes and the way she fidgeted with a coaster as if she couldn't sit still.

'The thing is, Hannah…' Ffion bit her bottom lip and closed her eyes. When she opened them they were red rimmed and glistening. 'Oh, it doesn't matter.' She waved a hand as if dismissing the thought.

'Of course it does.' Hannah placed a hand over Ffion's and squeezed gently.

'But see… we haven't known each other long and I don't want to offload on you. I'm meant to be showing you how wonderful the village is and celebrating the festival with you.'

'I'd like to think that we're friends now and that you can tell me if something's bothering you. I already think the village is fabulous and can still enjoy the festival.'

What was wrong with Ffion? Hannah suddenly felt cold, as if a cloud had passed over the sun, but when she glanced up, the sky was bright blue without a cloud in sight.

'I want you to enjoy being here and to write wonderful words about how amazing the cove is because I know how popular your articles are and how it will draw tourists to our gorgeous coastline.' Ffion was sitting up straighter now, a smile on her face, but Hannah knew that there was something she wasn't sharing. She could feel it in her bones with that primitive awareness of one woman observing another. However, never one to pry, she'd let Ffion share it if and when she was ready.

'I certainly will write many wonderful things about Cariad Cove, Ffion. It's just perfect here so don't worry about that.'

'I'm so happy to hear it. Anyway, shall we order some drinks and some cake and then we can have a good old chat about what you've been up to since I saw you last.'

They ordered lattes and slices of chocolate cake shiny with fondant icing and when they arrived at the table, Hannah's mouth watered. She raised the fork of cake to her mouth and moaned as she chewed. 'This is so good.'

'I know. They serve the best cakes here.' Ffion ate some of hers, closing her eyes for a moment. 'I used to come here as a teenager but forgot about it over the years, then Joe brought me here recently and now I can't stay away.'

'I'm not surprised.' Hannah took a sip of her latte. 'I'd be in here all the time. I mean… books, cake and coffee. It's perfect.'

They ate quietly for a few moments, the cake too good to resist.

'Tell me about your week, Hannah. What have you been up to?'

Hannah told her that she'd been relaxing in the hotel and on the beach, enjoying the delicious hotel menu, writing drafts of her articles and taking photographs for them.

'I'm assuming you'll have been to the festival stalls at the beach,' Ffion smiled. 'Seeing as how they're on your doorstep and it's one of the main reasons you're here.'

'I went on Saturday,' Hannah replied, wishing that her cheeks weren't glowing.

'Good?'

'Very.' Hannah lowered her gaze to her plate and pushed a few crumbs around with her fork.

'Did something happen?' Ffion put her own fork down and leant her elbows on the table.

'Kind of… Uh… On Saturday I was at the beach and I bumped into Will and Beti.' She looked up to find Ffion gazing at her intently.

'I see.' Ffion's eyebrows rose slowly.

The heat in Hannah's cheeks spread to her whole face and she sighed. 'I feel like a teenager confessing this to you.'

'Oh please go on. I'm intrigued.'

'It's just… Will is so nice.' She felt as if she should be twirling a lock of hair around her finger and chewing bubble gum but there was no judgement in Ffion's eyes.

'Nice as in *what a nice but boring guy* or as in *hot*?'

Hannah laughed. 'Be blunt, why don't you?'

Ffion was grinning. 'I'm teasing you. Well, just a bit. Do you like him?'

'He's quite different from other men I've met, and I just adore how he is with Beti.'

'He is nice and easy on the eye too. I can see why you'd like him. And as for Beti, she's an absolute sweetheart, isn't she?'

'She is. I can't get over how advanced she is for her age.'

'They spend a lot of time together and Will teaches her so much. It's such a shame that he's been on his own for so long.'

'Terribly sad. What happened to his partner?' Hannah wriggled on the chair, feeling bad for asking but wanting to know. 'He seems so down whenever she's mentioned and poor little Beti. Losing her mum must be so difficult, especially seeing as how she's so young.'

Ffion inclined her head. 'I know that she probably had her reasons for leaving but to abandon her child like that… I can't imagine doing the same thing.'

'Abandon? She *left* them?'

Ffion's eyes widened. 'Didn't you know?'

Shaking her head, Hannah said, 'I thought that she'd died.'

'Nope. I haven't known Will that long because I only came home in February and he's more Joe's friend than mine, but because he works with Joe and lives near Mari, I've got to know a bit about him. Will was with his ex-partner, Kayla, for a long time. Since college I think. She was, according to Joe, very much a free spirit type, never settling to one job and never wanting to have a family and traditional home life. Whereas, from what I know of Will, he's very much the family man.'

'He does seem that way. So Kayla left them?' Hannah was still surprised at what she'd heard and wanted to ensure she hadn't got it wrong.

'When Beti was very young; a toddler I think.'

'How tragic.'

Ffion picked up her latte. 'I don't want to judge anyone because none of us know what's around the corner, and we can't know what it's like to be in someone else's shoes, but I do feel terribly sorry for Will and Beti.'

'Being abandoned must have been very difficult, but on the upside… they do seem very happy.'

'They are. Will is very strong and the bond between him and Beti is the best.'

Hannah didn't know Kayla's reasons for leaving and, like Ffion, didn't want to judge anyone else. After all, she didn't know her own father, and as far as she was aware, he had no clue of her existence, but she did understand how difficult it was not having one parent around. If her father had been in her life, losing her mum would still have been awful, but at least she'd have had someone. However, she could attribute her father's absence from her life to ignorance; with Kayla, it seemed she had chosen to go. Relationships weren't perfect and Kayla must have been desperately unhappy to leave her partner and young child.

In spite of all that had happened, though, Will and Beti were OK. People could go through dreadful things and still make the most of life, still treasure the loved ones they had around. If they were lucky enough to have loved ones.

'Will has a lot of support from his parents and his sister, so I think he's lucky in that respect.' Ffion raised her mug to her lips and took a sip.

'That's good.'

Ffion blanched and she put her mug down, her top lip curling in disgust. 'Is your coffee OK?' she whispered, glancing through the doorway to the counter.

'It was lovely, thanks. Why?'

'Mine tastes funny and… it smells horrid.'

Hannah reached for Ffion's mug and sniffed. 'Seems fine to me.'

Ffion seemed to deflate on her chair. 'I don't know what's wrong with me. It's incredibly frustrating because when I came back from Scotland, I was struggling physic-ally and emotionally, but once I started running and eating properly, I got stronger and felt so much better.'

'You're feeling out of sorts, aren't you? That happens to people from time to time. It could be a virus or something similar. I'm sure it will pass.'

It will pass…

Something stirred inside Hannah, something that had flickered earlier when she'd been shocked at how poorly Ffion looked. Taking in the pale complexion, the shadows beneath her eyes, the exhaustion evident in her posture, she started to add things up. Hannah had seen this before. But when? Who?

It usually only lasts for the first trimester.

Her whole body tensed and she felt cold all over. She'd felt like this herself. Years ago… She shook her head, trying to dislodge the seed of a memory before it germinated and she experienced the full force of the pain again.

Hannah stood up suddenly, needing to get moving. 'I'll go and pay the bill.' Hannah went to the counter and paid, tipping generously, then she returned to the table. 'Come on. Let's get some air.'

'I have air here.' Ffion looked around at the walled garden.

'I meant some sea air.'

'Oh… OK.'

They left the bookshop and walked through the village to the gate that led to the fields, taking care to close it behind them. There weren't any animals in the field but Ffion told Hannah that the land belonged to a local farmer and he often let his sheep graze there. A few times, they'd escaped when someone had left the gate open and run through the village causing havoc, invading people's gardens and stopping traffic by trotting along the road as if they hadn't a care in the world.

At the far end of the field, they went through a turnstile gate and emerged onto the coastal path.

'This is one of the routes that the running club follows,' Ffion explained.

'I bet it's fabulous running around here.' Hannah could picture the scene, the air cool and fresh on her skin, the scenery breathtakingly beautiful, the sense of belonging to the club, of being a part of something important.

'You should run with me while you're here.'

Hannah averted her gaze. 'Oh... I don't know. I'm so unfit now.'

'You'd be surprised. Your fitness can improve quickly with running. I did the Couch to 5k and it was a fantastic way to get fit.'

'Maybe.' Hannah gave a tight smile. 'Shall we walk?'

They strolled along the path and Hannah gazed out across the water. The dark blue of the depths contrasted with the bright blue of the sky and the turquoise shade of the shallows around the rocks below. Seagulls soared over the sea like noisy winged clouds then swooped down, disappearing beneath the waves then shooting from the water with their catch in their beaks.

Star-like blue flowers of spring squill, mounds of green heather with their pinky-purple bell-like flowers, and the spiny leaves and burr-shaped metallic-blue flowers of sea holly grew along the side of the path. Hannah had encountered many different species of flowers during her time as a travel writer and appreciated the beauty and resilience of nature, how plants and flowers differed depending upon where they grew. She started to take photographs, enjoying the mossy, woody aroma of the heather that hung around the plants, temporarily lost in capturing the beauty and resilience of nature.

Pausing when she came across one she didn't recognise, she crouched down to take a closer look at the grassy clumps with thin stalks topped with delicate yellow flowers.

'That one is yellow whitlow grass,' Ffion said. 'It's a rare flower that doesn't grow anywhere else in the UK.'

'It's very pretty.'

'I think so too.'

'Shall we sit down?' Ffion gestured at a bench in what appeared to be a clifftop picnic spot.

'Sure.'

They sat on opposite sides of the table of the bench and Hannah set her camera down. 'How're you feeling now?'

'Not great but not terrible either. The fresh air has helped but I feel like I could easily take a nap.'

'Ffion,' Hannah ran a finger over the rough wood of the table that must have played host to hundreds if not thousands of picnics. 'I don't want to poke my nose into your business, but something's occurred to me… Is there any chance you could be pregnant?'

Ffion's eyes widened and she licked her lips. 'Why do you ask that?'

'Just a hunch.' Hannah folded her arms on the table of the bench. 'You're pale, tired, things smell funny to you… I know it could be something else but it could also be that you're expecting.' She swallowed hard, hating that she'd asked but feeling that she needed to because from Ffion's expression, it seemed like she hadn't entertained the idea.

'But we've been careful,' Ffion said eventually. 'I don't understand how it could have happened.' She rubbed at her cheeks vigorously, her brows meeting above her nose. 'Unless…'

'Unless?'

'The first time we were together.' Now her cheeks turned pink. 'After the sponsored run. We… were in a hurry… and we might not have been as careful as we should have been.'

Hannah lowered her gaze and folded her hands on the table. 'It happens. Sometimes things don't work as they should. Sometimes there's human error.'

'It's not Joe's fault. He was very considerate and responsible.'

Hannah smiled. 'I'm sure he was. But, as I said, sometimes things don't work.'

'Oh god.' Ffion pushed her hands through her hair. 'What if I am? Joe and I haven't been together long. Just over two months.'

'Do you love him?'

Ffion's face brightened. 'Deeply.'

'Well then, it's certainly not the end of the world and what's meant to be is meant to be.'

'I'll have to tell him.'

'You will.'

'But there's no point unless I know for sure, is there?'

'That's up to you.'

Ffion's eyes were darting around as she considered the possibilities and Hannah could see that she was torn. 'Why don't we head back to the village and get you a test then you can decide whether to do it or to wait for Joe?'

'That's a good plan.' Ffion covered her face for a moment as if to process the possibility that she could be pregnant, then looked up. 'Thank you, Hannah. You poor thing, having to help me through this when I'd offered to be your guide today. I was going to show you a good time, get you some food from the stalls and a few drinks too. There's a fabulous cider shack on the green and a Welsh gin one.' She laughed wildly. 'And if I am… pregnant… I won't be able to drink. Not that I've wanted to for the past few weeks anyway.' She slapped her hand over her mouth. 'At Mari's when we had Sunday lunch. I didn't like the wine.'

Hannah bobbed her head. 'The signs were there.'

'But…' Ffion's eyes clouded over. 'I didn't expect this and didn't plan it. I… I wonder what Graeme would say.'

'Graeme?'

'My husband.'

Hannah tried to conceal her shock. *Ffion was married?*

'He… I lost him… to cancer.'

'I'm so sorry, Ffion, that's terribly sad.'

'Eighteen months ago. We lived in Scotland and that's why I came back to Cariad Cove. I was broken, Hannah. But here, in my home, I began to heal. It wasn't an easy journey but something about this place helped. Being with my family, making new friends, meeting Joe… it all brought me back from the brink and I'm so grateful to everyone for helping me. Running too was my salvation. It made me stronger physically and mentally and helped fix me.'

'You have quite a story to tell, Ffion.' Admiration filled her chest for this brave and resilient woman.

'I apologise for pouring it all out now. I'm also very emotional at the moment and I guess that could be hormones. I'd thought that I'd missed two periods because of the running and how my body was changing and, to be honest, stress and anxiety over recent years meant that I wasn't regular anyway. I've been so busy and didn't dwell on why I was so late, but now that you've put the idea in my head... I'm wondering if it could be true. Goodness, what if it's true!'

There was silence as they both absorbed the possibility.

'How do you feel about it?' Hannah asked gently.

'I'm not sure. Is that bad?'

Hannah slid her hand over the table and took one of Ffion's. 'It's not bad at all. There is no right or wrong way to feel about this and if it wasn't planned, then of course it's going to be a shock. However, you might find that it makes you happy.'

Ffion's brown eyes were cloudy with a mixture of emotions, from doubt to shock to confusion and there was something else. Hannah could see it there, battling with the rest: the tiny glimmer of hope. If Ffion was pregnant then she had a feeling that it would be embraced with love and positivity. She'd seen how Joe looked at Ffion, as if she was the most important person in the world, the answer to everything he'd ever wanted. He loved Ffion and she loved him, they were young, fit and healthy so they had nothing to fear. There was the chance that it was something else, perhaps, and if so then a test would rule pregnancy out, but Hannah was fairly certain that her diagnosis was correct and that there was a baby on the way.

'Shall we go and get a test? The only thing is, that if I go into the shop and buy one then people might talk. They shouldn't but if anyone sees me buying it…' Ffion let her sentence trail off.

'It's fine. Not many people around here know me so I'll get it for you then you can go home and decide what to do.'

'Thank you so much.' Ffion squeezed Hannah's hand between both of hers. 'I'm so glad you're here.'

Hannah's throat tightened. Ffion was glad that she was here? Hannah had been able to help this amazing woman by talking her through something. Deep down, from the moment she'd laid eyes on Ffion today, a part of her had suspected that Ffion was pregnant. With her own history, this resonated inside her and made her think of how she'd wished she had someone to help her when things were difficult. A friend to talk to would have made the world of difference, someone to lean on would have helped her through one of the worst times of her life. Hannah hadn't had that but she would be there for Ffion so her new friend didn't feel alone. Talking was therapeutic, as was knowing that you weren't alone.

'It's no problem at all,' Hannah choked out, ducking her head so that Ffion wouldn't see the tears in her eyes. She'd come to Cariad Cove by chance, to get material for her articles, not expecting to fall in love with the location and certainly not expecting to find friends as well as an attractive man and his adorable daughter to care about.

But here she was.

Caring about the three of them.

Cariad Cove was proving to be so much more than a holiday destination and Hannah wondered how much more she'd encounter during her stay.

Chapter 16

Ffion waited in the street while Hannah went into the shop and picked up a test, a bottle of ginger cordial and some ginger and lemon tea bags. The woman at the counter didn't bat an eyelid as she served Hannah.

'There you go.' She handed the carrier bag to Ffion. 'I got you some things to help if the nausea gets worse too.'

Ffion peered into the bag as she accepted it. 'Thanks so much. You're very kind.'

They crossed the road and walked until they reached a pretty stone cottage with a front garden filled with flowers, white wooden window frames with small panes and a heavy iron knocker on the front door in the shape of a lion.

Ffion unlocked the door and they entered a cool hallway that smelt of beeswax polish and faintly of woodsmoke. The staircase was to the left and the hallway had two doors, one leading into a lounge to the right and the one straight in front led into the kitchen. Ffion led the way and in the kitchen she set down the carrier bag.

'This is a lovely place,' Hannah said.

'I know. Joe renovated it himself. He's very talented. Shall I put the kettle on?'

'I'll do it if you show me where everything is. I think you need to sit down.'

'I'm fine.' Ffion gave a wry laugh. 'I'm not an invalid, I'm just tired and… not quite right. But thank you.'

'Where's Odin?' Hannah asked, realising that the dog hadn't rushed to greet them as she'd have expected.

'With Joe. He takes him everywhere he can. He'd take him to school if he could.' Ffion leant against the worktop. 'I think I'm going to have to do the test now. It'll drive me mad if I don't.'

'Are you sure?'

Ffion chewed at her lip. 'No. But if I don't, I won't be able to think about anything else all afternoon.'

'Well, you go and do it and I'll make the tea. Unless you'd like to be home alone, of course. I don't want to intrude.'

Ffion grimaced. 'Please stay. If you don't mind, that is. I would call my sister, Mari, but she's taken the children out for the day and I don't want to worry her.'

'You and Mari are close, aren't you?'

'Very.' Ffion's eyes lit up and Hannah thought of the old yearning she'd had to know how it felt to have a sibling. 'OK. I'm going to do this. The bathroom is upstairs. Tea things are all there next to the kettle.'

'Great. I'll be here when you come down.'

Ffion gave a strained smile then left the kitchen and Hannah heard her padding up the stairs. She went about making two mugs of ginger and lemon tea, admiring the homely mugs with farmyard prints and the view of the back garden through the window over the sink. There were flowers in borders and pots, a long rectangle of grass and further along the garden was a wooden archway with climbing roses. Beyond that, she could make out what she suspected were fruit trees. It was a perfect home and she was happy for Ffion that she had somewhere like this, and that she had Joe because she'd clearly been through a lot in recent years. They might not have moved in together officially but it was on the cards she felt sure.

Hannah set two mugs on coasters on the rectangular oak table in front of bifold doors then sat down, leaning back in her chair to admire the view. She could imagine opening the doors and letting the sunny day into the kitchen, breathing in the scent of the flowers, grass and fertile earth. It would be a wonderful place to have break-fast with the sun warming the slate tiles of the floor and the birds singing outside.

Creaking overhead made her stomach clench. She was nervous for Ffion, understood the tension of the situation and wished she could make it easier in some way. This could be a good thing for the young couple and although it would be poignant for Ffion because of Graeme, it would also be a sign that her life was moving on.

Hannah knew that grief was a complex emotion and one that never truly went away. If you loved someone and lost them then they left a hole in your life and you would never be the same from that point onwards. She had learnt that when she lost her mum. The pain had been dreadful, she had cried until she was hoarse and until she made herself sick. As she'd got older, she'd run until her legs throbbed and her feet stung with blisters, she'd swum until her skin was dry and flaky from chlorine or salt and her hair was stiff and brittle. Sometimes, she'd drunk until she couldn't articulate her feelings, until she was numb, but the next day everything always seemed far worse, with darkness and a sense of hopelessness bringing her to her knees. As a child, she'd hoped that someone might take her pain away, a foster mother or father, a kind social worker, but none of them had been able to wipe her slate clean. Adults had no more power to wipe away grief than children did. The grief had been hers to deal with and she'd learnt to let it flood her system, to accept that it would hurt for as long as it hurt and that some days would be worse than others. Running and swimming had helped and then so had travelling, because while she was busy, she couldn't dwell on what she didn't have.

Ffion had lost the man she loved and Hannah couldn't begin to imagine how that would feel. Her mum had been her mum, but a partner would be different, that person you'd chosen to spend your life with and who had done the same with you. Ffion was an adult, whereas Hannah had been a child and she wasn't sure if either time was easier than the other. Loss would hurt whatever age you were and whoever you lost and that was how it was to be human.

On the flip side, being human meant that there were opportunities to be happy, to have friends, to fall in love and to enjoy the beauty of nature and Ffion had those possibilities now. She had a family around her and a man who loved her. She would be OK.

Hannah sipped her tea. The lemon and ginger complimented each other perfectly and she sighed as she cradled the mug in her hands. Coming to Cariad Cove had certainly been different to how she'd imagined it being but she was glad she was here and knew she'd be sad when the time came to leave.

She heard water running, a door opening then feet on the stairs.

Ffion appeared in the doorway, eyes like lumps of coal in her pale face.

Hannah stood up. 'Well?'

Ffion's mouth contorted and her eyes twitched. 'I… I…' Then she started to cry.

–

'There are so many, Daddy,' Beti said as she gazed at the bookshelf in front of her.

'I know. Exciting, isn't it?' Will crouched down next to his daughter. 'Can you see one you'd like to get?'

Beti ran a finger over the colourful spines, her small mouth open in awe. Will had decided that a trip to the bookshop in Cariad Cove would be a good start to a new week. Beti loved reading and loved Owlbert Einstein Books. It was, Will thought, like a curiosity shop with books new and old and a fabulous cafe where you could get delicious cakes and milkshakes.

Beti pulled a book from the shelf and held it up. 'I like this author.'

Will took the book from her and turned it over in his hands to read the blurb. 'Looks good. It's also the first in a new series so you can start with this one then when you've finished it, we'll get the next one.'

'They might have it at the library though, Daddy, and it would be free from there.'

'That's true and we will visit the library during the holidays too, but it's always nice to have some books on your bedroom shelves.'

'Yay! I was hoping you'd say that.' Beti took the book from him and held it against her chest. 'I can't wait to start reading it.'

'I'll see if I can find one I want to read then we'll pay for them and go and have a milkshake, shall we?'

'And a cake?' Beti's eyes were wide as she gazed up at him and his heart melted.

'Absolutely.'

While he browsed the thriller shelves, Beti stood next to him with her book and started reading. Will was delighted that she was such a bookworm because he knew how enriching reading could be and wanted her to be able to enjoy the escapism books offered throughout her life. There were so many benefits to reading and he wished that some of the pupils in school knew that too as he heard the words 'reading's boring' far too often in his job.

When he'd chosen a book, they went to the counter and paid then headed to the rear of the building to the cafe.

Sitting outside in the walled garden, Beti placed her book on the table. 'What shall we talk about, Daddy?'

'I know you want to read so carry on.' He laughed. 'I don't mind. I have my own book, remember.'

Beti rewarded him with a gap-toothed grin then slid her book towards her and opened it. While she read, Will sat back in his chair and gazed around. The garden was beautiful, the scent of the roses was heady and relaxing and he let his mind drift.

He hadn't seen Hannah for two days but that didn't mean he hadn't thought about her. Their time at the beach had been interesting to say the least and he was intrigued by her and what had happened in her past to make her the way she was. She'd dived into the water to save a stranger's dog without thinking twice, even though she'd confessed that she had reasons for not wanting to swim. What could those reasons be? What had happened to her to make her feel that way?

Will was also impressed by how well Beti and Hannah got on. They seemed so comfortable together and there was even what he could describe as affection in their relationship. It warmed his heart and simultaneously, it scared him. What if Beti grew to care for Hannah then she never saw her again? Hannah would leave once her work was done but would she make an effort to stay in touch with Beti? Her own mother barely bothered so why would a woman with no links or responsibilities to them?

A waitress arrived at the table and placed two strawberry milkshakes and two iced buns on the table. Beti lowered her book and waggled her eyebrows, making Will laugh, then she put her book down and reached for her bun.

'Thank you, Daddy, this is the perfect way to start the week.'

'I agree and you're always welcome.'

They chomped on their buns then washed them down with milkshakes and Will marvelled at his little girl and how resilient and sweet she was. Letting a woman into their lives would not be a simple decision to make and so he wouldn't rush a thing. He'd see how things went with Hannah because even if she was only around for a short time, that might be enough to open his eyes to the possibility of new friendships for him and for Beti. And as far as he was concerned, you could always make room for new friends.

-

Hannah sprang from her chair and went to Ffion's side. Ffion was shaking, her right hand clutching the test stick, her left one pressed to her chest. Hannah opened her arms and wrapped them around her friend. She stroked Ffion's hair and rocked her gently, and Ffion started to cry. Hannah didn't try to speak, didn't push Ffion to share the result, she knew that Ffion needed to let go.

When Ffion finally fell quiet, Hannah led her to a chair and sat her down then grabbed a box of tissues from the dresser behind the table. She pulled out a wad and handed them to Ffion.

Ffion wiped her eyes and blew her nose with one hand, the other still gripping the white plastic stick like it was a talisman against a darkness she was battling.

'Your tea might be cold. Shall I make another?' Hannah asked.

'It's OK. I'll still drink it.' Ffion picked up the mug and took a sip.

Hannah finished her own tea, gazing out of the window. She couldn't remember the last time she'd held someone while they cried. She kept her distance from people, afraid to open up to anyone, so what was happening with Ffion was both surprising and yet special. She didn't feel at all uncomfortable with Ffion; felt, in fact, as though she'd known her for years. But then, sometimes, people just clicked. She'd heard about that, read about it and now she was experiencing it first-hand.

'Sorry about that,' Ffion said, gazing at Hannah with swollen red eyes.

'No need to apologise. That needed to come out.'

Ffion raised the hand holding the test. 'It was such a shock. I wasn't sure how I felt about pregnancy until I did it and for a while, nothing happened. Then one line appeared, so I read the instructions and it said that meant the test was negative. I just felt… devastated. I didn't plan on being pregnant but the fact that I might have been changed something in me. But… I was about to throw the test in the bin when I noticed this…' She held the test out to Hannah.

'Two lines.'

'Yes.' Ffion's eyes were wide with wonder. 'Does that mean… Am I…'

'Those tests are pretty reliable. I think false negatives are more common than false positives. You could do another to be sure.'

'I will. Definitely.' Ffion set the test on a tissue on the table. 'I got upset because I was shocked and because I feel like I'm on an emotional rollercoaster. This is so… crazy. After everything that's happened over the past few years, this was the last thing I was expecting.' She snorted. 'Pardon the pun. *Expecting!* I might be expecting.'

Hannah smiled. Ffion was going to be fine.

A meow from the doorway made them both jump and a fluffy tabby cat stretched then padded towards them. It wound itself around Ffion's legs and she reached down and lifted it onto her lap. 'Hey sweetie.' The cat rubbed its head under Ffion's chin and started to purr.

'Who's this?' Hannah asked.

'This is our cat, Beatrix. I fell in love with her when I visited the animal sanctuary and Will adopted her for me. She's around ten now but she's the sweetest thing.' The cat settled on Ffion's lap and she stroked her, smoothing the soft fur from head to tail.

Then Ffion's face fell again.

'What is it?'

'Graeme.' Ffion pulled a tissue from the box and ran it between her fingers. 'He would have been a fabulous father. He was a wonderful husband and my best friend. I loved him so much, Hannah. I can't even begin to explain it… Seeing him get ill, seeing him change was unbelievably hard. The cancer took so much from him, and he battled it, he really tried, he was incredibly brave, but then… He became so terribly tired and it… diminished him. I wanted him to keep going but he told me he couldn't take any more and I had to let him make that choice.' She started to tear up the tissue, dropping tiny pieces on the table, creating a small white pile.

'I can't imagine what you've been through.'

Ffion blinked. 'The guilt at surviving was horrendous. I was physically healthy, carrying on with life while he drifted away. I held him in my arms that final day…' She covered her face with her hands. 'Oh god that day… I still can't believe it.'

Hannah got up and went to Ffion, crouching down next to her.

'He loved you and so he would want you to go on. He'd be so proud of you.'

'He… he left me a letter.' Ffion lowered her hands and placed them in her lap. 'He told me that he wanted me to go on… to live my life to the full.'

'And having a family is a sure way to do that, Ffion. I've no doubt that Graeme would be happy that you're getting on with your life, that you're in love.'

'The funny thing is that I know Graeme would have liked Joe.'

'I'm sure he would.'

They both turned towards the doorway at a sound from the hall then Odin bounded into the kitchen. Hannah stood up as the dog rushed at her and she stroked his head then he went to Ffion and placed his front paws on her legs, reaching up to sniff at her face and at Beatrix's.

'He knows,' Ffion said. 'He can sense when I'm worried.'

'Hello.' Joe entered the kitchen carrying a paper bag. 'Aunt Caryn sent supplies. She insisted on sending an apple crumble and chocolate muffins and—' Concern clouded his features. 'Fi?'

He hurried to Ffion's side and Hannah stepped back. 'I'll uh… I'll be going.'

Joe glanced at her then back at Ffion. 'What happened?'

'I'll explain in a moment, Joe.' Ffion placed a hand on his shoulder then peered around him. 'Thanks, Hannah. I'm so sorry for today. I promise I'm usually better company.'

'Don't be soft. It's fine. What are friends for?' Hannah said with a small shrug, liking how the words sounded. She was a friend of Ffion.

'I'll see you out,' Joe said, standing, confusion flooding his face when he spotted the test on the table.

'It's all right, honestly. You two have a lot to talk about.'

Hannah went to the kitchen doorway. 'Let me know if you need anything. I'll see you soon.' She waved then went to the front door. As she opened it, she heard the quiet murmur of voices from the kitchen, heard the words 'I love you, Fi, more than anything in the world', and her heart expanded.

Ffion and Joe would be absolutely fine.

Chapter 17

The next morning, Hannah woke early and couldn't drop back off to sleep. It wasn't worrying about Ffion that had woken her, although she did hope that her friend was OK today. It was restlessness, the feeling that had kept her travelling, moving from place to place, writing article after article after article.

But sometimes, she was coming to realise, a person needed to slow down. To stop. To spend time on self-awareness as they took a moment to look at themselves and their lives and to evaluate their direction.

Where was she heading? What was her ultimate goal? She might only be thirty now but before she knew it, time would pass and, if she was lucky, she'd grow older. And then what? As long as she was fit and well, she could continue to travel, to maintain momentum, but was that what she wanted?

Witnessing Ffion's distress had made her think. Ffion had been through so much, had been to the depths of despair yet here she was… grabbing hold of her life with both hands and creating a future, creating a new life inside her body, living and feeling and not shying away from all that she'd been through. If Ffion could do that, then there was a possibility that Hannah could do it too.

But where would she begin to make changes? She'd lived with her emotions shut down for so long, had buried all the pain she didn't want to feel and – most of the time – managed to shut it out by denying herself certain things that she used to enjoy.

Running.

Swimming.

Holding someone close.

Making love.

Dancing in the rain.

If she did any of these things then there was a chance that she would break wide open and release all of the darkness that she'd carried for so long. It was terrifying, the thought of letting go, of opening herself up, of crumbling to dust if she couldn't cope.

Just then her mobile buzzed with a message from Ffion. Hannah scanned it, a smile spreading across her face. Everything had gone well with Joe last night, in fact, he'd been delighted but they were both being cautious not to get too excited just in case the two home pregnancy tests were wrong. Ffion had booked an appointment with the GP and was going this morning to get everything confirmed. She ended by thanking Hannah for being such a good friend and promising to let her know how it went with the GP.

Ffion was brave, strong and fierce, and Hannah wanted to be able to find that strength in herself. She'd been mistaken thinking that not showing emotion equalled being strong, that it allowed her to be without a chink in her armour, because in reality, strength was opening up and showing the world who you really were and embracing all of your emotions. Ffion had felt guilt too, for living when her husband was gone, but she'd managed to overcome it. Not entirely, perhaps, because every time she encountered something new – like the pregnancy – there would be no doubt be some flashback or hang-up to overcome, but she would get there. It was inspirational and Hannah wanted to overcome her own guilt, her own sadness, and to embrace all that life had to offer.

But could she really do that?

There was only one way to find out and that was by taking a first step.

Today, the yearning to get outside and run was strong. When she was younger, she had loved to run, had woken some days filled with the craving to get out there and hit the pavement, to experience the buzz as endorphins flooded her system. Then her life had taken an unexpected turn and she'd stopped running, feeling that enjoying it so much was wrong. She had felt that something about her was wrong. After all, if she'd been doing things right then *it* wouldn't have happened.

Now she was questioning the beliefs that had held her hostage all these years. Cariad Cove, Ffion and her family, Joe and Beti existed wonderfully in the present and Hannah wanted to be right there with them.

She dressed in leggings and a T-shirt, slid her feet into her trainers and pulled her hair into a ponytail. It had been a very long time since she'd run, but she hoped that her body would remember its rhythm, just like she was starting to remember what caring about others felt like in her heart.

—

Will's feet pounded the sand. He inhaled deeply, exhaled fully, focusing on his body and how good it felt to run. Mari had invited Beti to hers for a playdate this morning and had said she'd give Beti lunch, then told him to go and do something nice. He'd laughed initially, wondering whether a morning in front of his computer making teaching resources would be considered *nice*, then he'd made a bargain with himself; he'd go for a run then do some work. Some teachers were able to work whenever it suited them during the holidays but Will had to fit work in around Beti. Whenever she went to his parents' house or to a friend's, Will had to use that time efficiently.

He pushed the thoughts of schoolwork away. This was meant to be his time out and he had the rest of the morning to focus on making resources and planning his schemes of work for the next year.

The air was still cool and there was a mist over the sea as if the clouds had sunk to rest on the water's surface. It made everything feel slightly muffled, but he also knew that it would probably burn off and there would be another beautiful summer day at the cove. Even though it was early, not yet eight, there were stallholders setting up in the car park and some people walking dogs on the beach. Every summer, he found it strange seeing other people going about their daily business as usual, because the six weeks away from the school building – apart from the times he went in to organise his classroom and for results – made him feel like he was in some sort of bubble. He worked when he could, but the rest of the holidays were spent focusing on Beti, whether that was taking her out for the day, going food shopping with her, visiting his parents and sister or taking her to get school uniform for September. While supermarkets advertised school uniform and 'back to school' supplies from the end of the summer term, it was only as August wore on that Will started to feel a bit gloomy. Not that he didn't love his job or the school he worked at, but because it meant the end of another summer and the start of another school year for Beti. Time was passing so quickly and he knew he'd soon turn around to find that she was all grown up. That thought made him sad but also hopeful; sad because he wanted her to be his baby girl forever, and hopeful because he wanted her to grow up healthy and happy. He'd had the opportunity to apply for a promotion at work but had decided not to do so because more work would mean more stress and more time away from Beti. When she grew up and left home, he'd have plenty of disposable time on his hands to pursue his career, but for now, Beti was his priority.

He reached the cliffs that separated Cariad Cove from Barddoniaeth Bay and slowed down before turning to head back the other way. He'd decided to run up and down the beach a few times today to check his pace and see if he could beat his 5k personal best.

Running in the direction of the hotel, he quickened his stride, glancing at his smartwatch to check his progress. Not bad. He could well create a new record. Up ahead, he spotted a figure running towards him, head down, arms flailing as if she was trying to propel herself along one minute, then wrapping them around her body as if she was trying to give herself a hug the next. Different people had different running styles – not that he was judging, although some people looked very strange when they ran – but this woman looked like she was trying to find her stride and losing the battle. If he kept going, he'd still make a new time for himself but a voice inside him was shouting at him to slow down and see if the woman was, as he now suspected, Hannah.

The voice won and he slowed down to a gentle jog, waiting for her to look up so he could assess whether or not she was all right.

-

Hannah had warmed up, stretched until her muscles groaned and then walked for five minutes, but even so, her legs felt heavy and her chest was tight. Looking at how far she'd come from the hotel, she didn't think she'd done two kilometres. That filled her with dismay. When she used to run, she often managed seven or eight kilometres before she started to feel tired. Her fitness had definitely dropped and her body almost felt like it belonged to someone else. Back then, in her teens, she'd loved the feeling during and after a run, but now, at thirty, it was different. Very different. Things had certainly changed.

She tried to suck in air but her chest was tight and her throat felt constricted. Her feet seemed to sink into the sand every time they landed and something was twanging in her bum cheek. The running bra she'd brought with her had seen better days and was not as supportive as it should be, so from time to time, she'd folded her arms across her chest to try to support her breasts. This was not a good thing because it distracted her from the run itself and she lost momentum. When something in her side started to burn, she knew it was time to call it a day.

She staggered to a stop then leant over, hands resting on her knees. Sweat poured down her face and her back and most of her hair had come out of its ponytail. She knew she must look a total mess. Thank goodness it was unlikely that she'd see anyone she knew down on the beach at this time.

'Hannah?' The voice was deep, sexy, familiar.

Oh shit.

She straightened up and met dark brown eyes filled with concern.

'Uh... hello... Will.'

She felt like her pulse was pounding behind her eyes and a ringing started in her ears, then everything went black.

–

'Hannah!' Will managed to catch her before she fell and he lowered her gently to the sand, resting her against his knees. Her eyelids flickered and then she was frowning up at him.

'What... what happened?'

'You fainted.'

'I fainted?' She tried to sit up but pressed a hand to her head. 'Everything's spinning.'

'Just rest for a moment and you'll feel better.' He pulled a bottle from his running backpack. 'Here, have some water.'

He helped her to raise it to her lips and she took a sip. Then another.

The colour was starting to return to her cheeks now. When she'd stood up to look at him, her face had gone white, her eyes had rolled backwards in her head then she'd fallen. Will had seen it happen before to other unfit runners, so knew what to do but it didn't mean he wasn't worried about her.

'I think I'm OK, now,' she said, easing herself up to a sitting position and crossing her legs in front of her. 'It's just been a while since I ran.'

'When was the last time you ran?' he asked.

'A long time ago. Many years in fact.'

'You should build up to it then.'

She glanced at him then lowered her gaze to the sand.

'I know. I didn't run all the way along the beach. I probably only did about two kilometres.'

'That's a lot if you're not used to running.'

'I woke with an urge to run and just had to go for it.' Hannah raised the bottle and drank. 'Thanks for this.'

'Well as long as you're OK, now. You gave me a fright.'

Hannah frowned. 'Where's Beti?'

'With Mari and her daughters. I thought I'd get a run in before I do some school work.'

'Do you have a lot to do?'

'Enough.' He laughed. 'Some people call teachers out for having such long holidays.' He air quoted *holidays*. 'It's time away from lessons but not away from the workload. There's always lots to do and it's the type of job where you never get on top of it all.'

'I don't know how you do it. I'd hate that. At least for me, I write an article and it's done then I move on to the next one.' She tilted her head. 'But you like your job, don't you?'

'I love it. Always have done. I feel privileged to work with young people and to help shape their lives, expand their knowledge and see them leave school and go out into the world excited about life.'

'That does sound wonderful.'

'Perhaps…' He swallowed.

'Perhaps what?'

'It doesn't matter.'

'Go on, please.' She smiled. 'Tell me.'

'I was going to say perhaps you could come in and speak to the pupils about your experiences as a travel writer. I know Beti asked if you'd do this at her school but I'm sure the pupils at the comprehensive would be interested too. They love learning about different jobs. But I guess that… probably can't happen.'

'Why not?'

'Well… you'll be leaving soon.'

'Oh… of course.' She sighed then set the water bottle down. She pushed her hands through her hair, pulling it back into a ponytail, catching all the strands that had escaped.

'Unless you came back at some point or even stayed a bit longer. I'm sure we could work something out.'

'I'd like that.' She moved to her knees then stood up and Will did too, holding out an arm in case she felt wobbly.

'OK?'

'Yes. I think so. I'll walk back slowly though… just in case.'

'I'll walk with you.'

'That's very kind of you.'

'We should get you checked out at the first aid station in the car park.'

'I don't need first aid.' Hannah's voice rose at the end of her sentence. 'I'm fine.'

'It would make me feel better if you did get checked over. Just in case.'

'Will, it's low blood sugar and being unfit that made me feel faint. Even I know that.'

There was a defensiveness to her tone, as if she hated having anyone worry about her.

'Well, it's not my place to insist and it's up to you, of course.'

She fell quiet for a moment and gazed up at the hotel. 'All right. I'll go to the first aid station but only for you. But I really am fine.'

'Thank you.'

They walked along the beach slowly, Will keeping a close eye on Hannah in case she looked like she was going to faint again, but his training told him that she'd probably be fine with more water and something to eat. Still, he didn't want her taking any chances.

Chapter 18

Hannah drove into the car park and cut the engine. She took a sip of water from the bottle in the cupholder then set it back down. It had been two days since she'd fainted on the beach and she'd been fine but she was determined to stay hydrated. She did, however, feel like an idiot. Poor Will had come along and found her puffing and panting with sweat dripping from her skin then she'd passed out, basically in his arms. It was embarrassing, and yet Will hadn't done or said anything to make her feel worse; he had been kind and attentive, understanding and concerned. She liked that about Cariad Cove, the fact that there were people here who cared about her. As much as she enjoyed being independent, it was nice to know that people had your back, that if something went wrong then they would be there to support you. It was, she guessed, what community was all about and when she wrote her articles, it would be one of the things she would ensure she stressed: Cariad Cove was a beautiful location with a warm and friendly community that looked out for one another and for their visitors.

She dropped her gaze to the steering wheel.

A visitor... a tourist... just someone passing through.

The thought of leaving the cove lost its appeal by the day. There was much here to love and enjoy and the thought of looking for a house of her own and settling here didn't seem bad at all. She'd be able to live in a place where she had friends like Will and Ffion and where she could continue to write but from home for a change.

Home?

To have a home of her own…

Would it be as bad as she'd always thought it would?

Movement caught her eye as another car pulled into the car park. When the door opened and Will got out, her heart leapt. He was wearing olive cargo shorts and a white T-shirt with a something printed across the chest, and he looked gorgeous. He was becoming so familiar to her and the more that she saw of him, the stronger her attraction to him grew. Not only was he her real-life hero, coming to her rescue when she fainted, but he was just so nice. There didn't seem to be anything about him to dislike and she could never imagine him being like some of the men she'd encountered in her past, the ones who'd wanted just one thing from her, who grew bored easily and who didn't let her close anyway. She'd always gone for men who weren't interested in commitment or more than a fling, men who often loved themselves so much they'd have no room in their lives for someone else. Had it been subconscious, that careful selection? A way of ensuring that she wouldn't care about them and they wouldn't pretend to care about her? The last thing she'd wanted was to bring anyone into her life and risk being hurt or abandoned again.

Again?

Her mum hadn't abandoned her deliberately but sometimes, as a child, she'd been angry that her mum had let ovarian cancer beat her. As an adult, she felt terrible for that mistaken belief because cancer didn't care about who it ravaged or who it left behind. Her mum had fought, clung desperately to life as she tried to be there for Hannah, but in the end, it hadn't been enough. Hannah knew it had shaped her, knew that her feelings as a child had been understandable, that anger was a stage of grieving, but her cheeks glowed now to think about the nights when she'd sobbed into her pillow and whispered to her mum that she hated her for leaving her all alone. There was no hate in her heart at all for her mum, only love and a longing to hear her voice, to feel her embrace and to smell her floral perfume that had lingered in the house long after she'd sprayed it on.

Rubbing her eyes, she made an effort to clear her mind. She had an exciting afternoon ahead with Will and Beti at the animal sanctuary. After he'd walked her to the first aid station two days ago, he'd mentioned that he was taking Beti there and invited Hannah along too.

Will, Beti and animals. What could be more appealing on a sunny afternoon?

Hannah grabbed her bag from the passenger seat, hooked her camera around her neck and slicked on some lip gloss. Opening the car door, the heat hit her like a wall. Away from the beach, it seemed to hover in the air, shimmering like it would in a desert because there was little breeze in the car park. She could imagine the sun heating the gravel like coals then that heat rising into the air and it made her long for the soothing air conditioning of the car.

'Hannah!' Beti had spotted her and she ran towards her, small arms outstretched. Hannah crouched down and accepted Beti's hug before standing up and taking her hand to walk back over to Will. He was getting a rucksack out of the boot and he hooked it over his shoulders then locked the car.

'Hot enough for you?' He grimaced and wiped at his brow.

'Makes me long for the beach.'

'Do you think the animals will be too hot?' Beti asked, her brow furrowing. 'What if they get sunburn?'

'I'm sure that Joe and the other volunteers at the sanctuary give them lots of water and special sunhats.' Will winked at Hannah.

'Sunhats?' Beti giggled. 'On the dogs and donkeys.'

'Why not?' Will gave a small shrug. 'Or sun umbrellas.'

'Sounds good to me,' Hannah said. 'Have you got your sunhat, Beti?'

Beti looked up at her. 'Of course I have, silly. Daddy packs everything but the kitchen sink.'

Hannah met Will's gaze and saw the mirth in his eyes. 'It's what my mam says.'

'Good to know you come prepared.'

'Did you bring a sunhat?' he asked her.

Hannah pulled a face. 'I meant to pack one but I think… actually I know, I forgot it.'

Will slipped the rucksack off and unzipped it then pulled out a small baseball cap with mermaids on that he handed to Beti as well as two adult baseball caps – one white and one navy.

'Here.' He held them out. 'I just happened to pack two. Pick a colour.'

Hannah accepted the white one. 'Thank you.'

'You're very welcome.' He put his own cap on before hooking his arms through the straps of the rucksack again. Hannah looked more closely at the slogan on his T-shirt.

'"I'm a history teacher, like other teachers but cooler",' she read.

Will laughed. 'A few of my students clubbed together and bought it for me last year. I wear it to wind other teachers up, especially Joe.'

'It's brilliant. The pupils must like you to get such a thoughtful gift.'

'Some of them do, I guess. There are a few who don't but you can't win them all round.' He shrugged.

'I don't like the naughty pupils who give Daddy a hard time.' Beti scowled. 'I'd give them pieces of my mind.'

'Lots of pieces?' Will winked at Beti. 'I don't speak about the pupils to Beti but I was asking Mam's advice one day about a particularly challenging group, because she used to teach too, and Beti overheard me. She wasn't impressed that not all pupils like her daddy.'

'That's not on, is it Beti?' Hannah shook her head. 'How could anyone fail to like your daddy?' She looked up as she said the words and caught something in Will's gaze. It made her heart beat faster so she lowered her eyes to Beti again, willing the heat in her face to subside.

'Just wait until I get to Daddy's school. I'll make sure everyone likes him.'

'I'm sure you will.'

'Shall we head inside?' Will asked. 'Before we all get hot and bothered.'

They crossed the car park and approached the gates, Beti still holding Hannah's hand.

'So your mam is a teacher?' Hannah asked Will.

'Was.'

'She's retired now?'

'Yes. She retired four years ago but you wouldn't know it.'

'What do you mean?' Hannah reached around with her free hand and placed it on the back of her neck hoping for some relief from the heat.

'She still speaks and acts like she's at school sometimes.'

'Nanny is a bossyboots.' Beti looked up at Hannah. 'But don't tell her I said that because she'll go on and on and Bampi will have it up to here all day and all night.' She rolled her eyes dramatically as she held a hand above her head to demonstrate how much her bampi would have to deal with.

Hannah wasn't sure how to react but Will chuckled. 'My dad has been known to say that. When Mam gets a bee in her bonnet… we all know about it.'

'Goodness.' Hannah grimaced.

'She's got a heart of gold and she'd do anything for me and Beti, as well as for Dad, so please don't think we're telling you that she's awful. I couldn't wish for a better mother. She has been incredibly supportive of me all my life but she does worry and sometimes her worrying takes the form of—'

'Nagging,' Beti whispered as if it was a criminal offence to say the words.

'Don't worry, I won't say a word,' Hannah said softly.

'You must come and meet Nanny,' Beti said. 'She's always telling Daddy to hurry up and bring a special friend home.' Beti pushed her tongue through the gap in her front teeth. 'Nanny says Daddy has been on his own for too long and it's not good for his mental elf.'

Will shook his head and Hannah bit her lip to stifle a giggle. Beti didn't miss a trick, although as for Will's mental elf, that was one she hadn't heard before.

At the gates, Will pressed a buzzer and gave their names. The gate opened and Joe was there.

'Hello!' He waved them through. 'So good to see you all. It'll be quiet around the sanctuary today but it means you can take your time and get lots of photos.' He gestured at Hannah's camera.

'Aren't you open to the public today then?' Will asked.

'No, with the heat and shortage of volunteers on shift because some of them have gone to the summer festival with their families, Gwyneth thought it was better to close for the day.' He looked at Hannah. 'Gwyneth is the owner. She set this place up.'

'Alone?' Hannah looked around her at the sprawling outbuildings and green fields beyond.

'She was an estate agent but she always loved animals. One day, she decided enough was enough so she quit her job and ploughed all her money into this place. She never turns away an animal in need.'

'That's amazing,' Hannah said. 'Before I forget to ask, how's Ffion?'

Joe glanced at Will then held Hannah's gaze for a moment. 'She's fine. Resting this morning because… you know… of the heat.' It was clear that he didn't want people to know about the pregnancy yet, so Hannah gave him a discreet thumbs up.

'It has been very warm this week.' She fanned her face.

'A bit too warm for my liking but it's meant to cool down a bit by the weekend,' Joe replied.

'Is it OK if I take some photos now?' Hannah asked. 'I want to include the sanctuary in the articles about Cariad Cove and I might even do one about the sanctuary itself at some point.' She didn't let on that the thought of that excited her. It could be the start of a whole other side to her writing, a way of branching into PR perhaps.

'Please carry on. Gwyneth loves free publicity. Let me know if you want any information about the sanctuary and I can send it to you. There's a fair bit on the website but I'm sure Gwyneth would be happy to speak to you if you'd like, by way of an interview.'

'That would be brilliant. I'll get back to you about it.' Hannah smiled.

'Where's Odin, Joe?' Beti asked.

'He's in the farmhouse with the other dogs.' Joe pointed at the building behind him. 'Want to go and say hello?'

'Yes please and then can I see the donkeys and the rabbits and the cats?'

'You can see them all.' Joe looked at Will. 'OK if I take her through?'

'Absolutely. We'll catch up.'

Joe and Beti made their way across the yard to the farmhouse while Will and Hannah looked around. It was cooler in the courtyard because of the shade from the buildings. It smelt how Hannah imagined a working farm would, of straw, leather and animals. The cobbled stones of the yard were weathered and the window frames of the buildings needed a lick of paint but the atmosphere there was calm and peaceful.

'You getting some good shots?' Will asked.

'I am. I'll take some of the animals and the land as we go round.'

'If you fancy taking some of Beti with the animals too, we'd be very grateful. She has to write about her summer holidays as homework and it would be amazing to include some photos.'

'Of course I will.'

Hannah raised the camera and pointed it at Will but he held up a hand. 'Please, no close-ups.'

'Why not?'

He laughed. 'You don't want photos of me on my own.'

'What, handsome single dad and history teacher poses in gorgeous sunshine? If I posted that online you'd have thousands of fans flocking here to find you.'

Will's face coloured. 'I doubt it.'

Hannah lowered the camera. 'Why?'

He scuffed the toe of his trainer against the cobbles. 'I hardly think of myself as handsome.' His voice became very quiet. 'Or as a catch.'

As his blush deepened, Hannah's felt a heaviness in her chest. This adorable man didn't think he was handsome or eligible? It was crazy. So many people swanned about as if they were the best thing since sliced bread and yet Will, who had so much to offer, lacked self-confidence.

She stepped closer to him and placed a hand on his arm, gazed up into his eyes. 'Will… you of all people should feel confident. You have no idea how incredible you are, do you?'

He held her gaze, his eyes intense, his body so close she could feel the heat emanating from him and smell his woody cologne. The urge to rest her cheek on his chest and close her eyes as she breathed him in was overwhelming and it wouldn't have taken much encouragement from him to do exactly that.

'Daddy!' Beti burst from the farmhouse and Hannah jumped back, heart pounding as she gulped in air. She wasn't used to this, wasn't accustomed to being so drawn to a man that she wanted to rip his clothes off and kiss away his sadness, to snuggle on the sofa with him and to make plans for a golden future. Will was unlike anyone she'd ever met and she felt a connection to him but she knew that nothing could come of it. He had a daughter and a life here and she was just passing through, would soon be forgotten as autumn and winter came to the cove and she jetted off to foreign climes to see out the colder months. Will and Beti would go back to school and to their lives and one day, she felt sure, Will would meet a woman who did deserve him and who valued him for the man he was.

That thought brought a sour taste to her mouth but she tried to hold it in her mind because the way her feelings for him were developing was scaring her. She seemed to be simultaneously falling for the cove, Will and Beti, and if she wasn't careful she'd lose herself and the protective wall she'd built around her heart would come tumbling down.

And then what would happen to her?

There would be no one to put her back together again.

Only herself, and she was getting tired of having no one to lean on when times were tough, no one to celebrate with when life was good.

'Come on, Beti and Hannah, let's have a look around, shall we?' Will said, snapping her from her train of thought. He reached out and gently brushed her arm, the touch was as light as a feather against her skin but it brought her back to the moment and gave her a warm glow inside. Perhaps the moment was all they had, and in that case she had better treasure it.

–

Joe led them around the sanctuary, taking his time to explain things about each area and its animals to Beti. Hannah took lots of photos and Beti posed with the donkeys, the ponies, the guinea pigs, the chickens and the cats. When they came to the kennels, Beti's excitement was through the roof and Will had to gently tell her to calm down.

'The animals will sense how excited you are, Beti.'

'Will they?' Her eyes were round, her cheeks flushed.

'And they might get excited too and then get too hot.'

'Oh.' She pouted. 'I will try to calm down a bit, Daddy. I just love the animals.'

'I know you do.' He ruffled her hair. She'd removed her cap as they were going inside the kennel building and she held it reverently against her chest as they went in, her hairline damp from the heat.

'This is actually converted stables,' Joe said. 'There are two dogs to a kennel because they like company... a bit like us humans.'

'Do they get lonely too?' Beti asked.

'Absolutely. They're pack animals.' Joe unlocked the first door and let them inside a small room with two low beds. Each bed had a mattress and colourful blankets. The room was cool and Joe noted that the building had air conditioning, essential with soaring temperatures like today.

Two dogs came through a dog flap in the rear wall, tails wagging, but one stayed back while the other trotted forwards.

'This is Bonnie.' Joe knelt down and let the small black and brown dog sniff his hands then his face. He rubbed at her ears and she wagged her tail harder. 'She's a rescue dog from Romania.'

'Romania?' Beti gasped. 'That's a long way away. We learnt about the romans in school and how they made roads and had baths and travelled a lot.'

Joe met Will's eyes and smiled at Beti's comment. Will gave a small shake of his head, knowing that now was not the time to correct Beti about Romania and Romans; it could wait until later when he'd explain to her.

'How did Bonnie get here?' Beti was gazing at Joe as if he had the answer to every question. Will knew that put people under a lot of pressure to explain clearly and accurately.

'It's part of a new scheme to get dogs off the street in Romania by homing them in the UK. Gwyneth has become friendly with a team out there and she's helping them by having some of the dogs stay here while they find homes. Bonnie is beautiful and will soon find a home, I'm sure.'

Beti sat on one of the beds and Bonnie ran over to her. She stroked Bonnie's head gently and the dog started licking her cheeks. Beti giggled and the dog started trying to reach her ears.

Hannah was taking lots of photographs and Will admired her focus and professionalism. He knew that she was a writer first and foremost, from what she'd told him, but she was also a good photographer. He was impressed by what a talented and creative a person she was. He doubted that he could visit somewhere then write about it like Hannah did. He'd never know how to start describing a place to make it appeal to others, but the work of Hannah's that he'd read made locations seem so inviting. He hadn't travelled much due to being at university, working and having Beti to care for but he could see the attraction for someone who was free and single. The world was Hannah's oyster and she could go wherever she wanted whenever she wanted. But pleasant as that might be, surely there must come a point when she felt tired and just wanted to go home? Back to people who cared about her. Back to someone who loved her and would be there for her no matter what.

'What's this one's name?' Beti asked as the other dog, fawn-coloured with a brown patch over one eye, eventually approached her, sniffed her hands then dropped a red ball at her feet.

'This is Patch and she wants you to play.'

'Patch?' Beti giggled. 'Because of her eye patch?'

'That's right.' Joe smiled.

'Do you want to play ball, Patch?' Beti stroked the dog's head.

'She thinks you look like fun,' Joe said. 'Shall we take them out to the field and you can throw the ball for her?'

'Oh yes please. Can we go out there, Daddy?'

'Sounds like fun to me.'

'I'll put their harnesses on for the walk to the field then they can run free because it's all enclosed,' Joe explained.

When the dogs were ready, Joe led them out of the kennels and across the yard then towards a large field. It had high fences and some well-established trees, as well as some jumps, tunnels and what looked like a knee-high maze.

'It's all designed to provide stimulation for the dogs. They get exercised several times a day and, when we can, we place them with foster carers so they get used to being in a home too. The journey from kennels to cuddles is not simple or easy but it's a very rewarding one. In lucky instances, we get failed fosters, which is when the people fostering a dog love him or her so much they feel compelled to adopt the dog.' Joe opened the gate and walked inside and Will closed it behind them then Joe unclipped the dogs' leads and they were off.

'I thought we were going to play,' Beti said, disappointment evident in her tone.

'We will but they probably want to go to the toilet first.' Joe pulled a roll of poo bags from his pocket.

'What are they for?' Beti asked.

'Come with me and I'll show you.' Joe winked at Will. 'Oh… and don't think I didn't notice the T-shirt, Will. PE teachers are by far the best.'

'Yeah, right.' Will laughed.

'Are you both this competitive at work?' Hannah lowered her camera.

'Always.' Joe nudged Will. 'I'm a PE teacher, so of course I'm competitive.'

'It's true,' Will said.

'Back as soon as we've picked up all the poos!' Joe took Beti's hand. 'Come on, missy, I'll show you how it's done.'

Beti glanced at Will as she jogged away, and knowing his daughter as he did, Will knew that Beti was disgusted by the thought.

Hannah watched as Beti threw the ball for Patch. Each time, the dog waited eagerly for Beti to throw it, then chased after it before returning it to Beti. Hannah captured the game with her camera; the joy on the dog's face as it bounded after the ball and the delight on Beti's as the game went on and on. She felt exhausted just watching them.

Joe was guiding Bonnie around the field, encouraging her to go through the tunnel and around the obstacles, and it occurred to Hannah that he would make a very good dad with his patience, energy and enthusiasm. The way he was with the dogs and the way he'd been with Beti were all very positive signs.

'You getting some good shots?' Will asked, leaning back against the fence.

'Excellent. You want a look?'

She stepped closer to him and held up her camera, clicked through the recent photos of Beti, Joe and the animals at the sanctuary.

Will was close. Very close. As she scrolled through the photographs, her eyes strayed from the screen towards him. The hairs on his forearms had been lightened by the sunshine, and there were faint freckles on his skin. Looking up, she saw more freckles in the hollow at his throat, on his cheeks, and a few on his nose that she hadn't been aware of before. The urge to trace her fingers over the freckles was strong and she dragged her eyes back to the camera, unsettled by her burgeoning attraction to him. It seemed that her desire grew with every passing moment, and she wanted to get closer to him.

'They're brilliant,' he said as she lowered the camera. 'You're very clever.'

'Oh… Well… I just do what I can.'

'Don't dismiss your skills, Hannah. Not many people have the eye for photography that you do. I might take the odd lucky shot but most of my photographs are awful… blurry, missing tops of heads or they're wonky so you have to tilt your head to look at them.'

Hannah laughed as he tilted his head and crossed his eyes.

'I'm sure they're not that bad. I thought everyone with a smartphone was a photographer these days.'

'I'll show you my phone sometime and you can see how bad I am.' He tucked his hands in his pockets. 'The ones you've taken of Beti are wonderful. My mam would really love those.'

'I'll email or AirDrop them to you.'

'Thanks.' He cleared his throat. 'My uh… my mam would like you. She's not easily pleased but you're the kind of strong, independent woman she admires.'

Warmth spread through Hannah's chest. No man had ever told her that his mother would like her before.

'Sorry if that seems a strange thing to say and… well… I know it doesn't really matter but it just occurred to me that if I shared the photos with her then she'd want to know more about you. She's not a nosey parent as such… she doesn't interfere or anything. I don't want to give you that impression… but she does like to know my friends.'

'She sounds wonderful.'

'You could meet her.'

'Oh?'

'Do you have plans on Saturday?'

Was Will actually asking her to meet his mother? In what capacity? As a friend? She wasn't used to situations like this and a whole host of emotions coursed through her. What if his mother hated her or thought she wasn't good enough to be his friend or what if she embarrassed herself or… or…

'No pressure,' Will said, 'but we're holding a joint party for Beti and Anwen at the hotel. Well, in the marquee in the hotel grounds and it would be great if you could join us.'

'I… I'd love to.'

'My mam has organised a cake and there will be games for the children and karaoke, I think, and my dad and sister will be there too. As will Mari, Bryn and their friends and family. It's a children's party but it should be pleasant enough.'

'Thanks for inviting me.'

'I don't think Beti would have been too happy if I didn't.' He gazed out across the field at his daughter, his eyes filled with love.

'I have a feeling that Beti is going to want to take the dogs home.'

He smacked his forehead. 'I have that feeling too. The thing is… with me working through the week during term time, it's difficult. I mean… I could ask my parents to have the dog while I was at work. It's one solution, I suppose, but I also don't like to impose on them. They're so good with me and Beti and always have been and I don't want to take advantage of their kindness. However, I also know that Beti would be delighted to have a dog of her own.'

Hannah leant against the fence next to him and raised her camera again. The dogs were gorgeous and she'd like to adopt one too if she had a home of her own. But that was all part of a dream that was probably never going to happen, even if it seemed to be a bit more within reach here in Wales.

Chapter 19

'It was so kind of Gwen and Aled to allow you to hold the party here,' Will's mam said as they entered the marquee.

'They're very generous people, just like Mari and Bryn for inviting us to have a joint party.' Will admired the layout of the marquee. There were long tables with plenty of chairs around the sides, a dancefloor at the centre and a stage at the far end where the DJ was setting up. The sides were open so the breeze flowed through making it light and airy.

'Can I go and play, Daddy?' Beti asked, pointing at where Anwen and Seren were standing on the stage near the DJ.

'Of course you can,' Will said.

'Don't get your dress dirty,' Will's mam said, making him suppress a groan. She'd taken Beti shopping for something for the party and they'd come back with an ivory dress with short sleeves, an embroidered bodice, and a full skirt. His mam had also bought Beti white sandals and socks with frills around her ankles. Beti looked pretty but Will could just imagine how she'd look by the end of the evening and he wasn't sure how his mam would take it.

'Now, now, Dorothy,' Will's dad said. 'It's Beti's party and knowing our granddaughter as we do, perhaps a white dress was not the most practical of choices. Therefore, if she gets a bit… messy, then we have to suck it up.'

'Suck it up? Goodness, Ifor, you sound like a teenager.'

Ifor rolled his eyes at Will then grinned. 'Forever young, my darling. Now, where's the bar?'

As his dad walked away, Will set the cake his parents had bought down on the table next to Anwen's then removed the covering. The unicorn shaped cake looked intriguing next to Anwen's pirate figure one, as if the pirate was about to jump on the unicorn's back and race off into the sunset. He was impressed by the pirate cake, knowing that if he'd tried to get Beti to have something other than a unicorn then all hell would have broken loose. Besides which, his mam and Beti had chosen it together and so he'd sat back and let them get on with it. When they got their heads together, they were both so strong-willed that he did his best to avoid trying to change their minds. He sometimes wondered what it would have been like if Kayla was still around. How would she have coped with that? But then, his mam had become more involved in Beti's life only because Kayla hadn't been there, and he felt sure she'd have taken a step back if there had been another woman in the mix. As he'd said to Hannah the other day, his mam worried about him and Beti and wanted to support them. She would, he knew, always worry about them, but he also believed that if he ever fell in love again then his mam would give him and his partner the space with Beti to adjust to becoming a family.

He looked around, suddenly keen to see Hannah, but his heart sank. She wasn't here yet.

Hannah…

He reprimanded himself inwardly. There was no chance that he could have a relationship with Hannah. Aside from the fact that he wasn't even sure if she liked him in that way, there was Beti to prioritise and the significant fact that Hannah would be leaving the cove once her work was done. A long-distance romance was definitely not on the cards for him and so, whatever he might think existed between him and Hannah, it was not going to last any longer than the summer.

Fact!

So when she walked into the marquee in a pale pink dress made of some floaty material, her blonde hair in soft curls, her eyes scanning the room for a familiar face, he cursed his heart for fluttering, his skin for tingling and his arms for wanting to hold her. Seeing her leave the cove was going to be hard enough without adding a romantic attachment. At least at the moment, he knew he liked her but didn't have any evidence that it was reciprocated – they hadn't even kissed!

He could not allow himself to even entertain the thought that he could be falling for her or that she might be falling for him.

–

Hannah spotted Ffion and Joe with Ffion's parents. They appeared to be trying to fix something to one of the supporting posts of the marquee. She turned her gaze in the other direction and saw Beti playing with Anwen and Seren. Mari and Bryn were near them, keeping a close eye on the girls. There were other people in the marquee too and Hannah's eyes skipped over them: families, couples, individuals with friends, two women – one of them elderly and in a wheelchair – cooing over a tiny baby as if the rest of the world had ceased to exist.

These people were getting on with life: falling in love, getting married or moving in together, having babies, raising children, supporting their adult children and caring for grandchildren. They were brave, Hannah thought, creating their families without fear or hesitation. For them it was about continuity, forwards momentum, and they seemed to embrace it without hesitation. Look at Ffion and Joe, standing together, his arm around her shoulders, her leaning on him, certain that he would be there for her no matter what, while inside her body a new life was just beginning. This glorious cycle of life played out every day and Hannah had felt for so long that she was not a part of it, that she was, actually, somehow outside of it, in a bubble of her own making where only the time of her flights, the size of the minibar and the batteries on her laptop, phone and camera mattered.

Was she living or simply existing?

If she ceased to exist then who would notice? Who would care?

The thought sent an icy chill down her spine and goosebumps rose on her skin. She didn't want to be insignificant; she wanted to matter to people, to have people who mattered to her.

And then she saw him.

Will.

As if her eyes had deliberately ignored him until the final moment, the moment when she needed to see him the most.

He was laughing at something the woman with him had said. She was almost as tall as him even in flat sandals, slim with toned arms shown off by a sleeveless navy dress. Her dark hair was pulled into a low bun and even from across the marquee, Hannah could tell that she was attractive.

Who was that? A friend or colleague of Will's? A date?

The latter thought made her stomach plummet like she'd jumped off the top board at a swimming pool.

Will looked up and spotted her then waved her over.

Hannah sucked in a deep breath and approached them, fixing her lips into a smile that she hoped would appear friendly yet reserved, just in case she found out that the woman was someone important to Will.

'You made it.' He reached out a hand and touched her arm. 'Thanks for coming.'

'Thanks for inviting me.' Hannah tried not to notice how his hand felt on her skin, how his proximity made her heart race.

'It's a pleasure.' Will turned to the woman. 'Hannah, this is my sister, Alice.'

'Hello.' Alice held out a hand and Hannah took it, feeling the assurance in Alice's grip, sensing that she was being assessed.

'Nice to meet you.' Hannah felt on edge, like an intruder, although she wasn't sure why. But Alice was looking at her without expression, as if she was scanning her for a microchip with her laser vision, or waiting for Hannah to make a wrong move so she could wrestle her to the ground.

'Don't worry about my sister,' Will said, gently squeezing Hannah's arm. 'She's a lawyer and she looks at everyone that way.'

'What way?' Alice turned her steely gaze on Will then her expression changed and she laughed.

'Like you think they're guilty of some heinous crime. She's been looking at me that way since I was toddling so I'm used to it, but it can...' Will frowned at Alice, '...be quite unnerving.'

Alice turned back to Hannah. 'I'm so sorry. I don't realise that I'm doing it half the time. I guess that my non-judgemental face can actually seem a bit *judgemental*.'

'It's fine, honestly. I don't mind.' Hannah swallowed, realising that her mouth was suddenly very dry.

'Would you like a drink?' Will asked.

'Yes please.'

'What do you fancy?' He pointed at the bar near the entrance. 'They have wine, beer, juice—'

'Champagne!' Alice interrupted. 'We should have some bubbly to celebrate Beti's seventh birthday party. I'll go and get us some glasses.'

Alice headed for the bar and Hannah looked around, trying to compose herself. It was ridiculous feeling so nervous around Will's sister but she couldn't shake the unsettling feeling that Alice might think she wasn't good enough to be Will's friend.

'Alice seems like a bit of a tough nut but she's a sweet-heart really,' Will said as if reading her thoughts. 'She's devoted to her career but also a fabulous aunt to Beti and she's been a brilliant big sister to me.'

'You're lucky having her to look out for you.'

'I am.'

'And your parents.'

'They're all wonderful,' he agreed. 'Although, sometimes, like now… I wish they didn't come across as quite so protective.'

'I'm sure it's just because she doesn't know me.' Hannah gave a small shrug. 'I could be anyone and your sister needs to know more, I suppose.'

Will took her hand, making her gasp. 'But you're not anyone, are you, Hannah. You're you and—'

'There you go.' Alice was back with a tray of flutes filled with sparkling champagne. 'Only the best at my niece's party.'

'Thank you.' Hannah took a glass and sipped the cold drink, wrinkling her nose as the bubbles tickled. What had Will been about to say to her? He'd looked so serious and sincere.

'Cheers to you, Will, the best daddy a little girl could wish for and to Beti, the best daughter and niece in the world… and…' Alice smiled knowingly at Hannah. 'To new friendships. May they bring joy, plenty of sunshine and no more rain.'

'Cheers.' Hannah clinked her glass against Alice's then Will's before knocking back half her glass. She wasn't quite sure what Alice meant by *no more rain* but suspected that it was a comment on how Will had been treated in the past.

'Right, I'm going to check on our parents, Will, so see you shortly.' Alice sashayed away.

'Again, I apologise,' Will said, raising his eyebrows.

'There's no need.'

'The thing she said about… no more rain. It's nothing to do with you, just… linked to my past.'

'It's OK, honestly. You don't need to explain.' Hannah drained her glass, trying not to burp as the bubbles rushed up into her throat.

'I find that I want to explain though... to you.' Will peered at her from under his dark lashes in a way that made her legs wobbly.

'I brought my camera,' she said, pulling it from her bag and holding it up, trying to shake herself from the way longing rose inside her when she was this close to Will. 'I thought I could take photos of the celebrations.'

'That's very kind.' Will looked at his glass and seemed surprised that it was empty. 'But then... you are very kind.'

Hannah raised the camera and started snapping.

'Hey! I hope you're not taking photos of me.'

He came to her side and looked at the screen. 'Now look at that... you got both my chins in.'

Hannah giggled. 'Don't be silly. Your chins look great.'

His mouth fell open and he covered his chin with his free hand. 'I'm mortally offended.'

'Sorry... I couldn't resist.'

'Tell you what... come and meet my parents and perhaps you can take some photos of us all. See if the double chin thing is hereditary.'

Hannah laughed then sucked in a deep breath, steeling herself. 'I'd like that.'

She knew she should be feeling apprehensive about meeting Will's mam and dad, but all she could focus on as they crossed the marquee, was how his hand felt where it rested in the small of her back. How much she liked being with him surrounded by his friends and family.

–

Will's body felt twitchy as he approached his parents with Hannah, almost like he was about to introduce a new partner to them. It had been a long time since he'd taken anyone home. In fact, since Kayla there hadn't been anyone, so introducing them to a woman he really liked was nerve-wracking. Although the difference was, of course, that Hannah wasn't his girlfriend.

Alice had been all right with Hannah, a bit colder than he'd have liked, but that was his sister for you. She didn't gush around anyone, was always cautious with praise and Will knew that in this case, Alice was wary of Hannah because she was aware that Will liked her. He'd tried to deny it but his sister knew him better than anyone and she would no doubt be worried about Will and Beti and about them getting hurt.

Clearing his throat to get their attention, Will realised he still had his hand on Hannah's back, so he removed it, knowing that his mam wouldn't miss a trick. 'Mam, Dad, this is Hannah.'

She shook their hands.

'Hello Mr and Mrs Hopkins.' Hannah's smile wavered and he realised that she was probably anxious. Meeting anyone's parents could do that to you.

'Nice to meet you, Hannah.' His mam's smile was cool, her eyes alert. 'So you're a writer?'

'That's right.' Hannah licked her lips. 'I'm writing about the summer festival at the cove and I might write a separate piece about the sanctuary too.'

Dorothy nodded. 'Will said that you travel a lot.'

'I do. For work.'

'Lucky girl,' Ifor said. 'Sounds like a dream job.'

'It has its advantages.' Hannah rubbed the back of her neck. 'I've seen lots of exotic places and get to stay in some gorgeous hotels.'

'So you can work anywhere then?' Dorothy asked.

'That's right.'

'And what do you think of Cariad Cove and the Gower Peninsula?' Dorothy sipped her wine.

'It's one of the most beautiful places I've been to.'

'Really?' Dorothy cocked an eyebrow.

'Absolutely. I mean… I'll be honest with you… I didn't expect it to be so wonderful. I hadn't been to this part of the world before and although I'd seen photographs, I had no idea what it would be like.'

Will saw something in his mam's eyes change, a kind of softening that meant she was warming to Hannah. Perhaps she'd expected a cold, hard journalist out for what she could get and instead she was finding Hannah. The Hannah he was getting to know, growing to care about.

'Oh yes, it is a beautiful place. The whole of the Gower Peninsula is gorgeous. We wouldn't want to live anywhere else would we, Ifor?'

'Never.' Will's dad grinned. 'What about you, Hannah? Where are you based?'

'In Watford.'

'Is that where your parents are from?' Ifor asked.

Hannah glanced at Will, uncertainty in her eyes, and he found himself moving closer to her as the need to protect her rose inside him. 'My uhhh… my mother's dead… she died when I was ten and uhhh… I never knew my father.' Tiny spots of colour appeared high on Hannah's cheeks and Will wanted to pull her into his arms.

'Oh bless you,' his mam shook her head. 'I'm sorry to hear that.'

'I grew up in foster care.' Hannah lifted her chin in what Will suspected was a small unconscious defensive act. 'As some people do.'

'Yes they do,' Dorothy said. 'But that must have been difficult at times, dear, and you must have missed your mum.'

'I did. I do.' Hannah had folded her arms around herself now and seemed to shrink in front of Will's eyes. 'Very much.'

'So will you go back to Watford when you're done here?' Will's mam tilted her head on one side.

'Probably. But not for long. Always on the move, me.' Hannah gave a strange, strangled laugh, then said, 'Excuse me for a moment.'

She hurried away and disappeared out of the marquee.

'She seems nice enough,' Will's mam said.

'Hannah's *very* nice.'

'Poor girl though,' his dad said. 'Sounds like she doesn't have anyone. Unless she has extended family there.'

'I don't think she does,' Will replied. 'From what she's told me and what I've picked up on, I think her childhood was tough and she's a bit of a loner.'

'She could do with a family around to care about her,' his mam said. 'Let's hope she falls in love with the right person and that she can have that family one day.'

Will met his mam's eyes and she placed a hand on his arm.

'You be careful, Will. I don't know how much you know about her but she's vulnerable. I can see it in her eyes. She's been through a lot and it will take her time to trust people. I saw it over the years with children in school who were in foster care or who had been adopted and they need a lot of love to feel secure.'

'Hannah's just a friend,' he said, his voice unconvincing even to his own ears.

'Darling, I can see that you like each other.' His mam squeezed his arm. 'But you're vulnerable too and you have Beti to consider.'

'I know that!' Will snapped then dipped his chin. 'I will always put Beti first.'

'We know,' his dad said, coming to his rescue. 'But you're entitled to have a life too, Will. It's been a long time since Kayla upped and left. Hannah seems like a good one.'

'How can you tell that from speaking to her for five minutes?' Will gave a nervous laugh but his dad tapped the side of his nose.

'I have an instinct for these things, son. After all, I knew within five minutes of meeting your mam that she was the woman I'd marry.'

'He did. And so did I.' His mam smiled fondly at her husband. 'But even so… things weren't so complicated for us. We didn't have painful break-ups behind us and neither of us had a child. It's a bit messier for you, however…' She held up a hand as if to prevent him from remonstrating. 'It's not impossible and if you like Hannah a lot then you should see where it goes.'

'She'll be leaving the cove soon,' he said, the reality of his statement sinking in.

'Unless you give her a reason to stay.' His dad winked. 'She could be happy here.'

Will looked at his parents in turn. 'Will you keep an eye on Beti?'

'Of course. Go and find her, Will.' His mam kissed his cheek then he hurried after Hannah, hoping she hadn't gone too far away because he couldn't leave his daughter's party for long, but he couldn't bear the thought that Hannah might be scared, sad and all alone.

Chapter 20

Hannah had left the marquee and gone around the side to the fence that overlooked the beach. The tide was in and it lapped at the rocks below, froth foaming on the surface.

She rested her hands on the fence and closed her eyes, breathing slowly in and out, in time with the ebb and flow of the tide. Will's parents had seemed nice but their questions had been difficult. It was natural for people to ask about her family, especially when they had their own family circle around them, but it had always been challenging for Hannah when people asked about her background. She usually saw either pity or awkwardness in their eyes, a bit like when some asked her if she had children or if she wanted to have them one day. It wasn't that they were being insensitive, she knew that, but those who were happy wanted everyone else to be happy too. And Hannah had been happy with her lifestyle and her choices, or at least satisfied the majority of the time. She hadn't pined for what she didn't have although she did sometimes wonder how it would be if things had been different. But if they had been then maybe she wouldn't be such a successful writer, perhaps she would have been content to do something else and wouldn't have seen so much of the world. There were pros and cons with everything – every decision, every flight taken, every job accepted – and she couldn't waste time regretting where she was and how she'd got there.

What would be the point in that?

'Hannah!'

She opened her eyes.

'Are you OK? I was worried. My parents… I know they can be a bit full on at times but they don't mean any harm… they just… they wanted to get to know you.'

'It's fine. I just needed some air.'

'I'm so sorry for everything you've been through.' His eyes searched her face.

'It's certainly not your fault.'

'But you've lost so much and not knowing your father… it's just… I'm so lucky to have both my parents and siblings, even if I don't see much of my brothers because they're both in the army, but growing up I had a family around me.'

She gave a wry laugh. 'My childhood was definitely different. But people's lives are. Everyone goes through good and bad times.'

'But…' He raised a hand then let it fall to his side. 'I wish I could make things better for you.'

'You're a good man, Will.'

'Come back inside?' He held out his hand. 'We have to sing Happy Birthday soon and then there will be a disco and karaoke.'

'I don't know… I don't want to impose.'

'I invited you. How's that imposing?'

She wavered. 'I… You have your family and friends and I'm just an outsider. I'm passing through… I'm not a part of all this.' She gestured around her at the marquee, the hotel and the cove itself.

'You are if you want to be.' He stepped closer and took her hand, held it between both of his. 'You don't have to have been born here or to have grown up here to belong here.'

'To belong?' Her voice cracked. Had she ever belonged anywhere?

'I think you belong here.' His eyes were dark pools of emotion, his Adam's apple bobbed in his throat, his hands were warm around hers.

'How? How could you know that?'

'I just do. I've never met anyone like you, Hannah, and even though it seems crazy… I feel like I know you. Like something inside me recognises something in you.'

'Will… I wish it could be as easy as just letting go but there are things about me that you don't know. Things in my past that are… messy and complicated.'

'Everyone has messy and complicated in their pasts. It doesn't matter. What's important is who you are now and who you want to be. Look… come inside and enjoy the party. Don't stay out here alone.'

'I am alone, Will. I've always been alone.' A tear squeezed from the corner of her eye and trickled down her cheek. Will gently wiped it away with his thumb.

'No, Hannah.' He placed both of his hands on her shoulders then pressed his lips to her forehead. 'You're not alone anymore. You have family here now.'

'I don't understand.' She shook her head, her eyes glistening.

'Friends are the family we choose for ourselves. Choose us now because we've already chosen you.'

-

Will held Hannah's hand as they went back inside the marquee. Outside, he'd seen the vulnerability in her that he'd sensed beneath the surface like an underground river but he hadn't known how deep it ran. Hannah had been alone for a long time and while she was braver than anyone he knew, she was also scared and wary of letting others in. Will could understand that because despite having his family, after Kayla had left, he'd felt isolated and lonely, like no one could understand what he was going through. Being a single parent was lonely however many family members you had to rely on because at the end of the day, he went to bed alone, woke up alone and wondered if he would spend his future alone. He had Beti but she would grow up and spread her wings and then Will could still be alone, rattling around in their lovely home, filling his days with running, baking, work and waiting for Beti to visit or phone him. He'd thought that he'd volunteer at the sanctuary or elsewhere when he had more time on his hands but then he'd still be going home to an empty house and falling asleep without someone to kiss goodnight.

Kayla had been his first and only love and when she'd hurt him, he'd thought he could never feel that way again. Will wasn't like some of the men he knew who could flit from woman to woman; for him there had to be a connection, a depth in a relationship before he could open up and be close to someone. He had to genuinely like someone and since Kayla, he hadn't found anyone he felt that way about. Part of it had been self-preservation, he suspected. He'd been reluctant to allow attraction to anyone to develop because he didn't want to be hurt again and didn't want Beti to get hurt. But now, gradually, like the fragile petals of a flower opening to the sun, things were changing. And it was because of Hannah. She was unique, a beautiful soul. She'd been hurt, damaged, but she was still fighting on, still moving, still creating.

Will wanted to help her to heal, so she could be free of the pain of her past and he hoped that he could make a difference even in the short time they had.

Inside the marquee, everyone was gathering around the table with the birthday cakes, so Will led Hannah over to Beti and stood there while Mari lit the candles on both cakes. Hannah was still holding on to him, and he didn't care who saw it. He wanted to be there with his daughter and with his friend. It was a special day and he wanted Hannah to feel a part of things, to be reassured that she wasn't alone and that any time she wanted she could come back to Cariad Cove and to the love that waited there for her – the love of friends who could be her new family.

–

Hannah laughed as Beti twirled around her on the dance floor. She was hot and her feet were aching but she'd had a brilliant afternoon. There had been cake, more champagne, more cake and karaoke. Hannah hated singing because she had a terrible voice but Will and Ffion had dragged her on stage and they'd sung together: ABBA, Beyoncé, Queen and more. After the first few songs, Hannah had relaxed and let go. It was liberating belting out songs and afterwards she felt elated by it all.

Will had been incredibly kind and encouraging, a true friend, and the things he had said to her were kind and reassuring. Could she really have a family here in the friends she'd made? She'd never been that close to people, not even the college friends she'd had as a teenager. They'd been the same age and into the same things but even back then Hannah had kept a distance from them, watching them and pretending to be the same, while knowing that she never could be. Their lives had been too different, their understanding of what she'd been through limited because she never let anyone in by telling them about her past. Then there had been that awful holiday in the intense heat of Greece after finishing college... She'd drunk heavily every night, slept through the days, then gone out again to drink and lose herself in the packed clubs where alcohol was cheap and where she could find someone who'd take her back to a hotel room and help her forget about everything.

The memory made shame crawl over her skin. How could she have been so rash, so careless? But all she'd wanted was to feel close to someone for a while, to be held and to push away the loneliness. The holiday had come to an end and she'd gone back to her tiny bedsit with damp on the walls and ceiling and the fridge that didn't keep things cool. She'd felt unwell: the drinking, the sunburn from the day when she did make it to the beach (and fell asleep on the sun lounger) and the exhaustion of trying to keep going had drained her. It took some time for her to get back on her feet and to go after the job on the local paper. That job had been her salvation and she knew that if she hadn't gone for it then life could have worked out very differently indeed.

The song ended and Beti grabbed her hands and grinned up at her.

'I'm very happy that you came to my party.'

'I'm happy I came too.'

'I'm not seven until tomorrow though.'

'Aren't you?'

Beti shook her head. 'Will you come to my house tomorrow and have pizza with me and Daddy?'

'Oh… Won't he mind?'

'He likes you.' Beti peered at Hannah's hands. 'I'll paint your nails for you and give you a unicorn makeover if you like.'

'A unicorn makeover?'

'Yes!' Beti hopped from one foot to the other.

'I think we'd better check with your daddy first though because he might want some time alone with you.'

'He'll be fine. You can have a sleepover too! I'll go and tell him.'

'Beti!' Hannah's voice was swallowed by music as the next song came on. She stood there awkwardly as Beti ran over to Will and tugged at his hand and he crouched down to listen to her. He frowned slightly then looked up and Hannah held up her hands and shook her head. She didn't want him thinking she'd invited herself.

Beti hugged him then ran back to Hannah.

'Daddy said he'd love you to come but only if you want to.'

'OK.' Hannah waved at Will and mouthed *Thanks*. 'I'd love to come.'

'Yay!' Beti jumped up and down. 'Come on then let's have another dance. You are one of my bestest friends in the world and I'm super excited about tomorrow.'

Hannah allowed Beti to lead her back to the middle of the dancefloor, a lump in her throat at what the little girl had said. Hannah had never imagined that she'd come somewhere like Cariad Cove and develop feelings for a man and his daughter, but it was happening and she knew in that moment that she didn't want to do a thing to stop it.

Chapter 21

'Are you sure you're OK to run?' Hannah asked Ffion early the next morning when they met on the beach. She'd spoken to Ffion at the party about how she wanted to try to get running again and Ffion had said she'd run with her and show her how she started with Couch to 5k. Ffion had said that if they met around seven, the beach would be quiet before the stallholders started setting up for the day.

'The NHS website said it's fine to keep running and exercising during pregnancy for as long as you feel comfortable.'

'But what about the nausea?'

Ffion screwed up her face. 'It's not very pleasant but I figure that fresh air and exercise will help me feel a bit better and hopefully take my mind off the queasiness.'

'Well if you feel worse at any point let me know and we'll stop.'

'Same for you.' Ffion flashed her a mischievous grin. Tongue loosened after a few glasses of bubbly last night at the party, Hannah had admitted to Ffion that she'd gone for a run, fainted and been caught by Will. Hannah's cheeks had burned with mortification as she'd confessed but while Ffion's eyebrows had risen and a smile had danced on her lips, she hadn't teased Hannah about it at all, for which Hannah had been grateful. Was this what true friendship was like? You could tell someone your deepest, darkest secrets and they wouldn't judge you? Would support you and be there for you no matter what?

Of course, Hannah hadn't exactly shared her deepest, darkest secrets but she was beginning to wonder if it would be possible with a friend like Ffion.

'I'm hoping this will clear my head to be honest,' she said, knowing that Ffion understood.

'OK, well let's do some gentle stretching then we can start with the first run. It's quite an easy one...'

'What's involved?'

'You warm up with a five-minute walk then run for sixty seconds, walk for ninety seconds and repeat seven times.'

Hannah pursed her lips. 'I can do that. Sounds easier than just trying to run the length of the beach then collapsing because it was too far.'

'Believe me, it is. This is how Mari and I started running and it was the best way to build up to longer runs.'

'But don't you mind doing this with me? It's like going backwards for you.'

Ffion shook her head. 'I don't mind at all and it's a gentle way for me to train while not feeling my best.'

Hannah experienced a flicker of unease that felt like a cloud passing over the sun. Was this the right thing to do after so long? Her reasons for stopping running had seemed to make sense at the time and in some ways, they still did, and yet being in Cariad Cove had shown her that there was a different way to live. A different way to be. There was no telling how long grief would rule your heart and head; it had no time limit and she knew she'd always grieve for her losses but the pain she'd gone through was no longer as sharp as it once was and surely that was a sign that it was OK to take steps to move on with her life?

'OK then, let's do it,' she said, choosing to take hold of this moment and to be positive with it. They started to walk briskly along the sand. 'How will we know when to run?' Hannah asked.

'I've got the programme running through my smart-watch so it'll vibrate when it's time for each change.'

As they walked, they talked. Ffion told Hannah that she'd been feeling tired and weak but that Joe was being amazing. They'd also decided to move in together properly and that Ffion would have her name on the mortgage. It was a big step, Ffion said, but having a baby seemed like an even bigger one and they wanted to create a stable environment for the baby to be born into. They had also discussed marriage, but decided that the coming months would be busy and tiring, so they'd talk about it again after the baby arrived. Everything was looking good for Ffion and Joe.

'What about you?' Ffion asked.

'What do you mean?'

'Well… you and Will seem to be getting along well.'

'He's a very nice person.'

'And?'

'And?' Hannah tried to keep her face blank.

'It was obvious last night from looking at the pair of you that there's something growing between you.'

Hannah glanced at Ffion, intrigued. 'Like what?'

'Oh come on, Hannah. He likes you and you like him. You're both adults. Beti adores you. I don't see what's holding you both back.'

'Don't you?'

'Well… I know there's the risk of being hurt… and Beti, of course, has to be the priority, but you two clearly fancy the pants off each other and it would be such a shame if you didn't do something about that.'

'We do like each other.' Hannah was surprised at how easily the word fell from her lips. 'I *really* like him, actually, and I think Beti is an incredible child and… I wish I could just fall into Will's arms and become Beti's stepmum, but it's not that simple is it? I'm meant to be leaving soon.'

'Well don't.'

'Don't leave?' If only it was as simple as listening to her heart.

'I didn't think I'd stay permanently when I came back. I didn't have a clue what I was going to do and I was up to my eyeballs in grief. But with time, I decided to stay and to give love another chance and I'm so glad I did. If I hadn't…' Ffion placed a hand on her belly. 'This little one wouldn't be here.'

'How big is the baby at the moment?' Ffion's stomach looked flat to Hannah and she wondered when she'd start to show.

'About the size of an apricot.' Ffion beamed. 'Apparently my womb is the size of an orange and the baby is like an apricot inside it.'

'That's amazing.' A shiver ran down Hannah's spine as a memory teased at the edges of her awareness, so she pushed it away, focusing instead on Ffion. 'You have a little apricot inside you and it's changing day by day.'

'I can hardly believe it. Before long it will be the size of a grapefruit then a melon and so on. Funny how we think about the size of a baby in terms of fruit, isn't it?'

'Very.'

'My belly hasn't grown much yet but my poor boobs.' Ffion placed her hands over her chest and winced. 'I've already gone up a cup size and had to get a new running bra.'

'Your body changes rapidly throughout pregnancy. Sore boobs are horrid as is the heartburn.' Hannah bit the inside of her cheek and rubbed at her throat. 'So I've read.'

Ffion was smiling as they walked, seemingly oblivious to Hannah's slip.

'Right... here we go then, Hannah. Time to run.'

They set off at a gentle jog, feet landing on the sand in time as if their bodies were synchronised, and before Hannah knew it, the run was over and they were walking again.

'Anyway, as I was saying...' Ffion got a water bottle out of her bumbag and took a sip. 'I wouldn't have this little apricot and Joe in my life if I hadn't stayed. My whole life has changed because I came home and because of Joe. I did worry at one point that perhaps Joe was a kind of rebound relationship because he was the first one I'd had since I lost Graeme, but I was at the point where I'd started to heal and I fell in love with Joe because he's Joe. They're very different people and although I'll always love Graeme, I love Joe now too. The heart has the capacity for so much love and that's something that never ceases to amaze me. The same could happen for you and Will, if you give things a chance. Time to run!'

217

Off they went again until Ffion slowed down.

'But... I... have a complicated... past... and...' Hannah tried to slow her breathing. 'I... don't want to complicate Will and Beti's lives even more.'

'How would you complicate them?'

'I've never been in a serious relationship.'

'So what?' Ffion shrugged. 'That could be an advantage.'

Hannah smiled in spite of the turmoil inside her at the thought of bringing any negativity to Will and Beti. Ffion seemed determined to see Hannah and Will's relationship as a positive possibility and wouldn't be swayed. She had an answer for everything and Hannah was enjoying listening.

'And off we go...' Ffion laughed as they ran again, drinking more water when they slowed down to a walk.

'This is good. I'm tired but not about to faint like last time.' Hannah sipped her own water. 'That was so embarrassing. Will must've thought I was such an idiot.'

'The first time Mari and I tried running along the beach, I got a dreadful cramp and Joe came to my rescue, so don't sweat it.' Ffion winked at her. 'Looking back, I actually think he liked coming to my aid and it's probably the same with Will.'

'Ha! Ha! That's certainly a batter way to view it.'

'Isn't it just?' Ffion pointed ahead of them. 'Shall we do one more in this direction then turn and head back to the hotel?'

'Good idea.'

'If you check out the Couch to 5k app, you'll see that the runs progress gradually and if you follow it your fitness will increase quite quickly. It's a brilliant way to start running or to resume running after time off.'

'I'll take a look later. Thanks so much for coming with me today. I'm sure the encouragement helps.'

'Oh it does. I run with Mari and Joe and the Cariad Cove Running Club that we set up. It's always good for morale to have others running with you, as if you start to flag, they keep you going.'

'I'd love to be part of a running club.'

'Well that's another good reason to stay in the cove.' Ffion touched Hannah's arm. 'Plus I'll miss you if you go.'

You'll miss me? The words floated around in Hannah's head as they did the next run. She would be missed if she left. No one had ever said they'd miss her.

Before she knew it, they had completed the first run of Couch to 5k and elation buzzed through her veins. Tired and sweaty, but proud of herself for doing it, she also had the joy of knowing that Ffion liked her enough to want her to stay in the cove. If she did stay, it wouldn't simply be about Will and Beti and her feelings for them; it could be about new friendships and a fresh start too. When she really thought about it, what was there for her in her house share in Watford? Whereas here, in the cove, there was far more to stay around for.

–

Will placed a mug of coffee on the kitchen table in front of Alice then sat down with his own mug. Alice had arrived with Beti's birthday gift (another one, seeing as how she'd already given her one the previous day) and she was keen to get him to sit down and chat. After she'd accepted her gift – a unicorn stationery set that she was delighted with – Beti had gone out into the garden and was playing with some toys on a blanket on the grass. Will could keep an eye on her through the open French doors. One of the main attractions about this house had been the secure back garden with access to the kitchen because he'd always wanted a garden for Beti to play in and where he could grow flowers, fruit and vegetables as well as hang up bird feeders to enjoy watching the wildlife all year through.

'Your veg patch looks like it's doing well,' Alice said.

'I've got quite a selection in the raised beds and we eat what I produce from them regularly.'

'Healthy organic meals by Will. You'll be one of those flashy Instagram super dads soon with your own cooking show.'

Will nudged the plate of cupcakes towards her. 'Maybe. But then I'd have to plaster my photo all over those bloody Instagram squares and you know I'm not fussy on having my mugshot everywhere.'

'You'd have a million followers in no time, I'm sure. You're one of those handsome daddies that the ladies love and all the single women would be dropping into your DMs with their phone numbers and Insta handles.'

'No thanks.' He laughed. 'I like my privacy.'

'Talking of privacy…' Alice picked up a cake and peeled away the case. 'I know you probably don't want to say much but you and Hannah looked like you were getting on well last night.'

Will groaned loudly but a part of him was secretly delighted that she'd thought so. 'Not this again.'

Alice laughed, her lawyer mask slipping as she grinned at him.

'It's only because I care about you.' She took a bite of the cake. 'OMG, this is delicious.'

'Glad you like it.'

'I'm not glad I like it! I could eat about twenty in one go and then my designer suits won't fit. I try to watch what I eat for that very reason but when you bake like this…' She rolled her eyes. 'It's just cruel not to eat your creations.'

'I'll pack some for you to take home with you.'

'That's my boy!' Alice chuckled. 'I forgot to ask if you and Beti are doing anything special today. I know you had the party yesterday but with it being her actual birthday and all, do you have plans?'

'Mam and Dad are coming over in about an hour and Beti and I are going to have pizza and watch a movie later.'

'A quiet evening in… just the two of you.' Alice seemed to deflate before his eyes. 'I thought you might be having the company of a new friend. Never mind, eh. Shall I hang around and keep you both entertained?'

'It's fine.' Will shook his head vigorously. Alice was like a dog with a bone when she got going. 'We'll be fine. Probably get an early night because I'm quite tired after yesterday.' He yawned as if to make his point.

Alice put her cake down and licked her fingers slowly. 'It's no problem, I'm happy to hang around.' Her dark eyes drilled into him and he tried not to blush, not to look away, not to laugh under her scrutiny. 'It's not going to be just you and Beti, is it?'

Now Will dropped his gaze to his mug.

'Will?'

He raised his eyes and felt his lips twitching.

'Is *she* coming here later?'

There was no point trying to hide it any longer. Alice could sniff out a fib at fifty paces.

'OK. OK. Hannah's joining us for pizza and a movie.'

Alice clapped her hands. 'Well bloody hell, Will, I'm glad to hear it. Watching you together last night, I could see that there's a spark between you and Beti loves her to bits. I meet a lot of people in my job and I know a bad one when I see them and Hannah is not bad at all. There's something about her that suggests she's wary, but apart from that she seems genuine. I hope you have a good night, Will, I really do.'

She picked up her cake and polished it off then drank her coffee as if she was celebrating the news that Hannah was joining Will and Beti later.

'This might all come to nothing, you know.' Will was gazing out of the doors watching Beti as she moved a unicorn through the air so it looked like it was flying. 'I have to be cautious because I don't want Beti to get hurt.'

'I know. I don't want to see my darling niece hurt either.' Alice reached across the table and covered Will's hand with hers. 'And I don't want to see you hurt. You and Beti are far too special to be upset by anyone. However... I can't help feeling that it's time for something to change and you're not getting any younger so now's a good time. The right time, I think.'

'Perhaps.' Will raised his mug. 'Here's to finding out if taking a chance is worth it.'

'I'm sure it will be.'

They clinked mugs then sat back and watched Beti playing. If only life was as simple as being a unicorn in a child's game, but then the things worth fighting for never came without effort.

—

Hannah waited outside Will's front door, a bag of goodies she'd picked up from the local supermarket in one hand, a gift bag and a helium birthday balloon in the other. She'd been to the estate before when she'd come to Mari and Bryn's for lunch but seeing it again reminded her what a pleasant place it was to live. She'd parked just outside Will's driveway and when she'd got out of the car, she'd taken a moment to gaze at the view of Swansea. It was a clear day and she could see for miles, follow the coastline around to the Mumbles aware that beyond that Barddoniaeth Bay and Cariad Cove lay in one direction, and she could see right across to Port Talbot in the other. The estate was a very green place to live with its well-established trees, hedges and communal flower beds between the houses, and not for the first time she was filled with admiration for Will for choosing such a gorgeous place to live.

'Well hello there.' Will had opened the door as she'd been lost in her musings.

'Hi.' She felt suddenly shy that she was here, at his home, alone. It would be just Will, Beti and Hannah and there would be no-one to hide behind, nowhere to run if she felt the need to escape. She swallowed down her doubts because she'd hate for Will to see them on her face.

'Come on in.'

'Shall I take my sandals off?'

'No need.'

She followed him through to a kitchen diner then handed him the bag. 'There are some sweets, crisps and popcorn in there. I wasn't sure what you both like so I got a mixture.'

'Thanks very much.'

'Oh… there's also some wine if you fancy some and juice for Beti.'

Will's smile lit up his handsome face. 'You didn't have to do this.'

'It's the least I could do. And these are for Beti.' She held up the gift bag and balloon.

'She's in the garden.' He gestured at the open French doors.

'Is it OK if I take them to her?'

'Of course. I'll get you something to drink. What would you like?' He opened the fridge. 'I have wine, beer, cider, lemonade… tea, coffee?'

'Lemonade would be great thanks.' Seeing as how she was driving, Hannah would stick to soft drinks.

'One lemonade coming right up.'

Hannah went outside, looking around her at the pretty enclosed garden with a decking area just outside the door complete with table and chairs, a rectangle of grass and flower-filled borders. There was an area that looked like it had been reserved for growing vegetables and a few fruit trees with bird feeders hanging from the branches. It was all surrounded by six-foot wooden fences that made it private and secure. It was the perfect garden for a child to play in.

'Hi Beti,' she said as she crossed the grass to the little girl.

Beti looked up. 'Hannah Banana!'

Hannah laughed, surprised at the nickname but also quite liking it.

'Happy birthday, sweetheart. I brought you something.'

Beti put down the bright pink plastic unicorn that she'd been playing with. Hannah knelt down on the blanket and handed Beti the unicorn-shaped balloon.

'Oh my gosh, I love it.' Beti peered at the balloon. 'I'll keep it forever.'

Hannah smiled at Beti's excitement. She wasn't sure how long the balloon would stay inflated but doubted it would be forever. 'You might want to take it inside or tie it to a chair or the table though because otherwise it will float away.'

'I'll do that right now.'

Beti looped the string of the balloon around one of the chairs then ran back to Hannah and stood in front of her, hands clasped and an expectant look on her face.

'And I also have this for you.' Hannah passed her the gift bag. 'There's a card inside too.'

'Thank you, Hannah.' Beti opened the bag and took out the card, something that impressed Hannah because she knew that a lot of excited children would just go for the gift first. Beti opened it then set it on the blanket. 'It's beautiful. You have pretty writing.'

Then she sat down and peered inside the gift bag. When Beti pulled out the small box, Hannah held her breath. She wasn't used to buying presents for young children, not for anyone at all really, so when she'd popped into the city earlier that afternoon, she'd been a bit apprehensive about making the right choice. She'd asked Ffion's advice about it and Ffion had said her nieces liked toys, stationery sets, books and jewellery. As the younger sibling, Seren seemed to like pretty much whatever Anwen liked, so Ffion said that made buying them gifts a bit easier. Hannah had browsed a few toy shops then gone to the jewellery shop on the high street. When she'd seen the small charm bracelet and the range of charms, she'd felt it was the right choice.

Beti opened the lid of the box and her eyes opened wide and she gasped. 'It's exactly what I wanted!'

'What's that?' Will had joined them with a tray of glasses of cloudy lemonade that he set down on the grass beside the blanket.

'It's a bracelet, Daddy,' Beti said, holding it up. 'It's very shiny.'

'There are two charms in the bag to go on it,' Hannah said, reaching for the bag then holding up the two smaller boxes.

'Wow!' Beti accepted the boxes. 'Can I wear it now?'

'Of course you can.'

Will fastened the silver chain around Beti's wrist and she gazed at it like it was the crown jewels then he opened the smaller boxes and got out the charms. 'Look at these.'

Beti's eyes grew even wider. 'A unicorn and a mermaid! Hannah Banana you are the best! I'm going to wear this forever and ever and never ever take it off.'

Something bubbled in Hannah's belly. It spread into her chest and then her throat and she placed a hand over her mouth to stop it bursting from her. At the same time, her eyes stung and she blinked rapidly, determined not to cry. She'd hoped Beti would like the gift but not expected this reaction. What was happening to her polished veneer? Being around Ffion, Will and Beti was shaking her to her core and she was transforming inside in ways she'd never imagined. It was scary and yet exhilarating to care for others like this and to do things that made them happy.

When Will had attached the charms to the bracelet, Beti held out her arm. 'It's so pretty.' She turned to Hannah and flung her arms around her neck. 'Thank you so much. I will love this bracelet and always wear it.'

'This was very kind of you, Hannah.' Concern was etched on Will's face as he stared at Hannah over Beti's shoulder. 'Hannah?'

She nodded but she was biting the inside of her cheeks to try to regain her composure. 'I'm just… really happy… that Beti likes it,' she squeaked out finally, Beti's arms still tight around her neck. The effort of preventing herself from crying was making her tremble and the hug from Beti was all that was keeping her from losing control.

The little girl smelt of sunshine, strawberry shampoo and whatever fabric softener Will used. When Beti finally let go, Hannah missed the hug immediately.

'She loves the bracelet,' Will said. 'Excellent choice.'

'I'm so glad.'

'Here, have a drink.' Hannah accepted the glass of lemonade. It was ice cold, sweet and refreshing and she drank it quickly. It made her think of long summer days, sandy toes and barbecues that went on after dusk. 'Did you make this?'

'I prefer it to shop-bought ones.'

'It's absolutely delicious.'

'It goes well with gin and vodka too.' He laughed. 'Not that I have either very often but sometimes, it's nice.'

'I can imagine that drinking and being a parent don't mix well.'

'Having a hangover with Beti bouncing around on the bed at six a.m. is not recommended.'

Hannah laughed.

'Are you hungry?' Will asked.

'I could eat.'

'I'll pick some fresh salad for our dinner. I have some ripe tomatoes on the vine in the portable greenhouse that will be delicious.'

'Fresh organic produce as well as homemade lemonade, eh? I am very impressed.'

'Can I go and pick them, Daddy?' Beti stood up, still admiring her bracelet.

'Of course you can, but be careful not to squash them.'

'If I do they can go in the pizza sauce.' Beti shrugged then skipped across the garden.

'She's got an answer for everything.' Will raised his eyebrows. 'Never a dull moment with Beti around.'

'Has she had a nice birthday?'

'I think so. Obviously we had the party yesterday but she's seen my parents and Alice, and Mari popped round with Anwen for a cup of tea. It's been quite a busy day.'

'Oh… If you're tired, I can go.' Disappointment swilled through Hannah's gut.

'No!' He held up a hand. 'Please don't go. I didn't mean to sound like I was *that* tired. I'm not. I'm just looking forward to sitting in front of the TV with a pizza.'

'Sounds good to me.'

'You have any preferences about what you like on your pizza?'

'Not at all.'

'Great.' He stood up then held out a hand. Hannah took it and he pulled her to her feet but she lost her balance and ended up falling into him. Strong hands caught her and for a moment her cheek was against his chest and she could hear the beat of his heart. As she looked up, she found his eyes on her face and she saw something there that made her stomach flutter and her knees weaken.

'Stop messing about you two!' Will stepped backwards as fast as if he'd had an electric shock as Beti thundered towards them, holding out her T-shirt. 'I got lots of tomatoes in here.'

'Well done, Beti!' Will ruffled his daughter's hair. 'Let's go and wash them.'

Beti went first and Will turned to Hannah. 'You OK?'

She inclined her head. But she wasn't OK. She was all mixed up, filled with longing, confusing emotions and above all else, a yearning to be a part of this life on a permanent basis. It was all very well telling yourself to live in the moment but what about when you found something you really wanted – like a family and a place you could call home?

Swallowing a sigh, she followed Will inside, trying to smile but feeling like she needed to have a good cry to release some of the emotion swelling in her chest.

-

'Choose your toppings!' Will gestured at the range of pizza toppings on the kitchen table and Beti and Hannah started adding them to their pizza bases.

'There's so much choice.' Hannah added passata, grated mozzarella, onions, minced garlic, mushrooms and sliced red and green peppers to hers. 'It's like a TV cooking show in here.'

'Ha! Ha! Shall I keep shouting out how long you've got left?'

They giggled together, their eyes locking in a way that made Will's whole body tingle.

'Here, put some more cheese on top of all that.' Will passed her the mozzarella plate. 'It will be delicious.'

'Thanks.'

Will hoped Hannah was having a good afternoon because he'd been worried when she'd got upset in the garden. Beti had hugged Hannah and been over the moon with her bracelet and in turn, Hannah had seemed to become quite emotional and at one Will had thought she might start crying but then she'd seemed to pull herself together. When he'd helped her to stand up, she'd stumbled against him and he'd wanted to hold her against him, to feel how her curves fit against his body. Lucky that Beti had been there because if it had just been him and Hannah, he wasn't sure how he'd have managed to keep himself from kissing her.

They'd brought Beti's tomatoes inside and Will had made the passata while Hannah and Beti had sat at the kitchen table and gone through some photographs on his iPad that Hannah had AirDropped to him. Beti was overjoyed to see all the ones of her at the sanctuary with the animals and she'd asked Hannah to help her write her summer holiday essay for school. Hannah had agreed, so Beti had got a notebook and they'd made a plan of what she was going to write because Hannah had told Beti how she always planned her articles before starting them. It was lovely to cook while Hannah sat with Beti, the two of them chatting away, heads together as they made notes. Will had imagined that this was how a weekend with a family would be, three (or more) of them in the kitchen – the heart of the home – getting homework done and creating tasty and nutritious meals. Having another adult around was comforting and he felt himself relax because he wasn't trying to do it all himself. Beti was being entertained and cared for and Will didn't feel torn in the way he usually did; concerned about ensuring that she ate well but also feeling guilty for not spending the time he was cooking with her. Of course, he did try to involve her in meal preparation as well as other chores, like sorting the washing and vacuuming the house, so that Beti wouldn't feel that he was ignoring her, but sometimes it was so much faster getting those things done alone than with Beti's 'help'. It was the same with food shopping, where from an early stage he'd involved Beti as much as possible, giving her a list of things she had to find. That often proved to be exhausting as she'd often run off to find her items first and he'd have to chase after her so he didn't run the risk of losing her in the supermarket. Of course, once Beti had located the items on her list, she'd get bored and want to go home. Being a dad was the best job in the world but it didn't mean that it was easy or that it wasn't downright exhausting at times.

'And now they go in the oven, don't they, Daddy?' Beti asked, bringing him back to the present.

'That's right.'

'And you have to let your adult helper do that,' Beti explained to Hannah, 'or my teacher says you might burn your little fingers and nobody wants that to happen.'

'That's very wise.' Hannah nodded gravely. 'No one wants to end up burning their little fingers.'

Once the pizzas were in the oven, they cleared up then went through to the lounge. Will was conscious of Hannah looking around, and he hoped that she liked what she saw. He'd kept the décor neutral, with real wood flooring, two large grey sofas with a rectangular coffee table between them and the TV in the corner on a stand that matched the coffee table. He had wooden blinds instead of curtains and a mirror above the fireplace that housed the log burner.

Hannah hovered in the doorway and he realised that she wasn't sure which sofa to sit on. It was very considerate of her not to just sit down because although Will wasn't bothered, his dad was a stickler for keeping his own seat in his house and if anyone else took it, he huffed and puffed until they realised and moved. Growing up, Will and Alice had deliberately sat in their dad's seat to wind him up and many a time they'd ended up in a tickling war on the hearth rug. He'd had a good childhood and memories like that were pleasant reminders. His thoughts strayed to Hannah, as they seemed to do quite often now, who hadn't had that kind of upbringing and his heart ached for her and for what she'd missed out on. Was it possible that he could make things better by giving her all those things she'd missed?

'Sit wherever you want.'

She turned to him. 'Really?'

'There are no concerns about taking someone's seat in this house.'

Hannah went to the end of the sofa nearest the window and sat down. Will swallowed laughter as Beti predictably took the seat next to her and imitated exactly how Hannah was sitting right down to resting her hands in her lap.

'OK then, let's have a look through the movies available and see what we'd like to watch.' Will grabbed the remotes then sat on the other side of Beti and started to flick through the channels.

–

Sitting on the sofa with a plate of pizza resting on her knees, a glass of cloudy lemonade on the table and a movie that Beti had chosen (some animated story about a mermaid who was best friends with a unicorn) playing on the TV, Hannah felt a contentment she'd never enjoyed before. It wasn't just the movie, the pizza or the lemonade though; it was everything. Will's house wasn't just a building with contents, it was a home. The sofa was incredibly comfortable, the room was light and airy, the TV was just the right size and position for the room, the pizza was the best she'd ever tasted and the lemonade was moreish. But the best thing about the afternoon was the two people sitting on the sofa with her.

Will and Beti…

What amazing people they were. This life they had, the easy way they interacted, the love that was present in everything they did together… It was how Hannah remembered things being with her mum. The love her mum had shown her was unconditional and she saw that same love in how Will loved Beti. He would do anything for his daughter and that was how it should be, Hannah thought. He was also making Hannah feel very welcome and not like an outsider who'd come for the afternoon and would soon leave. Somehow, he'd made her feel a part of this family, incredibly relaxed in his home, and Hannah had not felt that in anyone else's home for a long, long time.

She bit into a slice of pizza and flavours flooded her mouth. She might have selected the toppings but Will had grown most of them, prepared them by hand and cooked them to perfection. She glanced through the corner of her eye and her heart expanded at the sight of Beti munching away, eyes glued to the TV, tomato sauce around her mouth. And next to Beti was Will, his face now so familiar because of the times she'd gazed at him: the strong jawline, the dusting of stubble, the dark eyelashes and brows, the hair that would curl if he let it grow longer.

And she knew in that moment that she could very easily fall in love with this man, if she could just be brave enough to open her heart.

Chapter 22

For the next few days, Hannah focused on writing her articles. It was challenging to sit down and write now she had people she'd like to spend time with – a problem she'd never encountered before – but she had a responsibility to meet her deadlines and so she settled down to work.

She certainly had plenty to write about from the beautiful scenery to the fabulous hotel to the summer festival and the bookshop in the village. As she wrote, she opened the folder of photographs occasionally and gazed at them, marvelling at the coastal path with its array of wildflowers and panoramic views, the walk through the fields to the village where she had met up with Ffion, and those of the pretty little village with its stone cottages and central green. Then there were photos of the stalls at the beach car park selling food and drink, sea-glass jewellery and clothing, inflatables to take in the sea like giant pink dolphins. But it was the photos of Will and Beti that she kept coming back to. How two people could have such a significant impact on her life in such a short time she didn't know, but it had happened and she was torn between relishing the fact that they'd opened up a part of her she'd thought lost long ago and wanting to get in the car and leave as quickly as possible so she didn't have to try to work out what it all meant. With love and affection came responsibility and Hannah wasn't used to being responsible for anyone other than herself.

She'd had a fantastic time with Beti and Will at their home, but leaving them at the end of the evening had been difficult. Will had even suggested that she could stay in the spare room if she wanted to have a glass of wine and didn't feel like driving back to the cove, but Hannah had declined – partly from politeness and common sense (it might confuse Beti if Hannah had a sleepover) and partly from the fear of what might happen. Not that she'd thought Will would try to jump on her; he was a responsible dad and a gentleman, but because she had feelings for him and the temptation to do more than drink wine and sit near him on the sofa after Beti went to bed would be strong. What if she'd got tipsy and tried to kiss him? What if she'd embarrassed herself and he really did only see her as a friend? Perhaps he did this all the time with female friends and had no romantic interest at all in Hannah. Even worse, perhaps he felt sorry for her and was trying to be nice to her because of that.

She ran a finger over his face on the computer screen. She found it hard to believe that he had no feelings for her at all because of the way he looked at her when they were together. No one had ever looked at her that way before and it made her heart race and her whole body tingle, it made her long to embrace him and to hear him ask her to stay in Wales. Never before had Hannah wanted to settle down in a location but with every day she spent at Cariad Cove, she grew to love the people and the place even more.

Her phone buzzed so she picked it up and checked the screen. It was Ffion asking if she was up for their run later on. She replied with a thumbs up emoji then set her phone down. She'd run with Ffion every other day and had been enjoying it. The Couch to 5k programme was excellent and she already felt fitter in just a week, something that surprised her. If she stuck with it then she could well end up running regularly again and that thought filled her with joy. Getting past the mental hurdle she had erected years ago when she'd denied herself the pleasure of running hadn't been as hard as she'd anticipated. She was certain it was because she was here in the cove, where she felt safe and cared about, where people recognised her and gave her the time of day and where there were people she cared about in return.

Tomorrow was the Summer Festival Fun Run, an event that Joe and Ffion had organised to raise funds for the animal sanctuary. It was being touted as the highlight of the festival, and all runners involved were to wear costumes. The run would only be 3k in total and would be completed in a circuit around the beach, but Ffion had told Hannah that it would be good fun and that she should join in.

Hannah had laughed and told Ffion that she didn't have a costume but then Ffion had told her not to worry as she'd take care of that. Hannah couldn't help wondering what her life might have been like if she'd had a friend like Ffion years ago. Putting her trust and faith in another person was a big jump for her but there was something so liberating about it too.

-

Against his better judgement, Will thought he'd let Beti decide on their fun run costumes. She wanted to do the run today with him and so he'd gone along with her choice of costume and now that he could see himself in his bedroom mirror, he was becoming a bit anxious. People would actually see him wearing this and there would be photographs that would be forever accessible on the internet; some of the pupils from school might be there and they would, no doubt, relish sharing photos of him on social media and refer to them years down the road. Many of the teenagers he knew were internet savvy and recently one of them had found some photographs of the deputy headteacher during his time away on a friend's stag weekend. He'd been worse for wear and at one point dressed up in a pink tutu and baby's bonnet, and the images had somehow found their way to a printer then the school's noticeboards. Luckily, the deputy head concerned had a sense of humour and had laughed at himself during the staff briefing then cleverly turned the situation around to give an assembly about the dangers of posting embarrassing photos online. But from time to time, the stag weekend photos resurfaced and Will had a feeling they always would do.

'Aww, Daddy, you look amazing. Just how I imagined.' Beti stood in his doorway, her hands clasped to her chest. She was still in her dressing gown but he'd thought he should try to get ready first – in order to mentally prepare himself for wearing the outfit – before helping her.

'Well as long as you're happy, I guess it's fine.'

'Think of the money we're raising, daddy. We'll be helping animals who really need it so a few moments of embarrassment will be worth it.'

'I know.' How was his little girl so wise? Sometimes she seemed far wiser than he was.

Will had set up his online sponsor form months ago when Joe had first told him about the fun run idea in school and he'd raised over five hundred pounds so far. Colleagues and pupils' parents had been generous and supportive, as had his own parents, contributing about a third of the total via an anonymous donation. He knew it was them though because his dad had chuckled when Will had asked if it was from him.

'Will you help me get ready now?'

'Of course.'

He gave his reflection one last glance then left the bedroom, bracing himself for the day ahead.

–

'And don't worry because you don't have to run all the way,' Ffion said as she helped Hannah fasten the bib with her race number around her chest.

'But I haven't raised any money.' Hannah chewed at her bottom lip.

'You'll help with our total,' Ffion said. 'We needed another on our team after Mari's colleague had to drop out.'

Hannah tugged at the front of her costume. 'Is Mari's colleague very small?'

'She is petite, yes, but so are you.'

'Not quite as petite as her I don't think. This could have been made for a child.'

Ffion had turned up at the hotel that morning dressed as a cheerleader complete with short red skirt, white top and big red pompoms. She was wearing knee-length white socks and had a red headband on. She looked fabulous but when she handed Hannah an identical costume, Hannah wasn't so sure.

'What made you decide to be cheerleaders?' she asked now.

'There weren't many costumes left in the shop. I wanted to be a zombie or a superhero but they didn't have any there so Mari thought it would be fun to dress as cheerleaders.'

'You could have been zombie cheerleaders.'

'Damn it! I didn't think of that.' Ffion grimaced. 'Never mind, it's all for a good cause and we'll have fun anyway, I'm sure.'

'What's Joe dressing as?'

'Guess.'

'Ummm.' Hannah tugged at the red skirt, trying to pull it down to her knees but it sprang up to her thighs again. She made a mental note to put her running shorts on under it.

'He's going as Odin.'

'As his own dog?'

Ffion giggled. 'He thought it would be fun to run as Odin with Odin.'

'That's so cute.'

'I know and he does look so sweet. He has the ears and everything.'

'Did he make them himself?'

'He did. He's pretty handy with a crochet hook it turns out.'

'Well that'll be handy when it comes to making baby clothes.' Hannah's eye went to Ffion's belly which was still pretty flat, even though she was around eleven weeks along now. Ffion caught her looking and pressed a hand over her stomach.

'Mam says it will pop out at twelve weeks. She didn't show until then when she was pregnant with Mari apparently and then her belly suddenly curved. I'm quite looking forward to having a little bump to be honest because at the moment I have all the symptoms and nothing to show for it. Except these.' She pointed at her chest and Hannah laughed. 'Bloody grapefruits already so goodness only knows what they'll be like by the time I get to nine months. And here I go with the fruit comparisons again.' She rolled her eyes.

'I hope your running bra is supportive,' Hannah said, checking that her own bra was fastened properly.

'It is. Best bra I've got right now.' Ffion turned Hannah around so she could look in the mirror. 'So, what do you think?'

Hannah looked at the woman in front of her. She looked like a cheerleader from an American movie with her outfit and bunches that Ffion had done for her, complete with red ribbons. Ffion had also given her bright rosy cheeks that she'd created with blusher and it made Hannah look like she was either very warm or had been in the sun for too long.

'Come here.' She held out her hand and Ffion stood next to her. 'I had no idea I'd be dressing up at my age and with a friend too, but it's actually a lot of fun.'

'I'm so glad you're here for this.' Ffion leant her head on Hannah's shoulder. 'At least when everyone else runs off I'll have you to keep me company.'

'What, because I'm so slow and unfit?' Hannah chuckled.

'Yes!'

Ffion turned and wrapped her arms around Hannah and hugged her. Hannah froze. She wasn't used to this, didn't know how to react, but then, as if she did it every day, her arms wrapped around Ffion and she hugged her back. Warmth spread through her; she had a friend who cared enough to hug her and those rogue tears that seemed to have been permanently waiting in her eyes since she'd arrived in the cove blurred her vision.

'Thanks so much, Ffion,' she said softly.

Ffion leant back and peered at her. 'Whatever for?'

'For being a friend. For making me feel so welcome. I… I've never had this before.'

Now it was Ffion's turn to get tearful. 'Oh Hannah… You are a wonderful person and I'm so glad we met. All I want now is for you to stay and then we can see each other all the time.'

Hannah smiled sadly. Ffion had no idea how much Hannah wanted that too.

–

Down at the beach, it was getting busy. Will ducked his head as he passed some pupils from his year ten class but the laughter he heard suggested that they'd recognised him regardless of his efforts. He gave a mental shrug; what did it matter? He could laugh at himself and he was doing this today for two reasons: for Beti and for the animals at the sanctuary. He could take a bit of ribbing from the boys at school if it was for a good cause, besides which, it would give him the perfect opportunity to speak to them about not taking themselves too seriously.

As he walked to the starting line, he looked around. Hannah had sent him a message to say that she'd be taking part today, which had surprised him. They'd sent a few innocuous texts this week and she'd asked after Beti, and Will had considered asking her if she wanted to do something but when she'd said that she had to get first drafts of her articles written, he'd thought it best to give her some space. He didn't want to, was conscious that she'd soon be leaving, and that time was precious, but he also didn't want to get on her nerves if she had work to do. However, today she would be here and he was looking forward to seeing her, hoping they'd be able to spend some time together after the race. At least taking part would give her something else to include in her articles, first-hand experience to share with her readers.

'Look Daddy, there's Hannah Banana!' Beti pointed at three women dressed as cheerleaders. Joe was with them, looking very much like Odin with large floppy brown ears, furry jacket and trousers, and a long tail trailing behind him. 'Oh Daddy, doesn't she look pretty? She's like the prettiest cheerleader I've ever seen.'

'She is.' Will found his eyes drawn to Hannah's blonde bunches, red skirt and long socks. She looked very cute and it made him even more self-conscious about his own outfit.

'Let's go and say hello.' Beti tugged at his hand but his mouth had gone dry and his heart was pounding. What would Hannah think when she saw him looking like this? It was one thing when it was the boys from school, but Hannah? Would she ever be able to take him seriously again? His positive thoughts of moments ago were fast disappearing as embarrassment took their place and he felt like a self-conscious teenager.

'Daddy, you look cool. Don't worry, Hannah will still like you.'

'What?' He frowned at his daughter. What was she talking about? How did she know?

'Daddy…' Beti rolled her eyes. 'I know you fancy her.'

'What?'

'Stop saying *what*, it's rude. My teacher says—'

'Sorry! It is rude. You're right. But… where did you get the idea that I fancy Hannah?'

'I've seen the movies where princes and princesses and cats and dogs and mermaids and mermen look at each other like you and Hannah do. I'm not a baby, Daddy.'

'No. I know that. But… but…'

Beti's eyes were filled with mischief now and he realised that she was teasing him.

He crouched down. 'Beti… you know you'll always be my number one, don't you? You are my world and I love you and I'll never let anyone change that.'

'Daddy,' Beti placed her hands on his shoulders, 'just relax.'

She pressed a kiss to his nose then turned and tugged his hand again so he followed her over to where Hannah was standing. Exactly how much had his daughter seen and understood about his feelings for Hannah? And in turn, how much had she seen in how Hannah reacted to him?

Were their feelings mutual? If a seven-year-old girl could work out how Will felt then perhaps she could see how Hannah felt too.

Chapter 23

Hannah's mouth fell open when she saw Will and Beti. The little girl was dressed as a mermaid in a shiny blue playsuit with the hem of the trousers cut to resemble a tail and made of a material that looked like scales. Her face and arms were painted blue and green and she was wearing a long purple wig. Next to her, Will wore what seemed to be a pink and white striped onesie with a unicorn's head for a hood. His face was painted white and he had rosy cheeks.

'Well hello there, Will, why the long face?' Joe asked then started laughing.

'I'm a unicorn not a horse,' Will muttered. 'Can't you tell from my horn?' He pointed at his hood.

'Of course I can tell, mate. Just teasing you.' Joe grinned. 'And what about this mermaid then? Has she come straight from the sea to join us?'

'It's me, Joe!' Beti giggled. 'Did I fool you?'

'Absolutely. I thought we had a real-life mermaid on the beach,' Joe said.

'You both look great,' Hannah said, smiling at Beti then meeting Will's eyes. 'Really great.'

'So do you.' Will looked from Hannah to Ffion and Mari. 'Are you going to cheer us all on from the starting line?'

'Ha! Ha! Your jokes are almost as funny as Joe's.' Ffion grimaced but she was smiling. 'You need to get your bibs on, Will, because they'll be starting the run soon.'

'Come on, Beti, let's get ready.' Will took his daughter's hand. 'See you soon,' he spoke to Hannah, making her feel like the only other person on the beach.

'You will.'

She watched as he walked over to the table where people were registering, wishing she was with Will and Beti and dressed as a unicorn too. At least the onesie would cover her up a bit more than the cheerleader's outfit, although she did worry that Will might get too warm in it later on.

Turning away, she gazed at the course on the beach. The way was mapped out with cones and at the halfway point along the sand was a table where runners could get water and have their photo taken before heading back to the finish line. The route took them in a circuit designed to ease any congestion that might arise. It wasn't a long run but it was for a good cause and should be fun because of all the costumes. She pulled her phone from the special pocket in her running shorts and snapped some pictures. These would be great to include in her articles and, she thought sadly, for her to remember the day.

Around the beach, waiting for the run to start, were all sorts of characters from film and television, from books and comics and some random ones that runners had invented. Ffion's parents had set up some refreshment stands for runners and other people on the beach who'd come to support the run and she could see several dog water stations too for the dogs like Odin that would be taking part.

'You ready?' Ffion asked.

'I am.'

'Don't forget to take it easy. You've only just started running again and you mustn't overdo it.'

'I won't.' Hannah shook her head. 'The last thing I want to do is to pass out in front of all these people or to sustain an injury that will hold me back from training in coming weeks.'

'Exactly.'

'Are you sure you're all right to do this, Ffion?' Mari pushed her sunglasses on top of her head and squinted at her. 'You do need to take care.'

'I know, darling sister, and I am fine, I promise. I wouldn't do the run if I had any worries or if I wasn't feeling up to it. Besides which, it's not a race and I can run as slowly as I like. However, I want to complete it to get the sponsorship money and because I want to run for as long as I can through this pregnancy.'

Mari's brow was furrowed but she inclined her head, clearly trusting Ffion to make the right decision. 'I've been so worried about her since she told me,' Mari said to Hannah. 'I think I'm more worried about her than I was about myself when I was expecting.'

'You always worry about me.' Ffion hugged her sister with one arm. 'But I promise I'm fine. Also, I doubt very much that I'll be running once my bump gets bigger so I want to enjoy it while I can.' Ffion had placed her free hand on her belly as she kept doing since she'd found out that she was pregnant. She was already so protective of the tiny life growing inside her and it was moving to see how much her friends and family cared. If Hannah had that kind of support back when she was younger, then things might have turned out very differently. She might not have spent so much time running from her regrets and from her pain.

They gathered with everyone else at the starting line and waited. There was a buzz of anticipation in the air and Hannah had goosebumps on her arms. Being a part of this, even without having a sponsor form, felt good. She'd sponsor herself, she decided, and make a donation to the sanctuary, but to do that, she had to finish the run.

She could do it, she felt sure.

And then, they were off…

–

Will jogged rather than ran because Beti was with him. She gave it her all, grit and determination etched on her cute face as she pounded forwards. At the sidelines, some of her school friends, including Anwen, cheered for her and she waved as she passed them. He'd worried about the distance but Beti had run with him before and he knew she was quite fit. Even so, it was a long way for little legs and he was prepared to carry her if need be.

When they neared the halfway point, Beti tapped his arm. 'Can I… have a drink?'

'Of course.' He slowed and grabbed a water for her then waited for her to take a drink. 'Not too much though, Beti, or it'll give you cramp.'

She took some small sips then threw the cup in the bin.

'You OK to keep going?'

'Yes, Daddy, this is for the animals like Bonnie and Patch and I want to help them.'

'Good girl.' He was so proud of Beti and her tenacity, her compassion and her desire to help others.

As they set off again, he glanced behind them, scanning the runners for Hannah. It would've been hard to find her in amongst all the runners if she wasn't dressed as a cheerleader, and when he spotted her, his heart leapt. She was taking it slow with Ffion, although he'd seen Ffion run before many times and she was going at about sixty percent slower than she usually did, so he suspected that she was taking it easy for Hannah.

As they ran, he felt Beti's hand slide into his and he squeezed it, love filling his chest. He was raising a wonderful human being and on days like this, he was able to tell himself that he was doing a damned good job.

As they neared the finish line, he heard cheering and spotted his parents and Alice up ahead, waving and taking photos. He waved back, pointing them out to Beti who laughed then flashed the V sign at them but with her palm facing her.

'Beti!' He almost stopped running because he was so shocked. 'What're you doing?'

'I'm giving them the winning sign.'

'Winning sign?' he was torn between laughter and horror. He suspected his mother was going to be furious.

'Yes, like that pine minster used to do. We watched a video of him in school.'

'Winston Churchill?'

'Yes.'

'He didn't do it that way around. That way is… Oh never mind.'

'Woo hoo! We're almost there.' Beti flashed some more Vs at the people on the sidelines and their eyes widened in shock. Will snorted, knowing he was going to have some explaining to do later to some of the locals.

'Yes we are. Let's do a thumbs up sign instead shall we?' he asked, keen to try to distract Beti from her current mad V flashing.

'OK, Daddy Unicorn.' Beti changed her hand signals and Will breathed a sigh of relief. For now, at least, Daddy Unicorn had saved the day.

–

'What's Beti doing?' Hannah could see the small girl signalling to the people at the finish line.

'Oh god!' Ffion sniggered. 'She's flashing Vs at everyone.'

'I thought so.' Hannah glanced at Ffion who was bright red and she wasn't sure of it was the running or because she was laughing. 'Why's she doing that?'

'Perhaps she's pissed off with everyone… who's watching… and not taking part,' Ffion said.

'I doubt it.' Mari sniggered. 'And Beti's usually a very polite little girl.'

'I'm sure… she's not… doing that deliberately.' A need to protect and defend Beti filled Hannah. 'Perhaps… she thinks… it means… something else.' She sucked in a breath, trying to get her words out with every exhale.

'Oh look… she's giving everyone the thumbs up now,' Ffion said. 'All is well again.'

'Thank goodness for that. I'm sure Will doesn't want to have to explain that to his mother.' Mari laughed. 'She won't stand for rude gestures.'

'Is… she… strict?' Hannah asked.

'She's quite old-fashioned in some ways, especially about manners. I've spoken to her on a few occasions when she's been at Will's or come to collect Beti and she's lovely but she has that primary school teacher air about her.'

'I don't think any parents would want their child... making rude gestures,' Ffion said. 'Especially in public like today.'

'The things my daughters do to embarrass me.' Mari held up her hands. 'When I picked Seren up from nursery the other day, her teacher told me that she'd had to confiscate a sanitary towel from Seren. Apparently she'd taken it into nursery... in her pocket... then tried to use it to bandage her friend's head when they were playing. The little boy was walking around with the towel stuck to his forehead without a clue in the world as to what it actually was.'

Hannah guffawed. 'I'd have... loved to... see... that.'

She'd been conscious as they ran that Mari and Ffion were taking it slow for her and she was grateful to them for it. Also, while she was struggling to talk, her friends spoke easily, barely out of breath. It was something she wanted to aim for and she made a vow to herself to get fitter over coming weeks so that she could run and talk just like them.

'Right, give me your hands!' Ffion held hers out and Hannah took one while Mari took the other. 'We're almost there!'

They raised their arms as they crossed the finish line to a round of cheers and applause and Hannah's whole body tingled with the exhilarating rush of achievement. She had done it. She had completed her first proper run in years and she was proud of herself for trying. Proud of herself for running again and making an effort to overcome her reasons for stopping.

After they'd had photos taken and a group hug, Ffion and Mari went to their partners and families. Hannah stood on her own, smiling at how happy everyone was, trying to squash the longing for a family of her own.

A hand on her shoulder made her jump and she turned to find Will and Beti.

'Well done!' he said, holding his arms open. Hannah moved into his embrace, sliding her arms around Will's back. He was warm and smelt of fabric softener, woody cologne and sweat but the combination wasn't unpleasant. In his embrace, a whole host of feelings rushed through Hannah and she wished they could have stayed that way for hours.

When he released her, a flicker of disappointment shot through her but then he took her hand and Beti took the other one and all was well again.

Just when she'd thought she was alone at the finish line, Will and Beti had arrived and claimed her.

Chapter 24

After the run, people had hung around for a while before heading home or up to the hotel to shower and change. Gwen and Aled had opened the staff shower facilities on the ground floor so that runners could use them. Rather than see Will and Beti have to wait to shower, Hannah offered them the use of her room. Will thanked her then insisted she go first then she went down to the gardens to wait for them. When they were showered and dressed in clean clothes, the three of them went back to the beach for the barbecue.

'That's a relief,' Will said. 'If I'd had to keep that costume on all day, I'd have been a bit whiffy.'

'What's whiffy, Daddy?' Beti asked.

'It means smelly.'

'Urgh! Daddy's a stinker.'

'Well… hopefully not now that I've showered.' He flashed a grin at Hannah. 'Thanks again for that. We could have gone home but it would have taken a lot longer to get sorted.'

'No problem at all.' With his hair wet from the shower, his skin fresh and clear from the run, Hannah thought he looked incredible. He'd brought shorts and a T-shirt to change into and had a rucksack with him that he'd got from the car, telling Hannah it had warmer clothes in it for him and Beti for later on.

'Shall we go and get something to eat?' Hannah asked. 'I don't know about you but I'm starving after all that activity.'

They made their way to the festival food stalls that had agreed to cater extra food for the runners.

'I don't know what to have,' Beti said, scrunching up her nose. 'I like lots of the food but I can't choose.'

'I have an idea,' Hannah took Beti's hand, 'Why don't we get some different things then share them all.'

Beti nodded vigorously and when Hannah looked up, she found Will gazing at her, something in his eyes that took her breath away.

—

The afternoon passed in a blur of eating, talking, taking photographs and building sandcastles with Beti. As dusk fell and the horizon was painted a beautiful burnt orange daubed with pink and peach, Beti yawned and settled herself on Will's lap. He'd brought a large picnic blanket and they were sitting on it with Ffion and Joe while Odin lounged next to them, snoring loudly but occasionally opening one eye to check on everyone.

'What a day,' Ffion said. 'I don't know about you but I'm exhausted.'

Joe placed a hand gently on her belly. 'That's because you're busy growing our baby.'

'Joe!' Ffion's eyes widened and she looked over at Will who had lowered his bottle of water.

'Are you… expecting?' Will asked.

'We are,' Ffion said. 'But we haven't had the first scan yet so we *were*,' she looked pointedly at Joe, 'waiting to tell people.'

'I won't say a word.' Will smiled. 'But congratulations. It's brilliant news.'

'We are quite excited.' Ffion gently stroked Joe's cheek, the love in her eyes reflected in Joe's.

'We certainly are. But...' Joe gave a nervous laugh. 'We really do want to keep it to ourselves and close family and friends until after the scan. I'm so relaxed I forgot where we were.'

'Your secret's safe with me.' Will placed a finger over his lips.

'What secret, Daddy?' Beti asked dozily. She'd been drifting as she sat on his lap, her eyelids fluttering. Hannah couldn't help wondering how it would feel to hold Beti that way, to cuddle her and let the little girl know that she was loved.

'Nothing for you to worry about.' Will kissed Beti's head. 'Go back to sleep.'

Beti snuggled closer to his chest and he stroked her hair back from her face.

'I guess we should be going or I'll be sleeping too.' Ffion yawned as she got to her feet. 'See you tomorrow?'

Hannah nodded. 'You will.'

'Come on then, Joe.'

Joe clipped Odin's lead to his harness and the three of them set off along the beach.

–

Will and Hannah sat quietly, gazing at the horizon as the sky changed colour, orange fading to a sandstone hue that waned to a dark denim laced with ebony. Stars pricked the expanse of sky and the moon shone above the beach, its pearly-grey light reflecting on the water. Small fires glowed amber across the beach, giving light and warmth to those gathered around them. Will had lit one and it cast shadows across the blanket, making him think of stories he read to Beti about what you could see at the heart of a fire.

Beti was snoring softly and Will had wrapped a fleecy blanket around her, knowing that he'd need to take her home soon but not wanting the evening to end.

'She'll sleep anywhere,' he said to Hannah. 'Although I do try to ensure that she's at home in her own bed.'

'She's so beautiful.' Hannah gazed at her.

'I think so. I do worry about her though.'

'I think that's your job as her dad, isn't it?'

He smiled. 'And because her mother left us.' He said this softly so Hannah could barely hear him.

'Being a single parent is challenging. I know my mum struggled at times.' Hannah hugged her knees to her chest.

'And you never met your dad?'

'I didn't.'

Will swallowed. 'That's a real shame.'

'Maybe it is and maybe it isn't. Perhaps I had a lucky escape.'

'Perhaps. But at least if you'd met him you'd know.'

'There is that. It's strange not knowing one of the people who made you. Like a part of you is missing. But Beti knows her mum, doesn't she?'

'She does. For all the good it does her.'

'What do you mean?'

He glanced down at Beti but she was still fast asleep. 'Beti would love to have more of a relationship with Kayla but the feeling isn't mutual.'

'How often do they see each other?'

'About once a month but that's not even face to face because Kayla lives in Australia.'

'So do they video call?'

'Yes but sometimes Kayla gets the time wrong and then Beti ends up missing her calls which leads to disappointment and her asking repeatedly about when Mummy will call again. I feel terrible that I can't make it better but… apart from giving Kayla a piece of my mind, which is like water off a duck's back, what else can I do?'

'It must be hard.'

'I just hope it doesn't have long-term effects on Beti. You hear about adults struggling with life because they were neglected by a parent and I worry constantly that Beti will be scarred by her mother's behaviour.'

'She'll be fine, I'm sure. She has you and knows she's loved.'

'My parents and sister are great and I hope that counters some of the hurt caused by her mum leaving but it doesn't take it all away. She's at that age where her mum would be the centre of her world.'

'You're the centre of her world.'

'You think so?' His chest was tight and he felt the dull ache behind his eyes that came whenever he worried about how Kayla leaving would impact upon Beti. But it was also good to talk about it to someone who hadn't heard it all before. To hear a different opinion.

'Never knowing my father has been tough at times but my mum's love was so strong and so encompassing that I don't feel I missed out. Not most of the time anyway. The worst thing for me was losing my mum when I was ten. If she'd lived then I'm sure I'd have been fine.'

'It's scary being a lone parent. The thought of what would happen to Beti if anything happened to me terrifies me.'

'You're fit and healthy, Will. I'm sure you'll be around for a very long time and Beti is happy and well-adjusted.'

'Thanks.' Will smiled. 'It's not easy to talk about. It's hard enough being rejected by someone yourself but when it's you *and* your child, it's a million times worse. I could cope with my own hurt but Beti's breaks my heart.'

'Oh god, Will, you're just… so… amazing.'

Hannah shifted her position so she could take his hand. She squeezed it and looked as though she was about to snuggle up next to him but suddenly she dropped his hand like it had burned her and moved away.

'What's—'

Hannah gave a brief nod across the blanket and Will turned to see his parents coming towards them.

'Hi Mam, Dad…' Will looked up at them. 'Have you had a good evening?'

'Wonderful, darling. We've eaten and laughed and eaten some more. I am stuffed.' His mam patted her belly. 'We thought we'd head home now because it's getting late.' She stared down at Beti. 'Look at her. What a cherub.'

'What time are you going home?' Will's dad asked.

'Soon.' Will kissed Beti's head. 'I'll have to get her to bed.'

'Tell you what,' his mam said. 'Why don't we take her back with us?'

Will glanced at Hannah but her face was impassive. 'Uh…'

'Go on, Will. It won't hurt. It's the summer holidays and you rarely, if ever, get to stay out late. We can take her out for lunch tomorrow and drop her home in the afternoon. And before you worry about it, we have some of her pyjamas and clothes at ours so she'll be just fine.' His mam was smiling, her face warm with the glow from the fire.

'Are you sure?' He knew Beti would be all right with his parents but he didn't often do anything like this; he didn't allow himself to be away from his daughter if he could help it. However, this evening was different… It was the penultimate night of Hannah's stay in Cariad Cove. He might never see her again when she left and as much as that thought was making his chest ache, he also knew that he wanted to be with her while he could.

'Absolutely, Will. Let your hair down and go for a midnight swim or something.' His mam ruffled his hair in the way she used to do when he was a boy. 'Ifor, can you carry our granddaughter?'

'Of course, my love.'

Will stood up carefully with Beti in his arms. 'Beti?'

'Mmmm.' She opened her eyes and peered at him. 'Nanny and Bampi are going to take you to theirs for the night.'

'I'm going for the night?' Her eyes were hazy with sleep.

'That's right. You OK with that?'

'Yes, Daddy. Will Nanny make me a special hot chocolate with marshmallows?'

'I will, my sweetheart,' Dorothy leant over and kissed Beti's cheek.

Ifor took Beti from Will's arms and she snuggled into him.

'Bye Daddy.'

'See you tomorrow,' he said softly.

'Now enjoy yourself and don't worry about Beti.' His mam gave him a hug then turned to Hannah. 'Lovely to meet you again, Hannah. Have a great evening.'

Dorothy tucked her arm through Ifor's and they walked away. Will watched them go, torn between feeling like he should be the one taking Beti home and wanting to stay with Hannah. He'd never been in this situation before and it was strange. He could understand his own feelings of parental guilt but stranger was how his mam had behaved. She'd been so understanding, as if she knew that Will wanted to spend time with Hannah, seeming to give him her blessing. Did she see that Hannah was special too and that Will already cared for her?

When his parents were just shadows moving along the beach, he turned back to Hannah.

'So... What would you like to do now?'

—

Hannah was alone with Will. On a summer night. On a beach. They had a fire and the moon was high above them, the sea spread out as calm and still as a glossy silver pond.

She chewed at her bottom lip before saying, 'I think I'd like to go for a swim.'

He raised his eyebrows. 'Really?'

'I think so. It's been a long time.'

'Why?'

She hesitated before replying. 'I had reasons for denying myself certain things that I used to enjoy. Complicated reasons and I... to be honest... I'd rather not discuss them now. I want to be here, in this moment... with you. Is that OK?'

'That's more than OK,' he replied, standing up. He pulled his hoodie over his head then his T-shirt, before tugging down his shorts. Hannah tried not to stare but the moonlight accentuated the hard planes of his body making him look like a sculpture, rousing a fierce desire that throbbed at her core. 'I don't have my swimming shorts so I'll have to wear these,' he gestured at his underwear.

'I don't either.' Hannah stripped down to her underwear and felt Will's eyes on her skin like a featherlight caress. Her heart pounded and goosebumps rose on her arms but she was certain that she wanted to do this. She wanted him to look at her with longing like this.

It was now or never. It was time to let go of the things that had been holding her back.

She took his hand and they ran down to the sea, doing their best to avoid clumps of seaweed and shells that glowed as if pieces of the moon had fallen from the sky. The air was fresher the closer they got to the water and it was invigorating, though the thought of plunging into the sea made her belly quiver.

When they reached the water, they came to a stop and turned to face each other.

'You sure? It'll be chilly.' Will was rubbing his thumb against her palm and the sensation was hypnotic.

'Yes.' She was trembling but not just from the thought of plunging into the cold water.

'Then in we go.'

As they waded into the sea, Hannah squealed. Cold enveloped her skin, soaked into her bra and knickers, caressed her everywhere, but still they went deeper. When the water reached her shoulders, Will turned her around and took both of her hands.

'OK?'

'It's not that cold when you get deeper.'

'Patches of it are colder than others.' His eyes were dark as coals, his skin ethereal in the moonlight and Hannah reached out to him, circling her arms around his neck and moving closer. Their bodies met and Will groaned softly, closing his eyes for a moment.

Hannah kissed him. Gently at first but when he responded and his tongue found its way into her mouth, she kissed him harder, wrapping her legs around his waist and moaning as need burned inside her and she felt his desire against her.

Then Will's hands were everywhere, running over her skin, finding places that she'd forgotten existed, and still they kissed, Will seeming to need this as much as she did.

Hannah forgot who and where she was, and gave in to sensation, need and their powerful connection.

Chapter 25

Waking in a strange room in a strange bed, Will was disorientated. He blinked at the grey light that seeped into the room through the gap in the curtains then reached for his phone on the bedside table and checked the screen. *Just after six.*

His whole body ached but in the wonderful way it did after a night of passion. And that was very unusual for him, so unusual in fact that he was surprised he could remember what a night of passion felt like. Heat rushed to his cheeks as he recalled the previous evening, how he'd gone into the sea with Hannah, how they'd started kissing passionately. The kissing had led to more and soon they'd been racing up the beach to grab their things and hurried back to her hotel room.

Will didn't do this; he didn't kiss women, he didn't embrace them in the sea and he certainly didn't spend the night with them. There had been no one since Kayla. He had been alone all that time, had wondered if he would ever make love to a woman again and suspected that he probably wouldn't. Beti was his everything and the idea of bringing someone into her life who could hurt her disrupt her routine or that she might not even like had prevented him from seeking out companionship.

But Hannah was different.

Hannah liked Beti and Beti liked her.

Will and Hannah had a connection that he had not believed possible in such a short time and with him being so set in his ways, and yet it had happened. He refused to regret it because lying here, gazing at Hannah next to him, listening to the soft sound of her breathing while he could still smell her on his skin could not be wrong.

This wasn't wrong.

Hannah was right for him and for Beti.

'Hello you.' She opened her eyes and touched his face, smiling lazily at him. 'How long have you been awake?'

'Not long.'

'Have you been watching at me?'

'Perhaps...' He winked then pulled her closer. 'Do you mind?'

'Not at all.'

He lowered his head and kissed her then lost himself in her embrace.

–

'I needed that.' Hannah wiped her mouth with a napkin. 'I was ravenous.'

'Me too.'

'It seems we both have a good... appetite.'

They giggled together like teenagers and Hannah had to stop herself from grabbing hold of Will again as thoughts of how good it felt to be in his arms flooded through her.

They were sitting on the bed in her hotel room, the window open to let in the sea breeze. It looked like another beautiful day and she sighed as she rested her head against the pillows and it hit her how much she was going to miss the cove.

'What is it?' Will took her hand and stroked her palm.

'I'm going to miss this place.'

'Do you have to go?'

She broke eye contact because looking at him while she said this would be too difficult. 'I've just had the most wonderful night of… of my life, but this…' She gestured at the room. 'Was only temporary.'

'Couldn't you stay a bit longer?'

'The room is booked from tomorrow afternoon.'

'You could find another room.'

'It's high summer, Will. I doubt there will be anywhere available and anyway… then what? Do I stay until you go back to school?' Her throat was tight and her stomach was in knots but she was trying to be strong. She hadn't slept much after they'd come back and made love, had lain in Will's arms and held him tight, thinking about what they were doing and how much she wished this could be different. She had wracked her brains as she tried to think of a way through this, a way to be with Will, but he had Beti to think of and Hannah had her past and the damage she carried. She didn't want that damage to infect anyone else, especially not Will and Beti.

How could she put all that behind her and start a new life here?

Perhaps it was the cold light of day or perhaps it was experiencing the pleasure of being with Will again this morning that made her think that this couldn't last. Will had responsibilities, a family and a life here and Hannah couldn't just expect to slot into all that. She didn't know how to be in love, how to be a part of a family, how to be a mum.

A sob burst from her and she slammed a hand over her mouth.

'Hannah...' Will moved closer to her. 'This doesn't have to end here.'

She rested her head on his chest, held him tight, wanting to believe him but knowing that he would probably see things more clearly when he went home and saw his daughter. But as he started to kiss away her tears and wrapped his strong arms around her again, she wondered if her resolve to leave was right, or if there could be another way.

-

Will had showered and dressed and was sitting on the bed waiting for Hannah. The morning had passed in a delicious blur of lovemaking. He'd tried to speak to her about the idea of staying or at least returning to Cariad Cove once she got things sorted in Watford but he couldn't shake the idea that something was holding her back. She hadn't told him everything about her life and the things that had happened to her and he knew that was to be expected; no one met someone then poured their heart out to them in one go. Such things took time – trust took time – and he knew that it would take him time to trust Hannah in return. She'd said she didn't really have a home or a long-term base to return to, but could he ask her to uproot herself and come to live in Wales? It was a huge ask and what if things didn't work out? What then? Would she stay in the cove and be just another friend or would she feel the need to leave again?

His phone started buzzing so he pulled it from his pocket.

Kayla was video calling him?

Why now?

He sighed, realising she'd probably got the time wrong again, so he'd tell her to call back later. He adjusted his position so there was just a white wall behind him, not wanting to explain his whereabouts to his ex, then accepted the call.

–

Hannah emerged from the bathroom to find Will pacing the room.

'What's wrong?'

He glanced at her then back at his phone. 'Nothing. Well… something, but… could we go for a walk? I need some air.'

'Of course.'

She slid her trainers on then grabbed her bag and they left the hotel room then headed down the stairs. She saw Will scanning the lobby, probably hoping to avoid being seen, which she understood because he wouldn't want the fact that he'd spent the night with Hannah to become common knowledge.

'Shall we head for the coastal path?' she asked once they were outside.

'Good plan.'

The walk along the tree-lined path was quiet but Hannah knew that Will needed that time to process whatever was on his mind. She might not have relationship experience but she'd been through enough to know that sometimes, silence was the only way to work through something. However, she was concerned about him because they'd been so close that morning, as close as two people could be, clinging to each other as if they were each other's life rafts. But they'd both known it was temporary and she had to respect Will's thoughts and feelings, even when she was dealing with her own.

When they reached the top of the incline, Will stopped walking and gazed out at the sea. It was choppier than Hannah had seen it during her stay and the breeze was strong, whisking her hair around her face and tugging at her T-shirt.

'Hannah...' Will turned to her, his brow furrowed. 'I want you to know that I've enjoyed getting to know you. I don't make a habit of this... haven't been with anyone in years and the way I feel about you took me by surprise.'

She watched his face, saw pain in his eyes and her stomach dropped to her feet.

'I... As you said, I have to put Beti first. When you were in the bathroom, I had a call from Kayla. She was expecting to speak to Beti but, as usual, got the time wrong and so I told her to call back later. But it was like being shaken awake for me. Kayla hurt me and hurt Beti. She...' He ran a hand over his face, pressed his fingers against his eyelids. 'I hate talking about this because it makes me feel like shit but I need you to understand. Kayla walked away from me and Beti and it was the worst time of my life. I thought that she would be my partner for life but I didn't see what was right in front of me. I was blind to how she really felt and I think now... that I didn't see that she wanted out because I didn't want to. I was deliberately blind to her true feelings, especially after we had Beti because I wanted Beti to have a home with her parents together like I had growing up.'

'That's understandable, Will. I know how hard it can be growing up with a single parent, but I also know that you're doing an amazing job—'

'Kayla just told me that she's… she's pregnant and that she's getting married.'

'Oh… How… does that make you feel?'

He turned red-rimmed eyes on her. 'Kayla didn't want me or our daughter but now she's making a new life with someone else.' He shook his head. 'What am I talking about? She's already made that life with him. Things are moving on for them while I'm here…' His voice cracked and he bent over and rested his hands on his knees. Hannah felt powerless, useless. She reached out to rub his back but he straightened up and marched away.

'Will?' She trotted after him, hurrying to keep up with his long strides until they reached the area of the picnic bench. He sat down so Hannah joined him.

'I'm sorry. I… I'm just struggling to process everything that's happening. It feels so unfair that this has come along now, when I want to speak to you about us and what I think we could have and… and then Kayla telling me her news has just stirred everything up. To be honest, Hannah, being with you had already unsettled me because for me, caring about someone comes with fear and I don't know if I'm strong enough to do this again. I can't risk falling apart because it's not fair on Beti. She's older now and she'd see far more than she did when she was just a toddler. I need to be strong for her, to be there for her.'

'Of course you do.' Hannah took his hands in hers, holding them tight, her heart breaking at his pain. 'Of course you do.'

Will was brilliant and she cared deeply about him, and knowing what she did, she couldn't ask him to risk his heart again.

'We need some time and space. It's been an intense time, a truly wonderful summer, but we both have things to work through. I need to go tomorrow as planned, Will, but can we… can we stay in touch?'

He met her gaze, a multitude of emotions swirling around in his dark brown eyes, confusion and fear etched on his handsome features. 'I hope so,' he whispered then a tear ran down his cheek.

Sometimes, she thought, it just wasn't the right time. Will had things to work through, and so did she. It was time for Hannah to go.

–

Early the next morning, Hannah carried her suitcase down the stairs and handed the key card to the porter at the reception desk. Outside, there was a mist hanging over the sea and the air was moist. When she wiped at her cheeks, she blamed the mist, refusing to admit that the dampness on her skin was from her tears.

She packed up her car then took one more look at the hotel, the beach, the cove. She had so many special memories from her time there and she knew she'd never forget this wonderful summer. Her stay had been eventful, she had found far more than she'd bargained for when she'd come here and she knew that she'd never forget Cariad Cove.

In the car, she fastened her seatbelt and started the engine, then she drove slowly away, telling herself that this was all for the best because how else had she really expected things with Will to go?

Chapter 26

A month later, Hannah was sitting a cafe in Watford. Her laptop was open on the table in front of her and she'd just ordered a latte and an iced bun to celebrate the praise she'd received from the editors about both of her articles about Cariad Cove. She'd also outlined one about the animal sanctuary that several publications were interested in seeing, one about the Gower Peninsula and one about her journey doing Couch to 5k. With just three weeks of the programme left to complete she was proud of her progress and aimed to keep running.

Since returning from Wales, she'd kept herself busy, tried not to spend time dwelling on what she had experienced in Cariad Cove and how she had been drawn to Will and Beti. But writing about the cove and the area, the summer festival and the sheer joy she had felt there, receiving texts from Ffion that talked about how much she missed Hannah and how she hoped to see her again didn't help her to forget.

Hannah had always been good at pushing things away but since she'd been to Cariad Cove, something inside her had been cracked open and she couldn't seal it up again. Nor did she think she really wanted to. Experiencing emotions, as challenging as it could be at times, was not as awful as she had expected it to be. To appreciate the highs, she now knew that she had to take the lows and she no longer believed that crying or feeling sad were signs of weakness. She was coming to terms with the fact that it was OK to cry. It was OK to grieve – for her mum, for the father she had never known and for her other loss, for the girl she had once been and for the family life she had never known.

The waitress arrived with the latte and bun and set them on the table, smiling at Hannah. 'What a beautiful family you have.'

'What?' Hannah started.

'Sorry, I couldn't help seeing the photograph on your screen. Your partner and little girl are gorgeous.'

Hannah's screen had locked and there, in vivid colour, several memories were displayed: some older ones – pretty beaches with white sand, one of the pyramids, the Northern Lights in Tromsø – and one from the day at the animal sanctuary. It was a close-up of Will and Beti, cheek-to-cheek, with wide toothy grins aimed at Hannah's camera. They looked so happy and her heart squeezed as it hit her how much she missed them both.

'They're wonderful,' she said.

'You're very lucky,' the waitress said with a smile before walking away.

After Hannah had left Wales, she'd tried not to contact Will but it had been hard. He'd sent a text to ask if she got back to Watford safely, so she'd replied briefly and asked him to send her love to Beti. There had been a few more polite texts back and forth but Hannah had known that if she rang him or video called him then she might break down and tell him how she felt. Will had needed space and so had she but now...

After a month had passed…

Shouldn't she be feeling a bit better?

If anything, she felt worse, her longing for him and Beti felt worse. It was an ache that she could only describe as homesickness, except it was for two people and a place she'd never lived in. As long as Will was fine, she told herself, and moving on with his life, then she could cope with her own messy emotions.

But what if he wasn't fine? What if he felt as bad as she did and he was leaving her alone because he thought that was what she wanted? What if they were both being cautious idiots and they should give this connection they had a chance? Life was short and happiness had to be grabbed when it came along.

She took a bite of the bun, a sip of her latte, packed up her laptop then went to the counter and paid. The time had come to stop running away and to start running towards happiness instead.

-

Will jogged across the beach, the wet sand sucking at his trainers, his breaths regular, his legs strong. He was tired after a Monday in work but he'd needed to get out so had asked his mam to give Beti her dinner. She'd jumped at the chance and he'd told her he'd pick Beti up later on.

The past month had been strange. He'd thought that returning to school would be a positive thing, that it would give him less time to think about the summer, but he often found himself gazing out of the classroom window, daydreaming about the summer days and nights spent with Beti and Hannah, about how he'd hoped the summer would last forever. Of course, he hadn't been naïve, he had known that Hannah would leave and life would go back to normal at some point, but the summer had been so magical that he'd found it hard to believe that something wouldn't happen to stop Hannah leaving.

Then that night he had spent with Hannah... It had been one of the most incredible nights of his life. To feel so connected to another human being was wondrous and he had known that he wanted to feel that way for the rest of his life. He finally understood what all the romantic songs, poems and movies were about. When you found a person who lit up your soul, who touched you inside in a way that made you feel that you were no longer alone then that was worth preserving, worth taking a chance on.

But Kayla's video call when he'd been in the hotel room had startled him, scared him back into the corner like a wounded animal. He'd felt the need to curl up and hide away, to close his heart to his burgeoning feelings for Hannah and he'd used his old reasoning: he had to protect Beti and to put her first. But was he putting her first by denying them the chance to have love in their lives? Not their love, of course, because that went without saying, but the love of another person who could come into their family and enrich their lives. Not just any person either; it had to be Hannah.

Hannah... She was the only one he wanted to be with.

He reached the cliffs of Barddoniaeth Bay then turned and ran back towards the hotel.

Hannah?

Was that her running towards him?

He scoffed at himself. It couldn't be. Hannah was miles away in Watford, a drive that would take almost four hours. She'd gone back to her life and Will had not tried to stop her leaving. He was an idiot for letting her go. She was the best thing that had happened to him and Beti in ages.

As the figure got closer, his heart fluttered wildly. It did look a lot like her. He slowed down, wanting to allow himself to believe that it could be her, just for a moment, even though it was the cruellest of self-deceptions. Pretending that everything was all right was not easy to do but it provided a moment of breathing space from the ache of loss.

And then he stopped.

Because it *was* Hannah.

'Will!' She waved both arms, her trainers pounding the sand, her cheeks rosy with the exertion and from the cold September air.

'Hannah!' His voice cracked as he opened his arms and she ran into his embrace. He lifted her off her feet and swung her round and round, both of them laughing and crying and holding on as if they never ever wanted to let go again.

'You came back,' he said into her hair, aware that his whole body was trembling.

'I couldn't stay away.'

'I've missed you so much.' He pulled back and looked at her then lowered his head and kissed her, cupped her face between his hands, needing to feel that she really was there, that she was with him, that she wouldn't float away like she did in his dreams.

'Will…' she said finally, holding his hands tight. 'We need to talk. There are some things I need you to know about me. We can't move forwards until you know what I've been through, what I've done.'

'Tell me,' he said, knowing that nothing she said would make him let her go again.

Holding hands, they headed up the beach to the sand dunes where they sat with their backs against the tufts of sandy grass, their feet planted in the sand, the beach and the sea of the cove spread out before them.

—

Even though just a month had passed since Hannah had been at the cove, it looked different. The light was changing as summer gave way to autumn and the late afternoon was already dusky, the sky dove-grey with hints of peach and pink. The air was cooler too and smelt different, laced with woodsmoke from chimneys of cottages around the coastline and near the hotel.

'How did you find me?' Will asked.

'You live in Swansea. I know your address.'

He laughed. 'I mean… How did you know I'd be down here?'

'I went to your house but you weren't there then I saw Mari and she said she'd seen you leave in your running gear. I took a chance on you coming here.'

'I like running on the beach… it gives me a chance to remember.'

Hannah pressed her palms to her cheeks. 'What… everything?'

'Everything,' he replied, his dark eyes on her face, drinking her in, making her feel as though she was the only other person in the world. He had a way of doing that and no one else she'd ever met did it; when she was with Will she could believe that she was important, that she mattered, that he cared. 'Now tell me what you need me to know. Trust me with whatever it is that has held you back from happiness.'

'OK…' She took a slow, deep breath and Will took her hand, giving her strength. 'You know that I lost my mum when I was ten. She had cancer and the thought that it could be hereditary has always terrified me. I paid to have tests done to look for the gene that causes ovarian cancer and they came back as no higher than most people, but it didn't fully erase my fears. Growing up without her meant that I missed out on so much and because I didn't have a father either, I became self-sufficient. I had to be. Some of the foster carers were kind but I never felt like a part of their families and that was tough.'

'You've been alone for a very long time.'

'I have but please don't get me wrong, I'm not feeling sorry for myself, though I have done at times over the years. I just want you to understand me. After I'd had a meeting with the local council and agreed a pathway plan, I got a job at sixteen in a shop and worked alongside doing my A levels while living in a scruffy little bedsit. I needed my own space and while it wasn't exactly a home, it was mine and I could come and go as I pleased. If I wanted a snack I could open a cupboard and get one, I no longer felt that I had to ask anyone if I wanted something.'

'I grew up in a home I loved but I can understand that feeling because I'd often get told off for helping myself to snacks.' He smiled then squeezed her hand to show he was joking. 'Sorry… I'm trying to use humour to cope with my emotions. I hate to think of you being so alone and… you should have had everything, Hannah. You should always have felt loved and secure.'

She swallowed hard, moved by his passion and empathy.

'I managed though. I got a job at the local paper after finishing college and it was wonderful. For the first time in my life I could write about things and I felt like I was making a contribution to society. My mum was always an avid reader and I suppose I thought that she'd be proud of me writing, even if it was for a paper and not historical novels like she used to read. But before I started that job... I went on a holiday with some college friends. They weren't close friends but girls I got on with and they invited me to Greece for a week. It was hot, chaotic and... well... crazy. There was a lot of drink and sun and...'

'It's OK. I know how those holidays can go.'

'I'd been so alone for years, so self-contained, and suddenly I was out and about, drunk and getting attention. It was intoxicating and I... did some stupid things, took risks I'd never take now.' She hugged her knees to her chest and pressed her mouth against them for a moment, scared of going on yet knowing that she'd started so she'd just as well finish. 'I... went back to my bedsit after the holiday and continued the drinking and staying out late. I don't know how I did it but I was so young and wild, I guess by that point, and in the day I'd work, run, swim and then I'd be at the pub again in the evening. It was like once I'd had a taste of crazy, I had to keep going.'

'It sounds like you were just doing what lots of young-sters do, Hannah. You can't blame yourself for going out and having a good time.'

'The thing is though, Will, I don't even know if I was having a good time. I was... self-medicating, I think. I hadn't ever drunk much but after that holiday, it was like I'd realised how it could set my mind free by creating a numbing wall. I didn't drink every day but I did drink a lot and then… one day… on my run… I collapsed.'

'God, Hannah…' His face contorted with pain and she bit her lip, trying to manage her own.

'I… was found by a member of the public and taken to hospital by ambulance and it turned out that I was… I was… miscarrying.'

'You were pregnant?'

She gave a brief nod as the old shame and sorrow threatened to choke her. 'Fourteen weeks along.'

'I'm so sorry.'

'I was eighteen. Legally an adult but still in many ways a child. I had no one to turn to. I lost my baby in a hospital bed, alone. I hated myself for it because I didn't know who the father was. It could have been anyone of the men I met abroad. My first chance at having a family since I lost my mother and I lost it. My own child didn't stand a chance because I didn't even know it existed. I made the same mistake my mum made by getting pregnant by a man who would never know he had a child, even though that child didn't take a breath.'

Will moved closer to her and wrapped an arm around her shoulders. 'You were so young, Hannah. You can't blame yourself for not knowing, for trying to find solace in going out and partying. You'd been through so much. I know because I see it with some of the kids at school. Even the ones with so-called stable home lives go through difficult patches. It's part of growing up, part of being human.'

She looked up at him, saw that he really did understand and it filled her heart with hope.

'I feel like a failure because of it and I still feel shame. If I'd known there was a baby, I'd have acted very differently. I see how you are with Beti and I like to think that I'd have been a good mum.'

'You would have been, of course you would. But Hannah... even if you'd done everything by the book, you might still have lost the baby. There are no guarantees, and many women miscarry.'

'I sometimes feel like I was punished for being young and foolish. For being irresponsible.'

'Stop right there.' Will cupped her chin and met her eyes. 'It's time to forgive yourself. You've taken steps in the right direction but you need to give yourself a break now. You are one of the most amazing people I've ever met and I want you to know that. I adore you and Beti adores you. I'm so sorry that you lost your baby and I wish I could take that pain away but I do know that you cannot blame yourself. You didn't know you were pregnant and even if you had... These things happen.'

Hannah raised a hand to her cheeks and found that they were wet.

'I've never told anyone about this. My shame has been so deep that I've been unable to share it. It was why I stopped running and swimming. I needed to punish myself in some way for what happened. They were things I enjoyed and after I lost the baby, I didn't feel that I deserved to enjoy them anymore. When I was running or swimming, I felt so alive and after the miscarriage it seemed so wrong, so I shut myself down and denied myself the things that had helped me to cope with living.'

'Hannah… I'm utterly devastated for what you've been through. And you did this alone. I can't even begin to imagine how you've felt but I can tell you that I am in awe of your bravery and resilience. But now… No more shame or punishment. You can cry, shout, scream and grieve but you are not to feel guilt or shame ever again. You're a good person and you don't deserve to put yourself through this.'

'I feel…' She sniffed, needing to expunge everything now that she'd started. 'So bad for repeating my mother's mistake. And since then… I've also been terrified of getting pregnant again in case the pregnancy was successful. Firstly, because I believed I didn't deserve to be a mum or to be happy, and secondly, because what if I got sick and then the child had to cope without me as I had to cope without my mum? What if… perhaps on some level, I was trying to get pregnant to escape from that cycle or perhaps I was deliberately rash in order to lose the baby I could have had and… and…'

Will pulled her onto his lap and held her head against his chest. 'Stop being so mean to yourself. I'm here for you and I'm not letting you go. You never have to manage on your own again.'

The tears came silently at first and then in big noisy sobs that wracked her body.

Everything that had been held inside for years rushed to the surface and Hannah released it while Will whispered that he was there for her, he had her back and he would never let her go again.

–

Will placed his phone on the bedside cabinet and turned to Hannah. He'd phoned his dad and explained that

Hannah was back and they needed to talk and his dad had told him he understood and that he'd take Beti home and put her to bed. She could have stayed at Will's parents' home but because it was a school night and because Beti wasn't expecting it, they thought it was better to stick to her routine. His dad had said he'd tell Beti that Will had a meeting because telling her that Hannah was back would only lead to her begging to see Hannah. After all, she'd talked about Hannah non-stop since she'd left and even shed a few tears when she'd told Will how much she missed her.

'All sorted,' he said to Hannah. 'I'll have to go home later but there's no rush now.'

'Beti will be OK?'

'She'll be fine with Mam and Dad.'

'Good.'

He sat back against the headboard and held out his arm and Hannah snuggled into him.

'Funny that you're in the same room as before,' he said, looking around.

'Lucky they had a room free at such short notice.'

'They probably want you to write more lovely articles about how great it is here at the Cariad Cove Hotel.' He kissed her forehead.

'I have no problem with that.' Hannah sat up and pushed her hair away from her face. 'Oh Will, it's been such a difficult month. I've missed you and Beti desperately.'

'We've missed you too.' He reached out and stroked the side of her face and she closed her eyes. After they'd talked on the beach he'd walked her back to the hotel where she'd managed to get a room and she'd asked him to come in. He'd agreed but said he needed to sort out arrangements for Beti as he was only meant to be going for a run and he didn't want anyone worrying. 'Beti has broken down a few times.'

'About me?'

'About missing you and wanting to see you, wondering if you'll ever come back.'

'That breaks my heart. I'd never do anything to hurt her.'

'I know. But it was circumstances and not you that made her cry. And now you are back.' He sucked in a breath as the reality of his words hit him.

Hannah was back.

'To stay,' she said, and he reached for her and pulled her to him, kissing her deeply as his longing for her surged.

When Hannah broke away from the kiss, he scanned her face, worried that he was moving too quickly. 'What is it?'

'I just want you to know that I'll never do anything to hurt you or Beti. This past month I've thought about everything a lot and I realised that I've been wasting time. Life is short and any time away from you and Beti is wasted. I want to be with you both so much. I've never wanted anything more.'

'I'm so happy to hear that because I want you in my life and in Beti's life. She loves you as much as I do.'

'I love you too, Will. Both of you.'

'Then that's settled.' He laughed with relief and happiness.

'What is? Tell me, please, because I need to hear it.'

'We're a family of three.'

'Oh Will.' A tear trickled down her cheek. 'I'm going to be a mum?'

'As long as you're happy with that?'

'I'm happier than I've ever been.' Her eyes clouded over. 'But what if… What if Beti likes me but feels put out by me being around permanently? She might feel jealous or that I'm butting in and taking your time and attention away from her.'

'Do you not know Beti at all?' He took Hannah's hand and squeezed it. 'When my little girl loves someone, it's for keeps. She fell in love with you at the same time I did and knowing you're back will make her day. No, it'll make her week. Scrap that, it will make her year. You won't be taking anything away from her, you'll be enriching her life and mine.'

'That's such a beautiful way to put it. And now I just can't wait to see her.'

Will cleared his throat then he slid his legs over the side of the bed and stood up. 'Come on then.'

'Come on what?'

'There's no time like the present.'

'You mean go to her now?'

'What're we waiting for? We can pick up pizza and ice cream and meet her at home. I'll drop my dad a text so he knows about the change of plan.'

'Oh Will… I can't believe this is happening.'

'Well believe it. Now grab your bag and let's go.'

Will walked around the bed and went to open the door but as he passed Hannah, she grabbed his hand and pulled him close.

'I love you so much, Will Hopkins. Thank you for wanting me.'

'Of course I want you. We're meant to be together. And... I love you too, Hannah Banana.'

Giggling, and hand in hand, they made their way downstairs, and Will knew that this really was for keeps.

Epilogue

'Look at us, Hannah Banana!' Beti squealed with delight as she raced across the sand with Patch and Bonnie, the bobble on her hat bouncing as she ran.

Hannah waved, happiness filling her chest at how much fun Beti and the dogs were having.

'It seems that adopting both dogs was a good plan, then?' Will had his arm around her waist as they stood watching the energetic trio.

'Definitely.'

It had been six and a half weeks since Hannah had come back to the cove to find Will and in that time a lot had happened. She'd rented a small cottage in the village that happened to be quite close to the bookshop, and she hadn't renewed the lease on her rented house in Watford when it had come to an end two weeks ago. After she'd gone to hand the keys over to the rental agency, she'd moved her few belongings to Wales, overflowing with excitement about starting her new life with Will and Beti.

Hannah and Will had talked a lot about the best way forward for them and decided that although they knew they were in love, they needed to take more time to get to know each other. Also, they wanted to give Beti time to adjust too, although the little girl seemed to have no qualms about Hannah being around and often asked her to hurry up and move in.

She'd already been invited to spend the holidays with Will, Beti and Will's family, and she was really looking forward to it. A family Christmas was something Hannah had dreamt about as a child and every time she thought about it, her belly flipped over. She'd already started buying little gifts for Will and Beti and couldn't wait to see their faces on Christmas morning.

On the work front, Hannah's articles about the summer festival had been published and she'd promised the two editors that she'd send them her articles about the animal sanctuary and the Gower Peninsula, as well as others that she had planned about a typical Welsh Christmas at the coast. Will's head teacher had invited Hannah into school to speak to the pupils about her travels and her writing, and been so impressed that she'd offered Hannah a job teaching an afterschool creative writing club two days a week. There was a grant from the local education authority for extracurricular activities, and while Hannah would happily have run the club for free, the head teacher had insisted on paying her for her time. In addition, she was also in talks with a publisher about an idea she'd had for a novel about a woman who grew up in care and then travelled the world. It would be loosely based on her own life story but with some additional fictional adventures thrown in. Hannah was feeling positive about life in so many ways now. There was a lot she could do to make money to live on but for now she had her savings and the inheritance from her mum, and if she wasn't travelling, her living costs were lower anyway. Hannah had enjoyed her years of travelling but knew now that any travelling she did would be with Will and Beti. She couldn't imagine going anywhere and being excited about it if they weren't by her side to enjoy it too. And that was how she knew that she had changed and could be the partner Will needed, the maternal figure that Beti wanted. She'd never take the place of Beti's biological mum, Kayla, but she'd put her heart and soul into the role as Beti's additional mum.

Hannah walked along the beach with Will, the cold sand crunching beneath their boots, the brisk October wind tugging at her hat and coat and creeping under her scarf. It made her shiver but it was also invigorating and she knew she'd want to walk there every day throughout the winter. She had begun her healing process in this beautiful, rugged location and she wanted to savour being there every day through the seasons. Healing from trauma didn't happen overnight. It was an ongoing process and Hannah knew that it wouldn't be without bumps in the road. The life she was embarking upon was new to her; the life she was leaving behind had been familiar but, in many ways, lonely and empty. Cariad Cove held a second chance for Hannah and she intended on grabbing that chance with both hands and giving it her all.

As for the dogs, Will's reason for not adopting one had been his job, but with Hannah moving to the cove and working from home, she'd offered to dog-sit through the day while he was in work. They'd initially gone to the sanctuary to adopt just Bonnie, but when they'd seen Patch standing in the kennel alone after Joe brought Bonnie out, they'd known that he had to come home with them too.

Patch and Bonnie had become as much hers as Joe's, spending most days with her in the village and some nights when Will stayed over. The nights they stayed at Will and Beti's, Hannah was often there anyway. The dogs' love was unconditional and they found joy in such simple things that Hannah was able to follow their example without feeling that she should be rushing around, achieving more. Lying on the sofa with one dog at her side and one warming her feet while she read a book and drank cups of tea was a wonderful way to start the day. For the first time in her life, she was able to know what it was like to have company, both canine and human, and it was one of the best feelings in the world.

As was being a mum…

The thought made her bite her bottom lip. Beti had a biological mum but she wasn't around for her, still calling just once a month, and although her circumstances were different, Hannah knew the hole that not having a mum left in a child's life. She'd been able to use her experience to be there for Beti and she loved how easily Beti had accepted her as part of the family now. They shared lots of hugs and laughter, lots of time outdoors and Will was teaching them both to cook, sometimes with hilarious results like the time when Hannah's Yorkshire puddings came out like rocks and when Beti used a tablespoon for the baking powder in her fairy cakes instead of a teaspoon and they tasted terrible. As a family, they were creating memories together and Hannah was finding that the hole in her heart was gradually filling in as love surrounded her and healed her from within.

'There's Ffion and Joe!' Will pointed at the concrete ramp that led down to the beach. Ffion's arm was tucked through Joe's while Odin padded along next to them. He rarely left Ffion's side now, as if he was aware that she was expecting and it was his duty to guard her and the baby at all times. Ffion's bump was evident under her coat. She was about halfway through the pregnancy and absolutely glowing. The morning sickness that had gripped her early on had passed and she was happy and healthy. She was also still running, albeit carefully, often with Hannah who had completed Couch to 5k and now ran several times a week. At the twenty-week scan, Ffion and Joe had found out that they were having a boy and they were both over the moon. Ffion had spoken to Hannah about the prospect of setting up a PR company together in the future, but for now, she'd said, she wanted to focus on her pregnancy and on her time with Joe. She would work again after the baby was born but not immediately because what she'd been through in her life had taught her that time was short and spending it with those you loved was the most important thing of all.

And Hannah had to agree.

She'd come to the summer festival expecting nothing other than to work then move on. She'd been shut down, shut off from doing things she had once loved and still, albeit unconsciously, punishing herself for a past mistake. But in Wales, she'd found friendship, love and self-acceptance, and in turn those had brought along peace of mind.

Finally, Hannah had found a place to call home, and she couldn't imagine a better place to be starting over than in Cariad Cove.

Acknowledgements

My thanks go to:

My husband and children, for your love, support and encouragement. You and the dogs are my everything.

My wonderful agent, Amanda Preston, and everyone at LBA.

The fabulous team at Canelo – with special thanks to my lovely editor, Emily Bedford, for your encouragement, enthusiasm and insightful suggestions, and also Fran Riccardi, Louise Cullen and Iain Millar.

My dear friends for your love and support over the years. You are my tribe!

Sally-anne Atkinson for helping me with English/Welsh translations for Cariad Cove (Cildraeth Cariad) and Barddoniaeth Bay (Bae Barddoniaeth). I know how busy you are and I'm very grateful for your help.

My very supportive author and blogger friends. You are amazing!

All the readers who take the time to read, write reviews and share the book love.

The wonderful charities Greyhound Rescue Wales and Hope Rescue for the incredible work they do every single day.

And finally, huge thanks to the NHS for the Couch to 5K app. This app helped me start running and the running, in turn, helped me to heal.